She was
about to die

Sophie plastered herself against Rio's back, aware only of fear as the motorcycle rocked and roared beneath her.

"How you doin' back there?" Rio shouted to be heard over the wind.

Pride made her holler back, "Fine. I'm doing fine."

"Could you ease off your grip a little, then? You're squeezing my belly into my backbone."

Sophie forced herself to loosen her hold a trifle, and he nodded his thanks and stroked her hand.

She continued to cling tight to Rio's body, and every now and then he reached a hand back and touched her, sometimes her arm or her thigh, a reassuring small caress that linked them in the vortex of rushing air and speeding traffic. And long before they reached the city, Sophie's attitude toward biking began to change.

She felt young and wild and free.

She felt dangerous and sexy.

She felt like Rio's woman....

Bobby Hutchinson's first Temptation is a story that is close to her heart. She had a boutique in Vancouver for eight years. And yes, the garment factory was affectionately known as the Sweat Shop. There was no motorcycle store next to Bobby's boutique, but her husband, Al, had a bike. She admits it was thrilling to roar down the highway holding tight to the man she loved. But one of the biggest moments of Bobby's life was when she learned to ride and she took Al for a spin!

Books by Bobby Hutchinson

HARLEQUIN SUPERROMANCE
253–DRAW DOWN THE MOON
284–NORTHERN KNIGHTS
337–A PATCH OF EARTH
376–REMEMBER ME

HARLEQUIN AMERICAN ROMANCE
147–WHEREVER YOU GO
173–WELCOME THE MORNING
223–FOLLOWING A WILD HEART
290–HOME TO THE COWBOY

Don't miss any of our special offers. Write to us at the following address for information on our newest releases.

Harlequin Reader Service
901 Fuhrmann Blvd., P.O. Box 1397, Buffalo, NY 14240
Canadian address: P.O. Box 603,
Fort Erie, Ont. L2A 5X3

Strictly Business
BOBBY HUTCHINSON

Harlequin Books

TORONTO • NEW YORK • LONDON
AMSTERDAM • PARIS • SYDNEY • HAMBURG
STOCKHOLM • ATHENS • TOKYO • MILAN

Published February 1990

ISBN 0-373-25385-0

Printed in U.S.A.

1

"MORNIN', SOPHIE. You're at work bright and early today."

It was barely eight o'clock on a warm summer morning, and Sophie Larson was swearing under her breath at the disgusting mess on the sidewalk directly in front of her store. For the sixth time in two weeks a dog had deposited there, and she'd have to clean it up. Her stomach heaved at the thought.

"Morning, Herb," she greeted the talkative mailman. "See that?" She pointed an accusing finger down at the fouled concrete. "So help me, if ever I catch that animal, or rather, his owner..." She curled her hand into a fist and shook it.

Herb screwed up his face in a gesture of sympathy. "Hate dogs myself. Nasty, dangerous animals."

He handed her a fistful of envelopes, most of them with ominous windows.

"Bills."

Herb frowned at her. "Whatever they are, see to it you don't lose 'em."

Herb often lectured on her tendency to stuff mail anywhere handy and leave it unopened until she felt emotionally able to deal with it. Mail, he was fond of reminding her in a scandalized tone, was sacrosanct. He, for one, believed in being organized.

Sophie groaned and stuffed this batch into the immense tote bag slung over her shoulder. The end of every month was a time of severe trauma, what with wages and rent and taxes and fabric expenses and fifty other things she never anticipated. She hadn't even realized June was almost over.

"Gonna be a nice day, anyway," Herb said, doing his unctuous best to add a positive note to the morning. "Just look at that sky." He pushed his hat to the back of his bald head and gestured at the blue canopy overhead and then down at the persistent sunbeams glancing off the dusty front windows of the old shops and dingy warehouses that lined both sides of the narrow, cobblestoned street.

The Vancouver waterfront district was quiet and nearly deserted at this early hour; most of the merchants in nearby Gastown didn't bother opening their shops until sometime between ten and eleven, and the shop owners in this less prosperous area followed suit.

There were three storefronts in the old warehouse that housed Sophie's boutique. There was Kelly's Quality Footwear on her right, a lackluster operation if ever Sophie had seen one.

Herb was gazing with curiosity now at the boarded-up front window on her left. "Any word yet on who's gonna rent the other side to you, Sophie?"

"It's already rented, Herb, but that's all I know. The management company came by and took down the sign last Friday. I only hope it's somebody half as nice as Jessica was. I'm gonna miss her something awful." She was trying to open her door. "Damnation, this key's stuck again."

After two years, she ought to know just how far to twist it in order to release the stubborn, rusted spring, but the mechanism seemed to have a mind of its own.

"Jessica was all right, I guess. A bit sharp-tongued now and then," Herb said. He moved far too close to Sophie and did his officious best to loosen the key for her.

She moved away.

"Good eye for antique jewelry, Jessica had," he went on. "Really too bad her nerves gave out after that last break-in. Guess the cops haven't caught the guys yet, huh?"

"Not that I've heard. And it wasn't Jessica's nerves so much as her bank balance that forced her to close her store. Her insurance shot sky-high, and of course she had to keep replacing stock."

Herb gave up on the door with an apologetic shrug.

"No dice. It's beyond me."

"Sooner or later, I'm going to have to replace the lock on this door." Sophie sighed in exasperation.

Herb shrugged. "For all the good it'll do, you might as well stick with this one. Way things go around here, you put a new lock on, somebody'll just come along and bust it for you."

He was probably right. Anyway, it seemed she'd already replaced ninety dozen other things in her less than modern premises, trying to make the Unicorn an appealing showcase for the handmade fashions she sold.

"These old buildings are one headache after another," Herb went on, not noticing the venomous look Sophie shot him. She adored the old building, and despite any problems it caused her, she grew defensive when it was criticized. So much of the city's history was being lost in the zeal for newer, bigger, fancier buildings. Not that this building had any claim to beauty or antiquity. It was plainly and simply a warehouse converted into cheap retail space.

"A new lock won't keep those vandals out, Sophie. If they can't get the front door open, they just smash in the back or through the windows. They went to the trouble of breaking in through the front window of that music store a couple blocks over, and the owner told me he'd even forgotten to lock the front door that night. Guess the culprits never thought to try it, so they smashed the window. Lot of broken glass, and all unnecessary."

They'd broken Sophie's window six weeks before, which was going to send her insurance premium soaring. At least they'd left her alone since, probably because there was less than ten dollars in her store for them to steal. But they'd taken some of her best handmade silk blouses and a stack of fragile lingerie she could ill afford to replace.

They'd broken into Jessica's four times in two months. Antique jewelry was a lot more appealing and easier to fence than distinctive handmade clothes, the police explained. Which was why the neighboring premises were now vacant, the wide shattered window boarded over and, Sophie thought, lonely looking.

Herb readjusted the huge mail sack on his shoulder, and with a wave, set off down the street just as an old blue motorcycle, followed closely by a van with "Broadway Glass" painted on the side pulled to the curb in front of Sophie's building.

A dark-haired, muscular man swung one long leg off the bike and strolled over to the window. He gave several boards a tentative tug, then stood back and said something to the two workmen who ambled over from the van.

They nodded and began ripping off the boards, making a huge clamor. The man thrust his hands into the back pockets of his jeans, legs far apart in a cocky stance, and studied Sophie with open interest. He gave her a long, appraising look accompanied by a jaunty, white-toothed grin and a silent wolf whistle.

She pretended to ignore him, but from the corner of her eye, she took stock of skintight blue jeans framing dangerously narrow hips and long legs. A sleeveless white knit shirt outlined what she could only label a magnificent male torso.

Whew. Some of these laboring types were built, Sophie thought.

She tried to snap her attention back to the key and the reluctant lock, but this man wore his sexuality like a blatant message emblazoned on a T-shirt.

He made her very aware of being the only female in the vicinity. He made her feel hot and rumpled and more annoyed than ever with her fumbling efforts to get into her own damned store.

She sneaked another glance. His head was still turned her way, and his coal-dark eyes skimmed once again down the length of her cotton jumpsuit and impractical high-heeled sandals.

She always wore shoes with ridiculous heels, because they made her feel thinner. And she needed all the help she could get as far as thinner went, Sophie concluded with a grimace, wishing right now that she was wearing army boots so she could land the lousy door a good one.

"Need any help with that lock?" he called in a conversational tone. Sophie didn't take her eyes from the door as she shook her head. "Curses on the stupid, obstinate bloody thing..." she muttered, and right then her door opened.

Sophie lurched into the shop. She left the door wide open behind her in an effort to banish the musty smell that always overpowered the subtle aromas of sachet and perfume when she opened the store each morning.

Bad smells bothered her, they always had, and she went to extreme lengths to make her environment sweet and fragrant. It was no simple task in this ancient building.

The phone on the counter was already ringing in strident bursts. Dumping her handbag on a delicate antique chair, Sophie snatched it up. "Unicorn, good morning," she purred into the receiver, belatedly remembering the dog mess outside, and realizing she ought to have left the door shut until she'd cleaned it. The smell was going to waft straight in....

"Sophie? Good morning, it's me." Sophie rolled her eyes heavenward and groped behind her for the stool she kept under the counter. It was wise to sit and try to relax, to strive for inner serenity when dealing with Bill Stanopoulis this early in the day.

It never worked, but she tried anyway. Bill was her part-time cutter and best sewer, a meticulous craftsman and creative genius who supervised the Sweat Shop three days a week.

The Sweat Shop was an attic loft in the old building just across the street. Sophie rented the space for a pittance, and Bill and an assistant cut and sewed her original creations amidst velour dust, fabric scraps and storms of cursing from Bill.

The man had a Greek temperament volatile enough to drive the Maharishi Mahesh Yogi to taking Valium. Sure, he was a marvel when it came to cutting more outfits than seemed possible out of one bolt of fabric, and he put them together flawlessly. But his demonic nature, especially first thing in the morning, made working with him next to impossible at times.

The reasons Sophie kept him on her payroll were simple: one, she knew her business would probably crumble without him; and two, ironically enough, during the two years he'd worked for her, he'd become her friend and sometime advisor.

When she needed someone to talk to, Bill listened and cared and gave good sound advice. He free-lanced as a cutter for other boutiques, as well as hers, and in the process picked up all sorts of business know-how that he passed on to Sophie.

Much of the time, however, he also did his incomparable best to drive her nuts.

"Sophie, my dear," he emoted now in his melodramatic fashion, "just we cut that special rush order, the blue silk with the hips, for this afternoon?" Bill's voice took on a martyred whine.

"Such hips, can those measurements be correct? One panel from each width of fabric is all I can get for these hips. I hope you charge this lady plenty more, Sophie, because I am using this whole bolt of silk to get this dress out, yes? And no sooner I finish cutting than would you believe it, there's a flaw, right in the front, just where her . . ."

Several anatomically descriptive words and a string of Greek curses followed. Sophie tried to remember if there was any more of that particular shade of blue silk in the back. She was almost certain there wasn't, and her heart sank.

"There's no more here, Bill, you'll have to go to the wholesalers. Pray that there's another bolt from the same dye lot down there."

Another burst of woe poured from the receiver.

"Bill, I'll check, but I'm sure that's the only piece I had."

He groaned, and Sophie shook her head at his dramatics. He could have had a wonderful stage career.

"We need another whole skirt length in order to make this dress, Sophie. Now I will have to go myself. This is a big waste of my time, and they won't sell two meters only. We will have to take at least seven." He made the journey sound like a three-day trek, when actually the fabric wholesalers were conveniently located a few blocks away from the Sweat Shop.

"I know it's a nuisance, Bill," she crooned in a soothing tone, closing her eyes and taking in deep cleansing breaths. "By the way, did Michelle come to work on time this morning?" Michelle was the latest young woman in the long stream of talented but elusive seamstresses.

It was at least enough to divert him from the blue silk. Bill raved on about Michelle arriving late today and leaving early yesterday, and the delivery from Leonard Fabrics not arriving at all. Sophie kept her eyes closed tightly and willed her shoulders to relax. After all, it was only shaping up to be a perfectly normal day in the boutique business.

"Hey, pretty lady." The deep voice interrupted the pathetic sounds Bill was making into her ear. "Think I could use that phone a minute, whenever you get finished there?"

Sophie's eyes popped open and she jumped. She stared into the mischievous twinkling eyes of the hunk who'd been on the motorcycle.

Up close, he had long curly eyelashes shading eyes almost, but not quite, black. There was a deep dimple in his square chin and a trace of five-o'clock shadow on his jaw, as if his beard grew in again the moment he shaved it off. He had a head of clean, shining, rumpled dark curls and a decidedly crooked nose.

The aura of sexuality Sophie had noticed before at a distance now wafted from him like potent male cologne.

Virile, macho, sexy her feminine instincts tabulated. Thirty-something and dangerous. Arrogant. Mocking. Earthy. Insensitive, her mind warned.

There was something a little intimidating about having him looming over her, and she got off the stool in a hurry.

He was much too . . . large . . . for her feminine store. Surrounded by silken clusters of rainbow-colored dresses and wispy lingerie draped in artful disarray on delicate chairs and old polished bureaus, he looked massive, although he was probably just over six feet tall. Which was massive enough when you were five feet five like she was.

"So what d'ya say?" His voice was pleasant, deep and sort of gravelly. "It's kind of an emergency, see, or I wouldn't bother ya," he added, sounding apologetic. Mock apologetic. His shining eyes still danced with suppressed humor.

She knew he was looking her over with careful attention to detail—little details like the way her smoke-gray cotton jumpsuit clung to her rounded curves. His gaze seemed to linger on those areas like fingers stroking. Sophie tried to hold her tummy in.

He was rude, staring like that. But Sophie couldn't stop her own eyes from wandering.

His pants were far too tight. It was scandalous. How could he even sit down in jeans like that...hadn't he read that tight underwear could make a man impotent? Or was it sterile?

Something told her that this particular man had neither of those problems. Maybe—she gulped—maybe he wasn't even wearing underwear. There was hardly room.

"Sophie? Sophie, are you still there?" Bill's aggrieved tones echoed out of the mouthpiece of the phone she still held, and Sophie realized he'd been sputtering off and on for several long minutes.

"The fabric, Sophie," Bill was snarling. "You want I should go for it now, then say so why don't you? Three times I ask you already, this is a big waste of my time."

"Uh, look, Bill, I'll have to call you back, okay? There's someone . . ."

With a final expletive, Bill hung up in her ear, and Sophie winced and replaced the receiver, sliding the instrument across to where the man lounged, his huge hands—dirty hands, she noticed with prim disapproval—propped on each corner of her fake marble counter. One thick eyebrow crooked as he ignored the phone and went on studying her at his leisure.

"My phone isn't hooked up yet next door," he confided.

"Your, uh, your phone?" The meaning of his words were slow to sink in. "You mean you're the one who rented the place next door?" She sounded just as dumbfounded as she felt.

"Yeah, I ordered a phone hookup two weeks ago, but you know B.C. Tel. They have a monopoly, no use arguing with them." He shrugged wide shoulders, making his astonishing muscles move beneath the white T-shirt. He talked fast, and he sounded tough. Street tough. East side tough.

"So you don't mind then, if I use your phone?"

Sophie shook her head, waving a hand with expansive generosity in the direction of the phone between them. He gave her another cheerful, lopsided grin.

"Thanks. By the way, my name's Rio, Rio Agostini. It's actually Mario, but only my grandmother calls me that." The devastating grin came and went. "Especially when she's mad at me."

Agostini? Italian. Ravioli, spaghetti. Was he opening a restaurant? Not in this building. He'd need clearance from the health department, which would be impossible.

Maybe a shoe store? He was wearing expensive leather boots. But there already was a shoe store. Adam Kelly, Sophie's business neighbor to the east, owner of Kelly's Quality Footwear, was under the delusion that he sold shoes.

"Pleased to meet ya," Rio said. He rubbed a hand down his pant leg and extended it to her. His grin widened.

"How do you do, Mr. Agostini?" Sophie's soft, manicured fingers were engulfed by rough calluses and smears of what she thought could only be grease. He didn't let go in what she considered an appropriate time, either.

In fact, his handshake was giving her goose bumps. She gave a slight tug, and another one, firmer this time, and he finally released her. But he looked more amused than ever when she stepped back too fast and banged an elbow on the wall behind her.

"I'm doin' just great, Miss-Mrs.-Ms . . . ?"

He was teasing her.

"Larson," she blurted. "Sophie Larson."

"Mrs. Sophie? Miss Sophie? Ms Sophie?"

"Ms," she said with firm emphasis. Sophie had always hated Ms as a form of address. It was clumsy, affected and hard to pronounce, but she used it anyway.

"What, eh, what sort of business are you in, Mr. Agostini?"

"Rio," he corrected. "We're gonna be neighbors, Sophie, so first names, okay? And anyhow, Mr. Agostini was my grandfather. I'm too young to be Mr. Agostini."

He flashed that grin again, but his eyes were saying something quite different and again Sophie felt hot. Flustered.

"I'm in bikes, sales and repairs. That's why I need to borrow your phone, see. I'm expecting a shipment any minute now, and I wanna tell them to use the alley entrance."

A bike shop next door. She felt keen disappointment for a moment. It wasn't at all what she'd hoped for. She'd wanted something that would complement her boutique, like Jessica's jewelry and old furniture had, but . . . oh, well. She had a five-speed herself that she rode now and then.

Bikes would attract a different clientele to the neighborhood, that was certain. A more sporty sort. Maybe she could put in a small line of Lycra stretch shorts.

"Bikes," she repeated like an idiot.

"Yup, bikes." He winked at her. With two long, stained fingers, he carefully lifted the receiver of her ornate white-and-gold candlestick phone and, with ludicrous care, tapped out the numbers.

She watched in helpless fascination as his eyes narrowed and grew serious. A brisk businesslike tone filtered into his deep voice as the connection was made.

"Frankie? Hey, Frankie, it's me, Rio. Yeah, you, too. Listen up, Frankie, I want you to come down Hastings and then turn onto Cardero with that load. And Frankie, get the lead out, I've been waiting half an hour already; time's money."

Sophie edged out from behind the counter, retrieved her handbag from the chair near the door and hurried through the back room to the tiny bathroom stuck far in a corner. The deep reverberations of Rio's voice grew fainter as she moved farther away.

She shut the door behind her and clicked on the overhead bulb, studying herself in the smoky mirror over the washbasin.

Her blue-gray eyes stared back at her, maybe a trifle wider than usual, but still just her own ordinary eyes, outlined with subtle care by brown liner and dusty pink eyeshadow. She could tell where she'd used the contouring powder that was supposed to make her cheeks look like Cher's. Damn stuff was a waste of money and time.

Her lips were still a natural rosy pink, just the way she'd glossed them earlier. Yup, her face was exactly the way it had been when she left her apartment. The thick brown mop of curls was just as hopeless as ever, looking as if a brush wouldn't begin to go through the jumbled mass.

Sophie stared back at the same Sophie she'd encountered in the mirror all of her twenty-eight years. Just for a minute there, when Rio'd looked at her that way, she'd had the definite feeling that she'd suddenly grown irresistible, gorgeous even, with bigger eyes, fuller lips, smaller nose, sunken cheeks; but here she was, as ordinary as ever. A reasonable face, but unremarkable.

What a letdown.

Rio Agostini had probably practiced that simmering, seductive look of his in a mirror from the age of three. He probably made an avocation of charming women out of their . . . socks. He'd sure managed to do something to her, right down to the toes of her tummy-control panty hose.

Having him right next door every business day was going to be a trial, she could see that already. Well, she'd just have to do the best she could and not get involved.

She'd have to make sure she was cool, professional and businesslike every single minute he was around. That way, he'd never suspect the effect he had on her. She searched for the proper word to describe what Rio affected.

Gonads sounded right. Did women have gonads? If so, Rio affected hers in a way they'd never been affected before.

A loud knock on the bathroom door scared her almost witless.

"Hey, Sophie? Sorry to bother you, but there's a lady out here in your store who needs something," Rio's voice boomed.

Sophie tugged her jumpsuit into certain areas and out of others and ripped open the bathroom door.

He was standing some distance away now, in the dim back room beside the battered old table. He was eyeing with curiosity the bolts of fabric, stacks of patterns and miscellaneous odds and ends her business accumulated, and he jumped a little himself when she bounded out the door.

He lowered his tone to a conspirational near-whisper.

"Sorry to bug you, Sophie, but I didn't want to just leave the joint with her in here. After all, your cash drawer's right there and everything, wide open. I've got to get back and check on my place, and you just never know with people."

He acted as if her customers regularly robbed her while she was in the bathroom.

What kind of people did this Rio Agostini associate with, anyway, she wondered as he moved away from her in that forceful way he had, talking all the while.

"Thanks for the use of your phone, Sophie. I'll be right next door from now on, so if anything comes up, just holler."

Now why didn't that give her a feeling of security?

"Also, there was one hell of a mess on the sidewalk outside your front door. Dog mess. I cleaned it up before somebody stepped in it."

He was so casual it took a moment to register, and then she was dumbfounded that he'd do such a kind thing for her.

Before she could even thank him, he was gone.

BY QUARTER TO ELEVEN, Sophie had calmed Bill down and sent him for the blue silk, sold a bias-cut linen skirt, size small, and taken an order for an eggshell camisole to match, size large.

Some women had all the breaks. Skinny little bottoms, generous tops.

She'd tidied two racks of satin blouses that refused to stay on their hangers and was boiling the kettle in the back room for a cup of lemon spice herbal tea to go with her muffin, when an outrageous racket began in the alley.

It sounded like several airplane engines being revved up over and over again prior to takeoff. The sudden intensity of the noise made her drop her favorite black enameled Chinese teapot.

The pot didn't break, thank goodness. It landed on a pile of fabric scraps, but Sophie's heart stopped for a moment when she saw it sailing toward the floor.

She tore open the back door and looked into the narrow alley, then stood frozen in disbelief.

A cavernous truck was parked a few feet away, a wooden ramp clinging to its open back end. Down the ramp three men were wheeling a parade of motorcycles, red, blue, black, silver, large, small, medium.

Motorcycles were leaning against the brick warehouse that backed the alley, leaning against her garbage cans, leaning against her wall.

A fat individual with greasy red hair in a braid down his back and mirrored silver sunglasses was perched on a long, sleek machine right there by her back steps, revving the engine into the ear-splitting cacophony of sound that had made her drop the teapot in the first place. Another skinny youth with a red bandanna tied around his head sat on a second roaring machine.

Dust was swirling everywhere, and the smell of exhaust and gasoline filled the hot summer morning, making Sophie want to retch.

Rio Agostini was nowhere to be seen, and no one even noticed her standing there. As soon as she could make herself move, Sophie stepped back inside and slammed her door, collapsing against it for a moment as she fully understood at last just what sort of business was about to move in and operate right next door to her Unicorn.

He sold and serviced *motorcycles*. Great, noisy, smelly, dirty motorcycles that attracted great, noisy, smelly, dirty men—motorcycle gang members, who were bound to frighten Sophie's small clientele of genteel female customers right out of shopping in her store.

Motorcycle gang members grouped in front of the building would be enough to frighten women right off the entire block. They'd whistle and leer and make crude remarks. There'd be dirt everywhere and disgusting odors. She struggled to add to the list, but her mind boggled.

All she could visualize with any degree of clarity was a scene made up of those two caricatures in the alley, lounging in front of the Unicorn instead of behind it in their soiled white undershirts and black leather pants, slouching against her portion of the brick wall, ruining the clean, green effect of the two tubs of geraniums she'd placed on either side of her door, destroying the sparse, elegant and sensual impact she tried for with her window display.

It was bad enough having Kelly's Quality Footwear on one side, with its unwashed window and general air of neglect. But this. Bad language, grease, wolf whistles. Noise, smell, chaos.

It was the end of an era. The end of her two-year struggle to make the Unicorn a quality place to shop.

With shaking hands, Sophie filled her teapot and sank into the comforting old armchair she kept in the back room, trying to figure out what to do and wishing she hadn't finished off the bottle of sherry a satisfied customer had given her last Christmas.

She unwrapped her extralarge blueberry muffin and took a comforting bite. With the first swallow, the phone rang. Sophie snatched up the extension beside her, hoping it would be someone she could talk this whole mess over with, someone with a cool head, a rapier-sharp mind. Or maybe it was Bill, who'd scream and rant right along with her.

She chewed and swallowed too soon.

She needed someone who knew a good, inexpensive lawyer. Was that a contradiction in terms?

"Unicorn?"

Her hopes disintegrated when her mother's well-modulated, businesslike voice said, "It's me, dear. It sounds as if you're chewing. Are you having an early lunch?"

It was ironic, but Harriet Larson did have a cool head, a rapier-sharp mind, and without doubt, she'd know a good, inexpensive lawyer if such a creature actually existed. The problem was, Sophie had never been able to talk over any sort of mess with her mother and feel relieved after the conversation. She always ended up feeling inadequate and responsible for the problem instead.

Harriet had been a good mother. She'd been a single parent, and she'd provided well for Sophie, but somehow conversations with Harriet always left Sophie convinced that the two of them had boarded separate trains by accident and were heading in opposite directions while they tried to wave at each other through the windows.

Sophie still couldn't help blurting out her feelings, however. She'd never been good at hiding how she really felt.

"Mom, this terrible thing is happening. The empty space beside me, where Jessica used to be? Well, a motorcycle gang is moving in, right this very moment."

Harriet made a sound somewhere between a sigh and an exclamation of annoyance.

"Well, Sophie, I did warn you when you insisted on renting in that area that the zoning wasn't nearly strict enough. Location is absolutely everything in real estate, and that area leaves a great deal to be desired."

"Mom." Impatience filled Sophie's voice. "I'm not talking about real estate. I'm telling you about this man called Rio Agostini who sells motorcycles. At this very moment, he's moving in right next door to my boutique. He's probably going to ruin my business."

"Have you called city hall?"

"Mom, for heaven's sake. What is city hall going to do about it? He'd have to have taken out a license, and there's no law against opening a business. The point is he's going to attract the wrong sort of people to the area."

"Exactly. Which is why I suggested renting space in a decent area with reasonable zoning laws instead of a downtown retail slum. Zoning would have prevented this from happening."

Sophie sighed. Her mother could turn a discussion about hem lengths into a real estate issue.

"Mom, you know I couldn't possibly afford the rent in another area, and this building suits me fine. It's near the downtown core of the city, all the fabric wholesalers are down here, it's easy for me to get to work on the bus, and Bill lives nearby. Besides," she added with defiance, "I happen to love it here. My place has more character than a dozen of those new concrete monstrosities developers keep putting up."

"Perhaps this is grounds for breaking your lease," Harriet said next, and Sophie rolled her eyes heavenward in exasperation.

It was the same old story. Her mother wasn't really hearing anything she said.

Sophie heard the bell tinkle over the front door. Two women had just entered the store.

Saved by the bell.

"Gotta go, Mom, customers. I'll call you later."

"There must be something we can do about this, Sophie. Leave it with me," Harriet advised.

Sophie found herself wondering why she'd said anything to her mother in the first place. Her entire body felt tense.

"Right, Mom," she snapped. "Bye."

The two well-dressed women now flicking through the clothing on the racks had been in several times before, although they had never bought anything. Sophie pasted a smile on lips that protested, and walked out front to greet them.

"Morning," she purred. "Can I be . . ."

A prolonged, ominous roar from the street drowned out the rest of her inquiry, sending her and the women hurrying to the front window.

Three motorcycles had just pulled up to the curb, motors thrumming. The noise died as the riders dismounted, propping their steeds with expert care on kickstands, laughing raucously and calling greetings to Rio, who came ambling across the sidewalk to greet them with handshakes and shoulder punches. A smear of grease now stretched diagonally across the back of his white T-shirt, and Sophie couldn't help noticing how narrow his waist and buttocks looked in comparison to his shoulders.

"Bikers," one of the ladies exclaimed in horror. Rio caught sight of Sophie in the window just then and waved before he and his companions disappeared next door.

"You don't actually know them, do you, dear?" Sophie's customer raised manicured eyebrows in disapproval.

"Do you think my car will be safe parked on the street in this neighborhood, Marge?" her plump companion asked.

Before Sophie could reassure her, two more motorcycles pulled up to the curb, this time right in front of the boutique. The riders got off, and turned to stare at something just out of range of Sophie's window.

A series of wolf whistles sounded.

A young woman in a miniskirt, making her way down the sidewalk, no doubt on her lunch hour and heading to the Unicorn to buy something expensive, now turned around fast, crossed to the opposite sidewalk and hurried away.

Another bike roared up.

"Well, dear, personally I think you should call the police," Marge suggested to Sophie. "They must be having one of those rallies. I saw something like this on TV about motorcycle gangs. They wrecked the building."

"Marge, let's go," the other urged. "George will have a coronary if my new car gets vandalized. Besides, I don't feel safe in this area now," she whined.

The sound of a hammer pounding on metal began next door and went on and on, resounding through the wall.

"There you go, now they're disturbing the peace, that's against the law, isn't it? I'm telling you dear, if I were you, I'd phone the police," Marge insisted much more emphatically to Sophie.

"I would, but I don't quite know yet what law they're breaking," Sophie said a trifle sharper than she intended. "Disturbing the peace has to take place after a certain time of night, I think."

"There must be a noise bylaw, or something. Surely there must be rules that keep riffraff like that off the streets." Marge sniffed. "I mean, this isn't exactly Gastown, but even in a rundown area like this. . . ."

Sophie's sense of outrage and anger at what was going on next door expanded to include irritation with Marge. The woman was beginning to sound like an echo of Harriet. Besides, Sophie had seen the disdainful way she'd lifted the corner of a skirt and then raised her eyebrows in significant comment at the price tag a few moments ago, as if Sophie had no right to charge fair prices for what she sold. And the skirt was fully lined raw silk, with beautiful detailing on the slash pockets.

"I think I'll have to wait until they actually commit a crime to call the cops, don't you agree?" she purred now.

"Well, you do whatever you like," Marge huffed. "It's your business, I'm sure. Although what kind of customers you'll get with that going on next door, I'd hate to say. C'mon, Sandra, let's drive over to that little place on Granville Street I was telling you about."

The two stout backsides waddled out the door, and Sophie's heart sank. There was more than a little truth in obnoxious Marge's comments about the kind of customers who'd now come to the Unicorn.

The hammering next door stopped, and the sound of an engine being revved up over and over came through the wall, punctuated with loud male laughter.

Sophie could smell exhaust. She could almost see it, wafting through the cracks and infiltrating every silken fold of every precious garment, smothering the subtle and delightful aromas of lavender sachet, perfumed oils and small jars of scent she secreted all around her store.

She balled her hands into fists, squared her shoulders and marched out her front door. It took only fifteen long, determined strides to reach the newly installed window that read Freedom Machines; Motorcycle Sales and Repairs.

Freedom machines. Sophie snorted aloud.

Two workmen were now fitting wide double doors into the hole where Jessica's lovely old oak door had been. Sophie sailed past the workers, squinting her eyes against the noxious vapor of cigarette smoke that hung in the air. Jessica's quiet, orderly, sweet-smelling store was gone forever.

Desecration was proceeding rapidly. Men were putting up metal shelves along the walls on either side. Others were ripping up the soft gray carpeting Jessica had laid. One man, high on a ladder, was busy installing horrible fluorescent track lighting. The back of the place had been transformed into a workshop, with a long tool bench and millions of foreign objects strewn over it.

That's where Rio was.

The hubbub of male voices quieted as Sophie marched the entire length of the building, straight over to where he crouched with his back to her, peering at something on the side of a dismantled motorcycle.

When she spoke, Sophie's voice was louder than she'd intended, but she was mad enough not to give a damn.

"You, Mr. Rio, Rio Agostini. I want to talk to you."

He turned his head, raising his expressive eyebrows and gave her that charming white-toothed grin, only now it looked more like a leer. He rose to his feet in one easy motion, rubbing his palms down the sides of his jeans.

"Sure, Sophie. Hey, my pleasure. You can talk to me anytime you like, my place or yours," he said, with such innuendo his male audience let forth a barrage of whistles and catcalls, and Sophie's hands tingled with the urge to sock Mr. Rio Agostini right on his crooked nose.

For the first time in her life, she truly understood the emotions that provoked physical violence. She felt the frustration of being a female who'd never socked anybody in her whole life and wouldn't know how to begin to do a good job of it.

She also realized that she couldn't take even a verbal strip off a man playing with such blatant confidence to this entourage of male morons.

"Outside," she spat through her clenched teeth. "I'll see you outside, Agostini."

The audience applauded as she stomped past Rio towards the back door.

2

RIO CLOSED THE BACK DOOR behind them and followed Sophie's engaging figure down the rickety wooden stairs and into the narrow alley, already sorry for what he'd done to her in there.

He should never have teased her in front of all those guys. It wasn't fair. He'd sensed earlier that she was shy, and he might have known she'd blush that way. Maybe he was just too used to females who enjoyed being the center of attention, enjoyed being the object of sexual innuendo.

This lady was different. He'd flirted in a mild way with her that morning, and instead of flirting back, she'd been almost bashful. None of the women he'd known recently were anything like bashful.

Bashful was a whole new breed for him.

Sophie intrigued Rio. There was an indefinable something about her that suggested a subtle, powerful sensuality.

Maybe it was the slow, deliberate way she moved, or the way her full bottom lip curved in a provocative pout. She wasn't beautiful, but he'd learned the hard way that beautiful wasn't always the way to go. He'd been married to, and divorced from, beautiful.

He found himself more than a little attracted to this lady.

She whipped around now to face him, and scarlet color stained her cheeks. Anger shimmered in her soft eyes, and Rio felt rotten all of a sudden.

"Hey, hey, Sophie..." he began, reaching out to take her shoulders, to touch her, calm her down, apologize.

But she stepped back out of his reach, and her voice was trembling with the force of her anger.

"Don't 'hey, Sophie' me. You haven't any right to do this to me, you know," she accused.

"Yeah, I'm sorry about what I said in there—" Rio began, rubbing a contrite hand through his hair.

"What you said in there was bad enough, but that's not what I'm talking about. It's what you're doing with this business of yours that's making me crazy, Rio Agostini." Sophie drew a deep and quivering breath and hurried on. "You're successfully ruining my trade in a single day with your—your idiotic freedom machines, or whatever you call them. Roaring up and down in front of my store all morning, whistling and catcalling at women who come to the Unicorn on their lunch hour . . . those Cro-Magnon friends of yours are scaring all my customers away. They'd scare away lady wrestlers, for heaven's sake."

Rio almost grinned at that, but he controlled himself.

Good thing, too, because it seemed that Sophie had only started telling him off.

"The stink, I can't believe that awful stink. It comes right through the wall, you know." She nodded twice. "Yes, and now all my stock is starting to smell of exhaust, and—and grease . . . and oil. . . ." She wrinkled her nose in disgust and waved a distracted hand at him, as if the offending smell was wafting from his body right this minute.

Rio moved back a step and caught himself surreptitiously sniffing in an attempt to find out how bad he really did smell.

"And the noise . . . it's like being next to an airplane runway. I can't even talk to my customers over the roaring of those motors you're testing. Or whatever you're doing in there." She stopped for breath. She felt as if she'd been running hard and couldn't get enough oxygen.

Rio stared at her in amazement. He hadn't given a moment's thought to the effect his business might have on hers. With the single-minded determination he applied to everything, he'd planned and schemed and pinched pennies to start a business.

He'd been racing around like a maniac today, getting the last-minute details ironed out so his dream would run as smoothly as he could manage. And right here, day one, he'd created serious problems with a neighbor, one of the very first things his professor in business admin had warned against.

Son of a gun.

"I'm sorry," he repeated again, but it sounded halfhearted even to him.

It was, too. He felt like a balloon with the air hissing out full speed.

She was panting, and she gave a sniff as if her nose was starting to run.

She sniffed, and sniffed again, and in a childlike gesture that reminded Rio with poignant force of his five-year-old daughter, Sophie scrubbed at her nose with the back of her hand.

All he could do was repeat, "God, Sophie, I am sorry. I had no idea, I guess I didn't think...."

She was glaring at him again. She placed her hands on her hips aggressively and drawled in a sarcastic tone, "So, besides being sorry, what are you going to do about it?"

She was infuriating and funny and ridiculous all at the same time, and he had an overpowering urge to kiss her, to find out what that sensuous mouth with its pouting lower lip felt like under his.

Careful, Agostini. High-handed macho wouldn't work on this lady.

He studied her. She wasn't very tall. The top of her head probably reached just past his chin, and her luxurious breasts moved against the thin gray material of her jumpsuit, nipples showing in clear relief through the cloth.

Man, she didn't stink at all. She smelled like... he sorted out different smells and settled on vanilla, remembering it from the favorite cookies his mother made. Her wild, curling hair reached her shoulders and seemed to stand on end with the force of her emotion. Bits of it were gleaming with golden highlights in the afternoon sun.

He wanted to touch it.

Rio's body reacted even as his brain was still wrestling with the business problems she'd presented. He registered the hot compelling urge of desire in his groin, and did his best to subdue it.

Terrific. He had a problem here and all he could do was lust after Sophie. This was strictly business. A good business relationship with his neighbors was essential if his working days were to be pleasant.

"Tell you what I'll do," he said with deliberation, while he sorted out possible solutions to the problems she'd outlined and shifted from one foot to the other, hoping his erection wasn't that noticeable.

"What I'll do first is put heavy insulation on the wall we share in the building, to cut down as much as possible on noise and, uh, smell."

Sophie looked surprised, as if she really hadn't expected him to do anything practical at all. She also kept her eyes above chest level, because an accidental glance lower had deepened the flush on her face.

"I can't very well order the guys to stop whistling at women. It's kind of a natural instinct, see, but I will warn them not to harass any of your customers, if you think that'll help, Sophie." He paused and waited, and she gave a tiny, tentative nod.

"And I'll put a sign in front that encourages parking bikes in the alley behind the store, if you think that might work? In fact, I'll tell the guys in there—" he tipped his head toward his back door "—to move their machines back here right away."

This time the nod was more definite.

"Today's sort of special, see, the place opening for business and all that, so a lot of buddies of mine're around today who won't be here on your average business day," he added in a confiding way. "It'll be lots quieter from here on in. Promise."

Her chin was losing a little of its stubborn thrust.

"See, I really want us to be friends and good neighbors, Sophie." He tried a small grin on her, but there was no response. "I'll do what I can about the things you've mentioned, and if anything else bothers you, just let me know."

This time his best smile brought a tiny, answering tilt to her full mouth.

"I can't promise miracles, but I'll do my best to fix any problems that come up."

She seemed to be thinking that over.

"I guess that's all I can ask for," she said in a small, husky voice. She met his gaze and their eyes locked for long seconds. Then she turned away and, without another word, hurried over to the steps leading to her own back door.

Rio watched as she climbed them, and when she disappeared into her store, he released his pent up breath in a protracted silent whistle.

She had the most beautiful eyes, soft and almost fearful. A guy could swim in eyes like that. They begged you to protect her, those eyes.

Ah, come clean, Agostini.

She also had the most beautiful ass, an ass with lush rounded curves like women were meant to have instead of the tight little angles and planes they seemed to aspire to have nowadays.

She was one hell of a sexy lady. The fullness in his groin was still an uncomfortable reminder that his body had known that even before it registered in his brain.

He told himself he'd have to start wearing looser jeans if he was going to be around Sophie Larson every single working day. And he'd better start using stronger deodorant, as well.

He pictured the way her nose had wrinkled in disgust when she complained about the smell.

Rio sniffed at his armpit, shrugged and took the back stairs into his premises in two easy leaps, whistling a cheerful tune.

Deodorant, great. But he'd be damned if he'd resort to any of those phony perfumes television ads were pushing all the time. He wouldn't use them, even in the interests of good business relations with Sophie.

Men should smell like men.

SOPHIE ENDED THE LONG DAY as she always did, watering the spindly geraniums in her outside tube, locking the front door and putting the sign up, running over the carpet with the sweeper, and then sitting down in the back room and beginning the dreaded task of recording the day's meager sales in the ledger, along with the copious expenses.

She made herself another cup of lemon tea, wishing she had a cookie or something to fill the emptiness in her stomach. Bookkeeping always made her hungry.

Grappling with the ledger was harder than ever tonight because her mind wasn't on the numbers at all. The handsome, mischievous face and hard-muscled body of Rio Agostini kept appearing in her mind's eye.

After their conversation that afternoon, there'd been a definite improvement next door, from Sophie's point of view. The noise level had dropped, although bursts of hearty male laughter and wisps of foul odors had continued to seep through the adjoining wall at intervals.

But the bikes strewn in haphazard disarray along the curb in front of the Unicorn had one by one been moved into the alley and carefully parked clear of her back entrance. There hadn't been any more catcalling at her customers. Of course, there hadn't exactly been a stampede to whistle at, either. Sales were down.

But Rio'd surprised her. She hadn't expected him to take her complaints to heart or do anything about them. It made her a little uncomfortable to admit even to herself how many preconceived and nasty prejudices she had about men who rode motorcycles and wore tight jeans.

Rio, at least, was beginning to seem both intelligent and reasonable, traits which, Sophie pondered, she hadn't found often even in the more sophisticated men she'd dated.

Who was she kidding? She wasn't an expert on the modern North American male by any standards. She'd dated only one man in the past year and had decided several months before that he wasn't worth the energy it took to turn herself into the kind of woman he'd seemed to want. The kind of woman Sophie had trouble pretending to be—svelte, sophisticated, upwardly mobile. A woman willing to turn herself upside down so she'd match his fantasy, who was ready at the drop of a lift ticket to take off skiing at some resort for a week just because he was suddenly free, while he thought nothing of canceling out on a dinner party she'd planned weeks in advance.

Why did men always seem to want her to do all the giving, all the changing?

It was obvious she attracted the wrong kind of men.

She took a gulp of tea, trying to get her mind off her failed romance and back to the messy page of figures in front of her.

She bit the end of the pencil and frowned. She should have known right from the beginning what a romance with a real estate man would consist of: canceled dates, weekends alone, everything dependent on the pager he took with him everywhere.

She ought to have known. After all, hadn't Sophie grown up with a mother who breathed, ate and slept real estate deals, who thought nothing of interrupting a birthday celebration for her daughter in order to go and show a house to a person who had no intention of buying it anyway?

Memories of her childhood always made her hungry.

Sophie tossed the pencil down in exasperation and reached under the stack of patterns on the corner of the table. She'd secreted half a candy bar there a day or two ago in case of emergency, under an empty box to keep it away from the mice.

There it was. She peeled back the wrapper and took a small bite, savoring the taste of chocolate and nuts and gooey sweetness, and the sense of comfort chocolate always seemed to provide.

A sudden banging on the back door made her jump. Swallowing fast, she stuffed the remaining candy bar back into its hiding place and swiped at her mouth with a fabric scrap to remove any telltale traces of chocolate.

The banging came again, and she pulled back the bolt and opened the door.

Rio stood there, looking self-conscious and a little embarrassed. In one large hand he clutched a bouquet of roses, some red, some pink, with three huge yellow blossoms completing the assortment. With the other arm he cradled a bulky brown paper bag.

"Here," he said, shoving the flowers at her. "An apology?" There was a boyish shyness in his voice and in his gesture.

She used both hands to take the bouquet, which had clumsy gobs of white tissue wadded around the stems. She couldn't resist burying her nose in the satiny petals, breathing in the delicate scent. She looked over the flowers at Rio.

He had tiny specks of gold in the pupils of his dark eyes.

"I love roses. How did you know?"

He shrugged and looked pleased with himself. "Lucky guess. So can I come in, d'you think? This's hot," he said, indicating the bag. Sophie hesitated, but then stepped back from the door. He strode in and plunked the bag on the table next to her open ledger.

"Doin' the books, huh?" He flipped the account ledger shut. "Time for a break." He reached into the bag and extracted a bottle of wine, two plastic glasses and several fat deli containers that began to fill the air with a mouth-watering aroma.

Sophie watched, spellbound, as he pried open the lids with a flourish, revealing a tempting array of small hot sausage rolls, miniature pizzas, tiny meat pies and a small container of olives, as well as thin slices of green melon.

He pulled a Swiss army knife from the back pocket of his jeans, extracted the corkscrew with one deft flick of his thumb and opened the wine with practiced ease. He poured several ounces into each glass, holding one out to Sophie.

She was still standing in a daze by the door, clutching the roses. Things were moving too fast.

She found a jar and went into the washroom to fill it with water, wondering what she ought to do next.

She was all alone with the front door locked, and she hardly knew this man at all.

It was the classic scenario her mother had warned against the whole time Sophie was growing up in the big city.

"Rapists don't always look like rapists, Sophie. They can look like someone's Uncle George; you have to be on guard. Don't put yourself in vulnerable situations."

Rio didn't resemble anyone's Uncle George by a long shot. And would a rapist with delusions of murder go to all the trouble of bringing flowers, food and wine?

It didn't seem logical, so when she came out, she set the jar of roses on the table and accepted the glass of wine he was still holding.

He'd turned a paint-stained wooden chair around so the seat was facing him. He was straddling it with casual grace, jeans tight on his thighs, boots propped on the rungs, and bare, muscular arms resting on the back. He had a small anchor tattooed on his right bicep. Sophie realized she was staring at it and forced herself to look away.

He raised his glass to her and then to the flowers.

"Nice posies, huh? I sent Elmer over to swipe them from my aunt's garden. She lives on Main Street, not far from here.

She never uses them for anything—they just end up rotting in her yard," he confided. "Anyhow, I phoned and told her I took 'em. Had to promise to fix the taps in her bathroom as payment, too."

He studied Sophie for a moment, and she was glad she'd brushed her hair and put on fresh lip gloss.

"I've caused you a rough day," he said in a penitent tone. "So tell me, do you figure we can ever be friends after this, Sophie?" There was both bravado and a touching kind of shy appeal in his words and in the expression on his face.

She stared at him, and at last something inside her relaxed. He was outrageous. He was honest and exciting. He'd knocked her so far off guard, she hadn't once pretended to be anything she wasn't around him.

She slumped into the old armchair, balancing her wine with care, and a tiny giggle escaped her, followed by another.

He'd sent someone called Elmer over to swipe flowers from his own aunt's garden? Maybe his uncle owned a deli, and Elmer had raided that, as well.

He gave her a wide smile and a questioning look, and took a drink from his glass.

"So what's funny?" he wanted to know.

"You're a crazy person, Rio Agostini, do you know that?" She took a large swallow of her wine, choking as the tangy dryness caught in her throat and then slid down in a cool rush.

One of his eyebrows shot up, and his grin grew more confident. "Hey, my sanity's not the issue here at all, lady," he drawled. "I asked you if we were friends, my mental state has nothin' to do with that. Some of my best friends are maniacs. So are we friends?"

He leaned over and picked up the Styrofoam container of sausage rolls. "Eat, it helps when there's a big decision to be made," he commanded, and she reached for one. He went on holding the box out to her.

"There's nothing to them, take three," he ordered. "I'm always starving at this time of day, aren't you?"

When she took one more, he added another and then scooped at least five into his own broad palm and transferred them to his mouth one after another as if they were peanuts, chewing and swallowing with such obvious off-hand enjoyment that Sophie was intrigued.

She tried to nibble with dainty little bites at the tidbits she held, but after the first wonderful taste, she gave up and demolished the rolls almost as fast as he did, taking sips of wine between bites and reveling in the combination of flaky pastry and spicy sausage.

Rio poured more wine for both of them, and together they shared several of the other delicacies without talking much.

Sophie had always been self-conscious and constrained when a social occasion with a man involved eating; she wasn't anywhere near fat, but she had ten or twelve pounds here and there that weren't necessary in a technical sense.

And she was aware—who wasn't these days?—that society revered a bone-thin silhouette on a woman. As a result, Sophie never ate anywhere near what her appetite demanded when she was on a date. She admitted to herself it was a deluded attempt at making the man believe she suffered a glandular imbalance, but she still did it. And without being obvious about it, none of the men had ever encouraged her to eat.

Certainly not the real estate salesman, anyway. He'd made pointed comments about diet groups.

But Rio seemed to expect her to share a good portion of the feast he'd brought. And for some weird reason, she didn't feel at all embarrassed about eating with him.

Maybe it was because she had positive proof that he found her attractive. Of course she'd noticed his reaction to her that afternoon, even through her anger. How could she not notice, given the fit of his jeans.

It had both shocked and pleased her, that visible sexual response. It was a silent admission that he found her desirable just as she was.

And so Sophie ate with him, relishing every bite.

When all the food was gone, they started talking, and Sophie lounged back in the comfortable chair, one leg tucked under her, shoes off and at ease.

Rio's chin rested on his crossed arms, and a peaceful, warm ambience seemed to permeate the tiny room.

"How long you had the store here, Sophie?" he asked.

"Just over two years. I signed a five-year lease, and told myself that's how long I'd give the Unicorn to be successful."

"And? How's it going?"

If her mother had asked that question, Sophie would have felt her defenses rise like battlements. But for some reason, Rio's question didn't seem threatening to her at all, and she answered him with an honesty that surprised her.

"Not well at all." She wrinkled her nose and shook her head. "There's so many hidden expenses in business that I didn't know about, taxes and shipping charges on my fabric and continual upkeep on my space in this building. It's hard to afford enough stock after all that's paid. Plus I have to rent part of the warehouse across the street as a place to get the clothing made that I sell, and I hire two people part-time to cut and sew, Bill Stanopoulis and Michelle Dover." She shrugged and sipped the last drops of her wine. "There never seems to be enough to go around at the end of the month. In fact, about the third week of each month I start having nightmares about having to declare bankruptcy because I can't meet all my expenses."

For heaven's sake, the wine must be loosening her tongue. That was more than she'd planned to reveal to anyone, much less a man she'd known less than a day.

But he understood. "When the rate of bankruptcy for small businesses runs about ninety percent the way it does," he commented, "nightmares are the norm, all right. But it's no disgrace to try and then fail, either." He glanced over his shoulder and through the doorway at her darkening store. "Looks like you're doing all you can. You've made this place real appealing. I don't know much about women's stuff, but the things you're selling look great to me. And the fact that you've managed to keep going for two years impresses the hell out of me." He shook his head. "I was shaking when I signed that five-year lease of mine, I'll tell ya. It's a big decision, opening a business. I wouldn't have taken the chance if I were still married, with a mortgage and everything. As it is, I worked at a construction job until I had enough put away to meet my support and alimony payments for a full year."

He'd seemed such a free spirit, Sophie hadn't given any thought to whether or not he was married. The casual reference to support and alimony shook her in a way she didn't care to examine.

"You're . . . divorced then, Rio?"

He nodded. "Yeah, long time. Five years now. I got a kid." He reached into his rear pocket and shuffled through his wallet, pulled out a plastic folder stuffed with pictures and handed it over to Sophie. Pride was evident in his voice. "Her name's Melissa. I call her Missy. She's five. I don't see her as much as I'd like."

Sophie loved looking at photos of children and trying to guess what kind of adults they'd become.

"Oh, she's gorgeous." The words were no empty compliment. The child in the pictures was adorable, with huge, questioning dark eyes and a sweet little triangular face. She had long curls cascading over the shoulders of a frilly white lace dress. She looked like a life-size doll.

"How come you don't see her much? Doesn't she live in Vancouver?"

"Yeah, in the West End. Her mother figures I don't take proper care of Missy when I've got her. I let her get dirty and all that. Carol believes a little girl needs to spend most of her time with her mother."

Sophie figured the woman was dead wrong, but she didn't say so. She went on looking at the pictures in silence. The thing that she found surprising was that in every single photo, and the assortment seemed to span her entire short lifetime, the child was inevitably dressed in ruffles, lace, pristine white leotards and shiny patent Mary Janes . . . including one candid shot taken at the zoo, of all places to go in a party dress. Not one photo showed a little girl in jeans with mussed-up hair or a dirty face. Or a little girl play-wrestling with her proud father.

In one of the last snapshots Sophie looked at, Missy, all dressed up as usual, was clinging to the hand of a tall model-slender woman dressed in a silk blouse and a flowing skirt. The shape of the child's face was identical to the mother's.

Rio's ex-wife was lovely, porcelain delicate and fragile looking. And skinny beyond belief. Perfect. Sophie felt a knot form in her stomach as she handed the photos back.

No wonder Rio hadn't married again. Outside of the movie industry, it would be difficult to match physical beauty like that.

"Your wife's beautiful."

"Ex-wife. Yeah, she is, but you tend to forget that in a hurry when she's nagging at you all the time to buy her a fur coat."

With a final wistful glance at Missy, he tucked the pictures back into his wallet.

"How about you, Sophie, you married, divorced?" He gave her a stage-wink. "Involved in a meaningful relationship with a significant other?" he drawled in an unexpected parody of yuppy speech that made her laugh.

"Nope to all the above," she said without thinking.

"And?"

"What d'you mean, 'and'? And I go out on dates now and then like anybody does, that's all." Sophie felt defensive, off balance and irritable. She found herself wondering for the first time in the past hour what on earth she was doing here in the back of her store after closing hours with a man she hardly knew, a man she'd spent most of the day quarreling with, besides.

"Sorry," he said, waving a hand in the air as if wiping the question off some invisible slate. "I didn't mean to get too personal. Blame it on the wine."

She felt petty, but the easy mood of a few moments before was gone. "It was super wine, Rio. And all that delicious food, and the roses. Thanks."

He sensed an ending just as she did. He got to his feet and stuffed the empty cartons back into the bag, shoving the wine bottle after them.

"Guess it's time I headed out of here. There's a dozen things to do before tomorrow morning." He paused, hand on the back doorknob.

"Well, so are we or not?" he queried, frowning back at her.

"Are we what?" Sophie got to her feet and smoothed her wrinkled jumpsuit down over her body. She was certain she'd gained at least three pounds in the past hour.

"Friends. You never did answer me, y'know. Are we friends?"

She stopped fussing with her outfit and stared at him in surprise. He was waiting for an answer. It seemed to matter to him.

"Rio, you really are something else," she said, and then she grinned at him. "Of course we're friends, you screwball. I ate your food and drank your wine and accepted stolen goods, didn't I? We're business neighbors, aren't we? Of course we're friends." Then she added, "As long as you keep your promise to insulate that wall."

"Consider it done." He gave her a mock salute, spoiled by the paper bag of garbage he held, and then, before she had any idea what he was planning to do, he dropped the paper bag to the floor and took her elbows in each of his warm hands, drawing her toward him.

He kissed her, innocently, quickly—first on the lips and then a huge, noisy smack on each cheek. She could smell strong soap and a lingering, not unpleasant, trace of powerful grease remover. His breath was warm and pleasing, with traces of wine.

The gesture was over before it fully registered, but the sensation of his lips lingered and sent warm shock waves cascading through her.

"See you in the morning, Sophia *mia*," he said, crouching down and repacking the bag with the things that had spilled out.

The door closed after him, and while she was still standing frozen to one spot, she heard the garbage can lid clang, and Rio started to whistle some cheerful tune. Then, his motorcycle roared to life and accelerated up the alley.

Sophie pressed her fingers to the burning spots on her cheeks where his lips had been. Sophia *mia*. Nobody had ever called her Sophia before.

She couldn't help smiling.

3

"IT'S STILL JUST A SMIDGEN too long, don't you think, Sophie?"

Constance Woodbaine frowned at her reflection in the full-length mirror and moved her slender hips to and fro so that the soft rose-colored chiffon swirled around her legs.

Please, no, Sophie begged in silent dread. Not again. She'd altered the hem on the full skirt three times, trying to please this fussy woman so she'd pay for the special order.

After writing end-of-the-month checks the other evening for her employees' wages and paying rent plus the dozens of other expenses month's end brought, Sophie needed this sale. But Constance was one of those women who believed ordering an outfit gave her the right to change her mind about details such as the hem as many times as she pleased. She had the power of the purchaser, and she knew it.

It looked, Sophie thought with morose acceptance, as if she was in for another full hour of unpicking and hand stitching the slippery, fragile material, just because this...bully...knew Sophie was vulnerable.

She knew Sophie didn't dare do what she longed to do—tell spoiled Constance in no uncertain terms that the hem was exactly, to the millimeter, where she'd last requested it, and that if she wanted to change it again then, damn it all, Constance would do so herself. Period. Transaction concluded. Get the heck out of my store.

After Constance paid the substantial balance owing.

"It's up to you, of course," Sophie said with nonchalant cheerfulness that almost choked her. "But I think this length is perfect for you. It keeps the total look in balance. You have such long, attractive legs, and the skirt shows them off so well . . ."

"You are a dear, Sophie, but I really think just another inch or two up would be so much more flattering. Just take it up a teensy-weensy bit and I know you'll agree. . . ."

The bell on the door tinkled and Rio's head appeared in the doorway.

"Hey, Sophie, I'm hosing off the sidewalk in front, d'you want me to give those flowers of yours a drink, or what?" he called in his cheerful fashion. "They don't look so healthy."

It was three days since Rio'd moved in next door, and Sophie was learning that as far as small courtesies were concerned, having Rio as a neighbor was wonderful.

The sidewalk with its overnight dog deposit was cleaned for her every morning, which was nothing short of a miracle.

And without asking, he'd washed the outside of her display window yesterday when he was doing his own. There hadn't been a recurrence of the wine, food and flower episode, but Sophie felt easy and relaxed with Rio as a result of that afternoon.

Easy, relaxed and constantly aware that some deep part of her was attracted to him. Just on a physical level, of course, she reassured herself. Those rampant gonads of hers, or whatever they were.

As far as having a motorcycle shop operating next door, that was still a major problem that set her teeth on edge fifty times a day. Despite the specific changes he'd made, motorcycles were motorcycles, and most of the men who rode them were intimidating, both to Sophie and to her female customers.

"Hi, Rio." She was too involved with the hem problem to give him her full attention. "Yes, water them, please, if it's not too much trouble. I forgot yesterday and it's so hot they're gonna die if you don't." She happened to glance up at Constance's expression just then and a wicked idea began to form.

Constance was giving Rio the full voltage of her cutest smile, and the blusher on her cheeks glowed in two artistic circles.

Rio seemed to have a general warming effect on any female in his immediate vicinity. If only he would play along with the scheme she was plotting. Would he understand what was needed here? What if he said exactly the wrong thing and Constance abandoned the dress altogether? But Rio was a salesperson, just like her, and Sophie prayed he'd understand what was required.

Was it worth the risk? Sophie could feel her fingers smarting from the needle pricks the last hemming effort had produced, and she could also feel the ache in her shoulders from hunching over miles of lousy chiffon all afternoon.

"Rio, do you have a spare minute?" Sophie heard herself saying, sweet as Aspartame. "Could you come in here and give us an impartial opinion on this?"

"Sure. Gimme a minute to turn the hose off...."

He was back before Sophie could get her fingers crossed behind her back.

"Now what can I do for you lovely ladies," he said, including them both in his megawatt smile.

"Rio," Sophie began, trying to convey a silent message with her eyes, "Constance and I have been struggling for hours to get this hem just right. I've redone it twice," she said with as much significance as she could manage in her tone. "Now, I feel it's just perfect on Constance at this length, but we do need an outside opinion. A male opinion," she cooed, hating herself for being coy. "What do you think?"

"About the dress?" He looked Constance up and down with a lot more attention than necessary, and Sophie felt like kicking him. She should have known better than to get into this.

"About the hem," she said with distinct emphasis, pointing a finger at the problem area in case he'd never heard of hems. "This hem, right here, Rio."

He looked a bit uncertain, but it was too late now to give him a crash course in terminology.

She caught his eye long enough to give him what she hoped was a meaningful look instead.

"Oh, the hem," he repeated, nodding like a sage and squinting down at Constance's legs, tilting his head to one side as if he were giving the matter careful consideration.

"Could ya maybe turn around?" he suggested, and Constance all but danced her body around in a full circle, spinning hard enough so that a lot more leg showed than necessary. For some reason, Sophie felt like driving a needle into the woman's kneecap.

"I really like that length," he said at last, with rather vague but positive enthusiasm. Then his voice deepened, becoming intimate and somehow suggestive. "In fact, the whole rig is perfect, far as I can see," he declared, and Sophie could have hugged him until he went on, "Maybe you ought to spin around once more, though, so I can be sure."

Constance obliged, making the skirt flare even higher than before. The tops of her panty hose and a touch of pink lace panties showed this time.

Sophie shot Rio a murderous look. Enough was enough.

He met her narrowed gaze with a sweet, innocent smile and said, "I wouldn't change it even a little. Not a single inch. It's great. That color really suits you, too, uh . . . did I hear Sophie say your name was Constance?"

The way Constance preened and giggled and flirted with him during the next five minutes was enough to make Sophie's blood curdle. At last Rio left, and Constance floated into a changing cubicle with not one more word about the hem.

When she emerged, she handed the dress to Sophie and wrote out a check. She left the store with an amused smile and an assurance she'd be back soon for another outfit, news that Sophie considered a mixed blessing. She watched from the window as Constance did a slow stroll past Rio's store.

It was obvious there were types not at all bothered by motorcycle men. Or rather, types who were bothered by them.

There were customers in and out during the next hour, and it was some time later when the phone rang.

"Unicorn, good afternoon."

"Is the coast clear? Did Madame Constance go for it?" Rio said in a rough whisper.

"There's nobody in the store if that's what you mean, Rio."

The connection ended without another word, and she was hanging up the phone, puzzled, when Rio strolled in the front door.

"Okay, doll, where's da vig?" he growled, sauntering over to the counter with his thumbs in his belt loops, doing his best to look tough.

"What's vig?" Sophie demanded, unable to keep from smiling at his nonsense.

"Vig, vigorish, da payoff for helpin' you sell da pink number. Ya didn't figure I'd work for nothin, did ya, lady? Us guys in the Mob, we don't come cheap, y'know. I practically had to compromise my virtue to convince her that dress was right for her," he went on, strutting back and forth like a cocky rooster.

Sophie snorted. "Somehow I didn't get the feeling any compromise was involved. And we made the dress specially for her. The only thing I needed help with was that infernal hem."

"I did think it ought to have been a foot or two shorter at least, but I sorta' figured maybe I shouldn't say so."

Sophie yelped in horror. "Darned right you shouldn't. If you'd said something like that I'd be tempted to use my needle on your mouth, Agostini."

She was unaware that her laughing soft eyes and sensual smile had Rio plotting quite different plans for her mouth.

They were grinning like idiots when the front door opened and closed. Sophie glanced toward it, and her happy expression changed to amazement.

"Mother. For heaven's sake, Mom, what are you doing here?"

It was insane, but Sophie felt like a guilty child, caught doing something indecent when all she was doing was enjoying a joke with Rio.

Harriet's cool blue gaze shot from one of them to the other, and frost seemed to billow through the warm air. She stopped a few steps away from the counter.

Rio had turned and was studying her.

Harriet was tall, five eleven, and she wore heels that took her over the six-feet mark. She had a wardrobe of expensive suits in neutral colors, with tailored silk blouses in pale pastels, and she had her champagne-blond hair colored and cut to such perfection Sophie often thought it looked more like a wig than a wig would. The total impression she conveyed was one of genteel elegance on a framework of steel.

In other words, Harriet was intimidating.

Sophie moved over to stand between her mother and Rio, as if she were shielding them from each other. She had a hunch they weren't going to be bosom friends.

"Mother, this is Rio Agostini. Rio, my mother, Harriet Larson. Rio has the motorcycle store next door," she added.

Her mother gave Rio an up-and-down look that stated just what she thought of someone who rode motorcycles.

"I believe you mentioned the problem at some length the other day," Harriet said, and Sophie remembered the interrupted phone conversation with Harriet during which she'd gone on about Rio, emphasizing the noise and the motorcycles. It was the day he'd moved in, wasn't it?

Why had she done that? Now her mother had a preconceived idea of what Rio was like, and it probably was a mile from the truth.

And Harriet was making it sound as if Sophie had run whining to her just to complain about him, which wasn't at all how it had happened.

"Pleased to meet you, Mrs. Larson." Rio held out his hand, smiling in a friendly way.

Harriet extended a well-manicured hand with obvious reluctance. "How do you do, Mr. Agostini," she said with frosty formality.

Sophie knew Harriet prided herself on her ability to get along with people if it was necessary, despite what she labeled "awkward differences in social background."

That always amused Sophie, because Harriet had no social background that her daughter knew of.

Being able to overlook those differences for the duration of a sale, Harriet often remarked, was an attribute that greatly enhanced her income, and one that Sophie had decided years before should net her mother an Oscar nomination for acting.

The simple truth was, Harriet was anything but liberal in her views, and it was obvious she didn't think even pretense was called for with Rio. After all, he wasn't a client.

Harriet drew her hand away in one sharp movement and glanced at it as if she thought it might be dirty. Sophie saw Rio's eyes narrow and his smile fade.

"Mom's a salesperson, too. She's in real estate," Sophie babbled as the tension between the three of them seemed to permeate the room.

"Guess ya don't get much dirt under your fingernails selling houses, huh?" Rio drawled with what Sophie could have sworn was total innocence.

Harriet looked at him. "No, it's not exactly like repairing motorcycles," she purred.

"Ah, well, dirty work, clean money, my pop always says. He's a cement contractor." Now why should an innocent comment like that sound so much like a challenge?

"It's so nice that people believe that," Harriet answered, giving Rio a long, measuring look and turning to Sophie, ignoring him. "I happen to have a couple of hours between appointments and I thought we could have a drink together," she suggested. "Why don't you phone over to the warehouse and get that girl of yours to watch the store for you for the rest of the afternoon?"

Sophie had done that before, on the very rare occasions when Harriet ever found a free afternoon to spend with her.

Rio said, "Well, guess I'll see you tomorrow, Sophie. Take it easy." He gave Harriet a curt nod. "Interesting meetin' ya, Mrs. Larson."

He disappeared out the door.

Harried stared after him, frowning. "I don't much like having that type hanging around, Sophie," she declared. "Surely you could discourage him more than you are? When I came in, you were actually laughing with him. Yet you said yourself just the other day that he was ruining your business."

Sophie thought of all the little, kind things Rio had done for her during the past days and realized she was feeling defensive of him all of a sudden.

"I said that having a motorcycle store next door was liable to ruin my business," she corrected. "Actually, I'm finding that Rio himself is all right."

Harriet waved a hand, brushing the finer points aside.

"Nonsense. He's a different sort of man than you're used to, dear. You're far too gullible." She glanced at her expensive watch. "Anyhow, we're wasting time. Get someone over from your workshop," she ordered in the bossy tone that Sophie hated. "I want to check out the new lounge at the Sheraton Plaza. It's the in spot for the money crowd this week. It never hurts to be seen in the right places."

Sophie, with some reluctance, dialed over to the Sweat Shop. Having Michelle run the store wasn't the best thing for business; she wore awful old jeans and faded T-shirts to work, which wasn't quite the image Sophie wanted a salesperson in the Unicorn to project. Neither was she at all adept at either selling or making change if the need arose.

Sophie knew she shouldn't abandon her store to someone like Michelle. But there wasn't money enough to hire a clerk, even part-time. It was one of the things that was starting to bother Sophie about having her own business. She was married to the darned thing.

Sophie made the call, listened to Bill's burst of protests and finally, with a mute show of reluctance and a put-upon expression, Michelle came ambling over, in dirty jeans and T-shirt with a direct and simple message blazed across her bosom.

It read WANNA?

THE SHERATON PLAZA had a new lounge called Tarzan's, done up in hanging ferns and vines, with lots of fake leopard skin. It was scattered this afternoon with stock broker types who looked as if they'd stepped off the pages of *Esquire* magazine. There were lots of red ties and eel-skin briefcases. Most of the men were talking just loud enough to be overheard, remarks about where the market had closed and how many points some obscure stock had gained.

Harriet greeted a number of people by name before she joined Sophie at a table by the window. Friends in the right places meant referrals and commissions, according to Harriet.

Sophie considered the people her mother admired ultra boring. The only thing that excited them as far as she could tell was a string of numbers on their pocket computers.

"I saw Greg Marshall this morning, at a walk-through in that new development Andre Leclair designed at Granville Island. You remember I mentioned Greg before," Harriet said after the socializing was done and they'd ordered drinks.

Greg Marshall was an ambitious salesman in his late thirties whom Harriet had decided Sophie ought to meet. Sophie was dragging her feet. It was an invariable rule that if Harriet liked the guy, Sophie would detest him on sight.

"Also, those units are a great investment. You should take a look at them, dear."

Sophie shook her head. "I've seen other buildings Leclair's done, and I hate them. There isn't room enough for both a bed and a dresser in the bedrooms, the kitchens make airplane galleys look roomy, and I feel as if I'm in a dentist's waiting room with all that chrome around."

"They're not intended as lifetime investments, Sophie," her mother explained with a pained expression and a sigh. "They're priced so that young, upwardly mobile people like you can get your head in the market."

Sophie mumbled that her head was fine right where it was, and Harriet sighed again. It was a familiar nondiscussion between them.

"A person just can't live in a place where one dirty bowl makes the whole apartment look like a slum," Sophie tried to explain, sipping her club soda and wondering what fabric the waitresses' jumpsuits were made from.

They looked as though they were wearing wet vinyl, so tight that Sophie was certain if the wearer swallowed an olive, it would show in clear profile all the way down.

Why was she the only one who looked as if she ever ate a decent meal? Even Harriet belonged to a fashionable gym, and her dress size was smaller than Sophie's despite the difference in their height. In fact, as Sophie studied her mother now, she was almost certain Harriet had lost some weight.

"I don't see how you can be so positive about this when you've never even lived in one," Harriet was insisting. "In all fairness, you should at least try living somewhere before you decide you hate it."

Fairness? There was no fairness. There ought to be a law that said mothers had to weigh more than their daughters, Sophie thought. Mothers ought to be a little fat just out of courtesy.

"Mom, you know I grew up moving from one place to the other because you couldn't resist a hot real estate deal, and now that I have my own apartment, I intend to stay in it until they tear the building down."

"Don't try guilt on me, dear, you know it doesn't work. Buying and selling kept us in groceries, and after I'm gone, you'll inherit enough, God willing, so you can afford a good analyst to deal with any neurosis you think I created. As for that rat trap you live in, it probably won't be long before they do tear it down."

Harriet considered the old, spacious apartment Sophie rented to be just one step up from the city dump, and Sophie's attachment to it confounded her.

On the other hand, Sophie hated her mother's ultramodern unit and was vocal about it, so they were even. They'd been over this so many times both of them knew their lines and neither took offense anymore. It gave them a common meeting ground in one area, at least.

"Either they'll tear it down," Harriet went on now with the usual heavy attempt at humor, "or the city will declare it a heritage building, it's so ancient."

Harriet sat back in the ridiculous safari chair covered with some fake animal skin and steepled her fingers under her chin in a gesture Sophie decided she hated. "Seriously," she said, "the money you now put into rent could easily go on a mortgage, Sophie. I've offered to put up a down payment as long as whatever you decide on has good potential. It's madness to go on rejecting my offer, dear. You have to think of your future."

"I'm not a client you have to convince, Mom, and I appreciate what you're saying, but I don't want a mortgage. No matter how good the deal is, it would still be at least double what I'm paying now." Sophie shuddered at the thought of one more huge debt to worry over every month.

"Besides, I hate moving, you know that."

Harriet sipped her drink and gave up until the next time.

"The closing went through on that business property I gambled on out in Delta. I made a bundle on it."

"You're one heck of a businesswoman, Mom." Sometimes it seemed unfair to Sophie that she hadn't inherited the clear-cut sense of intent her mother had. Harriet always knew what needed to be done in order to clinch a deal. Sophie, on the other hand, had no idea most of the time.

Well, she mused, she had pulled a good one with Constance Woodbaine, though. She wondered whether or not to tell Harriet the story and decided against it. It would probably just get her mother back on the subject of Rio, and Sophie would rather avoid that.

A moment later, Sophie wished she had told the story. Even talking about Rio couldn't annoy her as much as Harriet's oft-repeated suggestion that Sophie give up the Unicorn and take a real estate course if she really wanted to sell. That way, according to Harriet, the two of them could set up their own office.

"I think you'd really do well in the business, I've told you that," she stated now, not noticing her daughter's growing irritation. "If you just pay attention to those three major rules: location, location . . ."

Sophie finished the litany. "Lo-ca-tionnn," she groaned. "For gosh sakes, Mom, don't bring this up again. I only get to see you, what, once a month? And when we are together what do you talk about? Real estate. I'm fed up to the gills with real estate. Why the hell can't we talk about something interesting for a change, like hypnotism or who won the music awards or Ann Landers' column or something?" Her impatience surprised even her. Normally she'd never snap at her mother like this.

Harriet's eyes grew frosty and her jaw tightened. But she prided herself on self-control and patience.

"Fine, dear, what exact subject did you have in mind?"

Sophie's brain was blank. What the heck did most mothers and daughters talk about? She had no idea.

She drank her whole glass of soda to avoid having to say anything, knowing it was going to force her to find the bathroom in a minute or so.

It was an immense relief when Harriet's beeper sounded. She hurried off to find a telephone, and Sophie admired the skyline view outside the glass wall and decided to order a wine cooler. Maybe alcohol would sweeten her mood.

But when Harriet came back, she explained in a dignified tone that there wasn't time for another drink. Within an hour, she had to show a house she had listed in North Vancouver, and it was probably going to take most of the evening, because the client had already hinted he was going to make an offer. She'd been going to suggest she and Sophie have dinner together, but business was business, after all.

Sophie wasn't the least bit disappointed, which in turn made her feel guilty. Shouldn't a mother and daughter have more in common than she and Harriet?

SHE ARRIVED BACK at the Unicorn just before closing time. Michelle was lounging behind the counter reading a novel, paying no attention whatsoever to the young woman in the dressing room trying on skirts and blouses.

In a furious whisper, Sophie explained to Michelle that her purpose was to help customers find what they were looking for, and to do that maybe she ought to try talking to them.

Michelle nodded with a distant look in her eye, and the moment Sophie stopped talking, she flipped her book open again like some kind of addict.

Feeling disgusted, Sophie shipped her back over to the Sweat Shop where she belonged. No wonder Bill acted like a maniac at times, trying to get reasonable work out of this woman. Dealing with the likes of Michelle was enough to unhinge anyone.

Using every ounce of charm she could muster, Sophie managed to sell the customer a graceful and expensive rayon outfit and a wide leather belt by letting her emote for forty-five minutes about her husband. Her husband was having an affair with her gynecologist's nurse.

He wasn't even discreet enough to choose his own doctor's nurse, the woman sniped.

Sophie couldn't quite make the distinction, but she clucked with sympathy anyway, thinking that women went on shopping sprees for the damnedest reasons.

The woman finally left, after paying for her substantial purchases with her husband's credit card. It made Sophie sad. Women like that used credit cards as punishment, substituting material goods for love.

Why was love so difficult to recognize, to find, to hold on to, when it was what everyone seemed to really want?

For some reason, she remembered Rio's comment about not noticing his wife's beauty because she kept insisting he buy her a fur coat. Was she at fault in the marriage, or was Rio?

She locked the door and was about to flip her sign to Closed when Rio himself tapped on the window.

"Hiya, kid," he called. "You alone?" He pressed his face to the glass, scanning the empty store behind her, perhaps checking for Harriet. Sophie opened the door for him.

"Actually, three gigolos, one of whom is a male belly dancer, are in the back room waiting for me as we speak," Sophie told him. "But come in anyway, I'll introduce you. You might learn something."

"I doubt it, I been around," he said without even changing expression. "But you're a different story altogether, so I'll save you from a fate worse than death." And he scooped her up in his arms and walked right out the front door of the store.

Sophie was horrified. The last thing she wanted any male to do was actually pick her up and find out just exactly how heavy she really was. So far in life, it hadn't been all that difficult to avoid men who did things like that. In fact, Rio was the first she'd ever come across.

"Rio, you maniac, put me down, the door isn't locked, I need to . . ." her voice reached a high octave.

"Hang on, Sophia. Hang on, honey."

She was forced to put an arm around his neck and another on his shoulder, because it was going to hurt like hell if he dropped her on the sidewalk. Cars were going past and someone honked.

It was mortifying. What if they both fell?

Rio was grinning in an idiotic fashion, as if he were silly drunk, but she was enveloped in his unique man smell and there wasn't a single trace of alcohol on him. She could see where his whiskers were beginning to show on his jaw. She could hear the little noises he made in his throat with the effort of carrying her. She could feel his corded arms under her thighs.

"Put me down. I'm heavy. You're going to hurt your back. . . ."

He turned into his store, and several yards inside the door, he released his grip and at last her feet touched the floor. He slid his hands to either side of her waist, holding on and still grinning down at her like a man who'd taken leave of his senses.

Her face felt as if it were burning up. She glared at him and gulped several times with shock and anger and injured pride.

He just looked at her and laughed. Then he tipped his head back and let out an ear-splitting whoop of pure joy. He took his hands from her waist and grabbed her wrists instead, tugging her farther into the shop, over to where a gleaming red-and-chrome motorcycle was standing, propped on its stand.

"See that sucker?" he chortled, and Sophie, beginning to suspect that he'd gone absolutely berserk, stared at him and nodded, trying to guess what manic thing he'd do next.

Rio gazed down at her, and the elation he felt spilled from him so palpably that without even knowing why, Sophie began to feel excitement filling her, as well.

"I just sold that bike, half an hour ago. My very first big sale, Sophia; I was terrified you weren't gonna be back to share it with me. I sold her for . . ." he named a figure well in excess of ten thousand dollars, and Sophie stared at him in shocked admiration and utter disbelief.

"Is that how much one of those silly things cost?" she blurted. "Why, that's ridiculous. I don't take in that much in a whole month. I can't believe that anyone would pay that for a motorcycle."

But then she remembered in vivid detail how a woman had walked into the Unicorn the day after it opened and bought a dress for $84.98, and with that memory, she understood exactly how Rio felt right this minute.

You could open a business, give it a name, call yourself proprietor, but it felt as if you were playacting until that first real customer came along and bought something with honest-to-goodness money.

That's what had happened to Rio.

She clapped her hands and gave a happy little bounce.

"You made your first sale. Rio, that's great, that's super, I'm delighted for you . . . ."

Then his arms came around her, and the breath left her lungs in a whoosh. His muscles were like iron, and she was pressed tightly against his hard length in a crushing embrace, aware of his belt buckle and the incredible heat of his body.

His lips came down on hers, slanting first one way and then the other, fierce and eager, finding the perfect match, opening and encompassing her mouth in a kiss so adept and arousing she felt insistent desire churn to life in her abdomen.

His hand slid around to her buttocks, stroking her flesh, pressing her in intimate haste against him, and she could feel him adjust his stance so that his legs were apart and hers were between them, his thighs holding her body captive in a thrilling embrace.

Sophie shuddered and thoughts fled as the tip of his tongue flicked at her own, met and thrust and retreated in perfect cadence with the hard arousal pressing and releasing against her own throbbing, burning center.

There was nothing innocent about this kiss, the way there had been about the one in her store. This one was real, a prelude to seduction, right there among the freedom machines.

4

THINGS THREATENED TO GO right out of control, there in the middle of the motorcycles

Sophie's arms were locked around Rio's neck, and her body and mouth molded themselves to his. Both of them were breathing in sharp, short gasps when a taunting wolf whistle and a male voice from behind them made Sophie tear her mouth from Rio's and stagger backward.

"Hey, hey, Rio baby, way ta go, man...."

Rio's arms steadied her, and there was hot, dangerous anger in his eyes when he glanced over his shoulder at the short, stocky man in the Greek sailor's cap.

"Louie, the place is closed for the day, didn't you see the sign?"

"Hey, Rio, no offence, buddy, the door wasn't locked. I just came ta see the bike Harry bought offa you. He was down at the Fraser Arms, bragging his head off about the new Harley he's in hock for."

Sophie swallowed several times and smoothed her trembling hands down over her skirt. Her heart was pounding in her ears.

Rio gave her a long, slow look full of apology and frustration, and then let go of her and whirled on Louie.

For an instant Sophie thought he was about to attack the other man. His fists clenched and he seemed to give off angry sparks.

But then he let his breath out in a protracted sigh and gestured with his thumb at the machine on the pedestal. He sounded a lot less enthusiastic than when he'd shown it to Sophie.

"There she is. Look all you want."

Louie whistled again, a long appreciative sound, and moved so he could run an admiring hand down the side of the bike, just as if he were stroking the nose of a Thoroughbred horse.

"What's she redline at, Rio?"

"Fifty-five hundred RPMs." Rio gave Sophie's hand a final apologetic squeeze and began to move toward the bike himself, caught up in the mysterious fascination such things seemed to have on the male species.

It was past time for Sophie to leave. She moved toward the door and was through it before Rio even realized she was going. He came after her in long, impatient strides and caught up with her just outside the door of the Unicorn.

"Hey, Sophie, hold it, would ya? I was gonna see if you wanted to come out and celebrate with me, maybe some dinner and then a show or something? I'll get rid of Louie in a coupla minutes."

But she'd had time to collect herself, time to think. And what she thought was maybe it was wise to put some distance between herself and Rio Agostini now, while she still could.

That kiss had unsettled her, and her mother's words must have hooked on something Sophie sensed, as well, because it had dawned on her in the past couple of minutes that she and Rio were indeed very different, just as Harriet had pointed out.

It was hard to explain, even to herself. There were cultural differences, but they made him interesting. No, the thing that bothered her had something to do with the fact that he was easy with physical contact, with intimacy, in a way Sophie wasn't. He was expert at it.

The passionate kiss they'd shared had shaken her to her foundations, made her wonder now if she might have tumbled with him to the floor and had sex right then and there if Louie hadn't arrived.

It was shocking to contemplate now, but in all honesty she thought she probably would have done exactly that.

She was anything but promiscuous. Quite the opposite. She'd always prided herself on being cautious about intimacy, about planning ahead and taking precautions, about being certain well ahead of time that a sexual relationship was what she wanted, certain with her head, as well as with her body.

Sure, she'd had her share of fantasies involving being swept away in a passionate interlude with an irresistible stranger. The trouble was, the reality wasn't as easy to accept as the fantasy had been.

"Sophia? So what d'ya say? Wanna come out with me?" Rio was frowning down at her, waiting for an answer.

She hesitated, then shook her head. "Thanks, Rio, but . . . I've made other plans for tonight. Sorry."

The open disappointment that flashed across his features almost made her change her mind. But after a moment he shrugged and made an attempt at a grin.

"Can't win 'em all, I guess. Another time, then."

He turned back to his store, and Sophie went into hers, feeling let down and sorry for herself and, for no apparent reason, good and mad at her mother.

She flipped the sign on the door from Open to Closed and locked up, shoving the money from the cash drawer into a steel box and hiding it under a stack of fabric in the back room.

To hell with worrying all the time about being robbed. She couldn't face making out a deposit and walking six blocks out of her way to the bank. Besides, there wasn't enough in the till to make it worthwhile, she rationalized.

She also put off the job of entering the day's sales in the ledger. Those miserable lines of figures were impossible to contemplate right now. She just couldn't face much of anything this afternoon.

The evening stretched ahead of her like a toothache to be borne, with nothing to ease the loneliness that had somehow bitten into her like a tenacious rat the instant she refused Rio's invitation.

She grabbed the basket she was using as a purse and left the store, wrestling with the cranky lock until it clicked into place, swearing as she did so. But even shocking language didn't help.

With dragging steps, she started off down the sidewalk. As usual, she was concerned that Michelle had locked up properly at the Sweat Shop, and she glanced up at the second-story area wondering if she ought to check.

To her surprise, Bill Stanopoulis was standing in the dusty window, waving like a maniac.

She changed direction and headed over there instead of to the bus stop.

There were long flights of narrow, dark stairs to climb, and she was puffing when she finally reached the top.

Bill was waiting for her, a short, wiry little man with inky hair starting to gray at the temples and thin at the crown. His chiseled features, hooked nose and snapping black eyes made him look like an Indian chief masquerading as a Greek.

"Come in, come in," Bill ordered with an impatient wave of his hand, motioning her into the brightly lit, cavernous room with its makeshift cutting tables—large pieces of plywood on sawhorses—piles of dusty fabric scraps, and pattern pieces tacked to walls. Thread and tape measures and half-completed garments were tossed carelessly across chairs and sewing machines. Every available surface was cluttered with dressmaker's pins and dirty coffee cups, jackets and sweaters worn on cold mornings, grease-stained paper bags empty now of doughnuts and bagels Bill and Michelle used to fuel their days.

It was a mess. It was also homey and familiar, dear to Sophie's heart, and she felt a little better just being there.

"How come you're still working, Bill? It's after six o'clock," Sophie reminded him, setting her basket on the table and collapsing onto a rickety wooden chair.

"Just I am finishing this special order for tomorrow, the burgundy velour caftan with the hood. Michelle was supposed to do it, but . . ."

A stream of Greek curses told what he thought of Michelle's efforts. "That girl, she will not sew clean, no matter how many times I show her. There were lumps here . . . and here, look at this seam. . . ."

He held it up for Sophie to see the marks of Michelle's inefficiency, then resumed his place in front of a large complex industrial sewing machine that no one dared touch but Bill.

Sophie had bought the contrary thing for a song from a company gone bankrupt, and Bill oiled and polished and cursed it until he knew its every elaborate curve and capricious mood. He was the only one who could keep it from chewing up garments and spitting them out in tatters.

Holding the napped fabric between practiced hands, he sewed as he talked, the roar of the machine's motor like a wild animal.

Bill controlled it with the pressure of his right knee on the presser bar, violent threats and curses, and occasionally a blow with his fist on some part of its cantankerous steel frame just to reaffirm who ran the show.

Sophie was always reminded of a lion tamer brandishing a whip at an animal that snarled and balked but recognized its master.

And Bill was a master of his craft. He could turn out as many as a dozen garments a day, a feat no other sewer she'd ever known came anywhere near.

"So, this motorcycle man, now he picks you up in his arms and carries you down the street, Sophie? Michelle, she was about to leave, she screamed at me to come to the window, and oy oy oy. Such a scene."

Roar, pause, curse, roar as he whizzed one seam after the other.

She felt her face heat up. "It wasn't exactly the way you tell it . . . see, Rio was excited because he sold a bike. It was the first real sale he's made, and he just wanted to celebrate. . . ."

"Plug in the kettle, would you please, Sophie. We will have coffee." Bill kept the makings for his favorite thick Greek coffee in a wooden box over in one corner, and Sophie got up and plugged in the frayed cord to the kettle.

"You've ordered the red velour for Christmas, yes, Sophie? This pattern, just we should cut a good supply of these for Christmas. I know they will sell."

Sophie designed some of the patterns used for the garments Bill cut and sewed, but she also experimented with commercial patterns, taking a sleeve from one and adding a bodice from another, giving her stock a distinctive and unique character but cutting down the painstaking work involved in drafting patterns from scratch. The caftan Bill was referring to was a happy combination of three separate patterns.

But Sophie hadn't ordered the velour yet. She hadn't been able to afford it.

Bill's black head was bent over his work, bald pate gleaming, wiry body seeming an extension of the great machine in front of him. His attention seemed to be wholly on how many housecoats they ought to cut, but Sophie wasn't deceived.

Bill was a master at leading in one direction when he actually intended going straight back in the other.

The subject of Rio seemed to have taken a back seat for a while, but it would surface again.

The moment Sophie resumed her seat, Bill's commanding eyes caught and held hers with a long, knowing look.

"Just, Sophie, I think this Rio Agostini is not the gangster you thought he was that first day, yes? Michelle, who sees all that happens on the street because she pays no attention to what she's doing, she told me he washes your windows and cleans the sidewalk each day."

He let the velour drop for a moment and held out his hands in an expressive gesture. "So this is a good thing, no? To have a neighbor who takes an interest, who's tough enough not to be afraid of hoodlums breaking into his store."

The kettle was boiling, and Bill insisted on making the coffee himself. He got up and fussed with the tiny demitasse cups, handing her one at last with a gracious little bow.

The coffee was thick as molasses and so sweet it hurt her throat when she sipped it.

"Actually, my mother thinks I'm crazy to give Rio the time of day," Sophie confided. "What d'you think, Bill? I mean, he's sort of rough and ready, all right, but underneath . . ."

She thought of the kiss and shivered. She was the one who'd felt rough and ready.

Bill snorted. "So your mama doesn't like him. What do mamas know? We Greeks have a saying. . . ."

Sophie tried to stop the grin forming on her mouth.

No matter what the situation, Bill always came up with a "saying." Sophie suspected he made them up as he went along.

He rattled off something in Greek, complex, full of clicking sounds in his throat.

"What does that mean, Bill?"

He'd balanced his coffee on the edge of the nearby counter, and their conversation was again punctuated by the roars of the sewing machine.

"It means listen to your mother's advice and then say to hell with it and follow your own heart, because opportunities for happiness come seldom in this life."

"How is your mother, Bill?"

Mrs. Stanopoulis lived with her son and drove him berserk with her constant urging about marriage.

Bill rolled his eyes. "Just, she has found a girl for me from her village, she sent her picture to me, and she wants me to write to her. I ask you, do I need this?"

Sophie laughed at him, the way he intended her to, and by the time the coffee was done, the caftan was finished as well. She and Bill locked up the Sweat Shop and strolled to the bus stop together.

Sophie's mood had brightened. Bill was good therapy.

Vancouver's inner harbor was suffused in a rosy glow from the sun's final reflection on the water, and the early dinner crowd was wandering two by two toward Gastown and its selection of trendy restaurants.

Sophie watched them. She and Rio might have been among them if . . .

Bill kept up a steady stream of disjointed chatter about patterns and fabrics and what was selling in the other boutiques he worked for, and at last Sophie's bus arrived.

She boarded, and he gave a jaunty wave.

Sophie's apartment was in another part of the city, a twenty-minute bus ride across the Granville Street Bridge, in an area noted for old, genteel, crumbling mansions.

At the turn of the century the area had housed sugar magnates, diplomats and Vancouver's plain old filthy rich, but their time had come and gone again with fluctuations in the economy.

Now the drafty old monoliths were converted into apartments, home to scores of pensioners and a sparse sprinkling of young people like Sophie who appreciated dignity and character more than built-in dishwashers and garbage disposal.

She let herself in the heavy oak entrance door and checked her mail cubicle before making her way up the wide, curving staircase that led to her first-floor suite. For once, she was glad not to meet old Mr. Wanless, the caretaker of the building, who lived in one of the two ground-floor apartments. Mr. Wanless was seventy. He was lonely, and he often lay in wait for Sophie in the downstairs hall, just to pass the time of day for ten minutes or so.

The other apartment on the ground floor had been empty for several weeks; the old woman who'd lived there had had to move to an extended care unit, but it looked now as if someone was moving in. The door was ajar, and Sophie could hear a woman's voice.

She didn't feel like meeting a new neighbor any more than she felt like talking to Mr. Wanless. She bolted up the stairs.

Once inside her own door, Sophie dropped her basket, threw the mail on the old wooden tea crate she kept by the front door and began to remove her clothes. High heels first, then with a wriggle and a tug, her control-top panty hose.

It felt wonderful to strip off the layers and feel the coolness of the apartment's air on her skin.

The clothes fell in crumpled heaps on the faded hall carpet, wisps of panty hose followed by her shirtwaist dress and then her bra and finally her panties. Naked, and without a backward glance at the discarded clothing, she headed for the large high-ceilinged bathroom at the end of the hall.

In another five minutes, her hair was pinned up and she was in the bath, up to her neck in hyacinth bubbles.

She lay fully stretched out in the old porcelain tub for more than half an hour, wishing with each indrawn breath that she'd accepted Rio's invitation, and with each outgoing one, telling herself how wise she'd been not to get involved with him out of business hours.

But if only there was a next time, she'd go.

Nope. If there was a next time, she'd do exactly the same thing.

At last, she got out of the tub and toweled off, pulling a cotton-eyelet caftan over her head and padding back down the hall, grabbing the fistful of mail and heading into the kitchen.

All the rooms were spacious, high ceilinged and roomy, wasteful of space and ignorant of the massive amounts of heat required in winter to keep them even moderately comfortable.

It was now, in summer, that the rooms came into their own. They were cool and regal, filled with airy sunlight from the single-paned windows that reached halfway up each wall.

Sophie's kitchen was anything but efficient with its ancient gas range and stained old porcelain sinks, but it was her favorite room. It made up in character whatever it might have lacked in competence.

It had a fat old wheezing refrigerator set off in one inconvenient corner far from the stove, and Sophie had papered the wall behind it with a pattern of massive, outrageous sunflowers, each bloom two feet across. She'd made and hung ruffled yellow curtains on the high narrow windows and turned discarded coffee cans into matching canisters with several coats of yellow enamel. Her table was another version of the Sweat Shop's makeshift cutting areas; here, the wide flat surface was a plain wooden door, covered with yellow-and-white gingham-patterned plastic, stapled under at each edge. It was balanced on an old frame she'd found at a garage sale.

The door doubled as sewing table, eating surface, desk and cooking island.

She sat on one of the bright red folding chairs she'd bought, also at a garage sale, and examined her mail.

Three envelopes were bills, and she dropped them unopened into a tin cigar box kept on the table for just such a purpose.

The fourth letter had spidery black script on a lavender background, and she tore it open.

It was from Jessica Stanton, who'd had the antique shop next door before Rio moved in. Jessica was now living on a peninsula a half hour's ferry ride from Vancouver, on a small farm she'd bought years before as a weekend retreat.

Dear Sophie,

Greetings from the hinterland—love my new and different life here with the back-to-nature crowd, but if ever you can tear yourself away from the Unicorn, I'd adore a crash course in what's happening to hemlines this season. My neighbors, a young would-be hippie (male), living in a converted school bus to the west, and a peculiar old person of no determinate sex in the cottage to the east, are not the sort with whom one discusses Givenchy. Dear girl, do take a mini holiday and come see me—you're the only one I miss from my days in trade. We could have cups of Earl Grey and settle the thorny question of shoulder pads.

Fondest love, Jessica.

Sophie read the letter twice, homesick all of a sudden for the proper-seeming Englishwoman with the wicked, earthy sense of humor.

Damn, she missed Jessica.

Jessica would know just what to do about Rio Agostini, too.

Maybe one of these days she'd do exactly what Jessica suggested and run away from the city for a holiday.

In the meantime, there was supper to prepare. She made a big Caesar salad with lots of garlic and anchovies in the dressing, and ate it with leftover cold chicken and a large quantity of French bread, wondering the entire time she ate it where Rio was having dinner, what he was eating and with whom.

Usually, being alone didn't bother Sophie one whit. She loved her home; she didn't have to make apologies for her messiness or make adjustments for another's taste in food or decoration. But tonight, she was plain old lonely.

She went on a long, rambling walk just before dark, wandering the quiet sedate streets and torturing herself by imagining that behind each lighted window were two people, talking, laughing, making love.

When she let herself into her building, the new tenant's door burst open.

A child of about five planted herself in front of Sophie, hands on her minuscule hips. She wore blue jeans with a pink flannel pajama top over them.

"You gots a hammer we could borrow, please? My mommy needs to put my night picture up so I can go to sleep."

It was a surprise to see a child in the building, and Sophie smiled down at this one. Till now, Sophie had been the building's youngest tenant, which at times had made her feel as if she'd bungled into an extended care unit by mistake.

She liked her older neighbors, but it would be nice to have other young people living here, as well.

"Sure, I've got a hammer. Come on up and I'll get it for you."

"My name's Tara Mills, what's yours?"

"It's Sophie Larson."

"My mommy's name is Betty; we're 'vorced."

That took a minute to decipher, but Sophie soon got the drift. Tara was telling her that Betty Mills was a single parent.

Sophie opened her own door and found the hammer, as well as a canister of cookies she'd baked a few days before.

She dumped a generous amount of cookies into a bag and gave them to Tara.

"Tell your mommy I said welcome to the building, and for you both to come have coffee with me when you get settled."

"But we can't tonight; I gotta go to bed right away and there's a helluba mess down there. Mommy says she can't find her hair dryer anywhere and she's gonna look like a hag in the morning."

Sophie stifled a laugh. Betty Mills had no secrets with this kid around, that was certain.

"Not tonight, no. Another day."

The little girl agreed, and with a thank-you, hurried downstairs. The last Sophie heard was her excited voice telling all the news to her mother.

It had been an eventful day. Sophie ate some cookies herself and went to bed, to dream that Rio was working for Bill, and the two of them turned the old sewing machine into a motorcycle. But when it came time to ride it, Bill faded into oblivion and Sophie got on behind Rio. She wrapped her arms around him, and he wasn't wearing any clothes. She could feel the tantalizing combination of smooth and rough as she ran her hands through the thick hair on his chest, and then she let her fingers slide down and down until she encountered the intimate part of him she'd been searching for all along. . . .

SOPHIE WAS AT WORK earlier than usual the next morning, and she'd made a cup of lemon tea and was drinking it at the counter when Herb arrived with the mail and all the gossip at ten o'clock.

"There was another break-in last night, that little grocery store two blocks over," he announced with relish, setting her bundle of mail down on a bare spot on the counter and lining up the edges of the envelopes so they were in a neat stack.

Herb fussing with her mail irritated Sophie this morning, and she moved away from him, pretending to be involved in tidying blouses and skirts on a rack at the other side of the store.

But Herb was hard to discourage.

"The owner told me he lost mostly cigarettes and tinned meat, and some cash he'd left under the money drawer. The cops were still there when I did my rounds, but they didn't seem to be making much headway. Makes you wonder about the general mentality of the police force these days, eh?"

"I don't suppose there's much they can do, really, except patrol this area and hope eventually they catch the crooks in the act," Sophie snapped, wishing Herb would pick up his sack of mail and leave instead of hovering this way.

She hadn't slept well. Or rather, she'd slept too well early in the night.

After the ride on the sewing machine, her dreams had been increasingly unsettling, peppered with still more erotic scenes, all starring Rio as the male lead. And in those dreams, Sophie hadn't had a single inhibition, if the raunchy details she remembered when she awakened at five this morning were accurate.

Those vivid details were shocking to her conscious self, and she hadn't been able to get back to sleep again for thinking of them.

Was she turning into some kind of pathetic sex-starved bimbo, just because an attractive man had kissed her almost senseless?

"So what d'you think of your new neighbor?" Herb was determined to gossip this morning, and his choice of subject was the last straw. "I notice he's made lots of changes over there. Must have plenty of money to start right off remodeling that way, and he's got quite a stock of motorcycles in, as well."

"I haven't had any problems with him," Sophie lied.

"No? Funny, I would've thought—"

The phone rang, and for once Sophie blessed the interruption, because at last Herb shouldered his bag of mail and headed out the door with a final wave.

It was Harriet.

"Dear, you remember I mentioned Greg Marshall yesterday, the man who recently joined our office?" Harriet's tone of voice told Sophie that Greg Marshall must be standing right beside her.

Sophie suppressed an exasperated sigh.

"Yeah, Mom, I remember."

"Well it happens he has an appointment in your area of town this morning, and I mentioned to him that he should drop in and meet you."

"Oh, Mom, not today, it's—"

"He'll be there in about an hour then, dear. I'll tell him you'll be expecting him."

"Mother . . ."

Dial tone.

Sometimes Sophie wished she'd been an orphan.

During the next hour, the woman who'd ordered the burgundy velour caftan arrived to pick it up, and Sophie called over to the Sweat Shop and had Michelle bring it over.

The garment was a huge success, the middle-aged customer delighted. Sophie could see why Bill thought a stock of them would sell come Christmastime.

She made a mental note to phone her velour supplier in Montreal before noon and order bolts of the sensual fabric in bright Christmas colors.

First, she realized with a sinking feeling in her stomach, she'd have to call her bank manager to get an extension on her meager line of credit.

She double-checked her books to make sure, but there wasn't enough available in her business account right now to make a major velour purchase. And if she waited until business picked up in the fall, the velour wouldn't arrive in time to do the cutting and sewing for the holiday market.

The store was empty, and Sophie wandered into the back to nibble on a few nuts while she worked up the courage to make the bank call. She'd just filled the teapot and poured a mug of Red Zinger when the bell sounded over the door.

"Sophie, hey, I got somebody here I want you to meet."

Her heart skipped a beat at Rio's cheerful voice. Sophie hurried out front and then wondered why she'd bothered.

Rio had an arm around the shoulders of an amazing-looking woman. She was almost as tall as he, thin to the point of gauntness, with straight dark hair caught up in a huge pouf on one side of her head. She seemed to be somewhere in her early twenties, but it was hard to tell for sure, because of an air of both supreme sophistication and pouting childishness.

She was wearing a red leather mini so short one dip of the knees would result in indecent exposure, and her legs went on forever in their opaque hose.

Her features were large and dramatic—strong nose, huge eyes, square jaw—but at this moment, she looked totally bored. She was chewing gum.

"Sophie, this here's my baby sister, Gina." Rio gave the girl a shake, as if to wake her up and force her to respond.

Sophie felt like falling to her knees with gratitude when she heard that Gina was his sister.

"Gina, say hello to Sophie Larson, who makes all these nice—" he waved a hand around in a vague manner and searched for an appropriate word, finally settling for "—eh, things."

Gina nodded, looking as if she'd like to yawn instead, and went on chewing her gum, rotating her shapely jaw in rhythmic circles. Her eyes were a clear, innocent blue, fringed by sooty thick lashes that couldn't possibly be real, and her makeup was nothing short of amazing. It contoured, emphasized and concealed without being garish.

But even the spectacle of Gina couldn't hold Sophie's attention for long.

The instant she set eyes on Rio, all she could think of were the explicit sexual dreams she'd had about him for half the night, and in some insane way she felt convinced that he would know about them just by looking at her.

"Hi, um, Gina," she said at last in a high, unnatural voice when the other woman remained silent.

And then nerves took over and Sophie began to babble. "I don't really make everything myself, oh, I did in the beginning, but you see I couldn't keep up with it and I had to hire people, first Bill and then several more girls. It's hard because you just get them trained and then they leave for one reason or another, and you start all over again. Right now there's Michelle, but—" with horror, Sophie heard herself give the phoniest laugh imaginable "—ha, ha, it won't be long before she's gone as well, I'm sure . . . where do you work, Gina?"

Rio was staring at her with a puzzled frown, but Gina wasn't impressed one bit by the flood of words.

At least Gina now showed a few signs of life. She switched her gum to the other side of her jaw and said, "I'm not working right now. I'm laid off."

Then she moved out from under Rio's arm and moved in what Sophie could only describe as a sinuous slither over to the racks against the wall. There she started a professional examination of Sophie's stock, taking it rack by rack and looking at each garment with swift and certain movements before she moved on to the next. She didn't look bored anymore. In fact, her whole body had taken on an electric tension that Sophie recognized.

It was the aura of a committed and serious shopper who wouldn't tolerate distraction. Gina loved clothes, that was obvious.

Rio was still frowning, his dark eyes on Gina.

In a rapid, low voice he said, "I gotta talk to you, Sophie. I need a favor. You free after work for a while?"

Before Sophie could answer, the bell sounded, and a tall blond man in a blue summer suit, tailored to perfection, strolled in the door.

Sophie felt like groaning aloud.

Without a doubt, this was her mother's candidate for man of the month, arriving at just the wrong moment.

He looked around the shop in an appraising way, even squinting up at the ceiling, before he made his way over to where Sophie and Rio were standing.

His smile was an advertisement for Vancouver's dentists, and his cologne wafted into Sophie's nostrils. He was the type who would make certain he stayed thirty-nine forever.

She wasn't certain, but she thought Rio gave a tiny grunt of disgust and moved a half step closer to her as the visitor extended a well-groomed hand in her direction and said in a melodious voice, "Hello there, you must be Sophie. My name is Greg Marshall. Nice little place you've got here."

Sophie had been right in assuming that if Harriet liked this man, she wasn't going to. He gave her a definite pain behind her ears.

5

SOPHIE OFFERED HER HAND and Greg shook it, a firm, practiced handshake. His hands were softer than hers.

"Hi, Greg," she said without much enthusiasm. "This is my neighbor, Rio Agostini, and—" she twisted around to locate Gina, now examining the lingerie in the opened drawers of the old chest "—that's Rio's sister, Gina, um, Agostini?" She lifted an eyebrow at Rio. He hadn't said whether or not Gina was married.

"Yeah, Agostini." Rio somehow made it sound like a warning directed at Greg Marshall.

Greg wasn't daunted at all. "Great to meet you both. So you run that little shoe store next door, Rio?"

Sophie caught the look of horror on Rio's face. It wasn't exactly a compliment to be considered the person responsible for the dusty window and dreadful stock displayed by Kelly's Quality Footwear.

"Nope. I'm on this side." Rio jerked a thumb at the wall he shared with Sophie. "Freedom Machines. I sell motorcycles."

"That a fact? How fascinating. Not that I ever had the yen to drive one, of course, but friends of mine used to, when we were all young and foolish." Greg was the only one who laughed at that.

"Riding a bike doesn't have anything to do with age. It's a state of mind, sort of a spiritual thing," Rio said in a deadpan way, pinning the other man with a cool, long stare.

Sophie was now a spectator, watching the interplay between the men. It was interesting to compare them.

Greg was tall, about the same height as Rio, but that was where the resemblance between the two ended. Greg's blond hair was expertly cut and styled to look windblown and disheveled, while Rio's curls were plain old riotous.

Sophie would bet that Rio went to an old-fashioned barber on the rare occasions he had his hair cut.

"I've never heard anybody claim motorcycles were spiritual," Greg was saying in a cynical tone, with another attempt at a laugh and a knowing glance at Sophie that tried to indicate she and he were the only sane ones around.

But Sophie ignored the glance, curious as to what Rio would say next, and still engrossed in her mental comparisons of the two.

Greg was older than Rio, but not that much. He was picture-book handsome—deep-set blue eyes with golden lashes, a straight nose, nice lips, firm chin.

Rio's nose was crooked, his macho-rugged features irregular.

Greg was tailored to the nines. He'd never tolerate—well, an erection, for instance, at an inconvenient moment.

Rio's tailoring was all by Levi.

And as for erections . . .

Sophie came out of her reverie with a guilty start.

What on earth was her problem, anyway, dwelling on men's personal parts like this?

The discussion about motorcycles was reaching a peak.

"Guess you never came across a classic piece of literature called *Zen and the Art of Motorcycle Maintenance*, by Robert Pirsig," Rio was saying. "It explains a lot of the prejudice about bikers, as well as the true philosophy behind riding. But you gotta have an open mind to start with, or it wouldn't mean much."

"I've always prided myself on being open-minded," Greg bristled. "And furthermore—"

Without waiting for the rest of Greg's answer, Rio called, "Hey, Gina, I gotta get back to the store. You comin', or what?"

Gina didn't even look up from her study of a shell-pink satin teddy. "No, you go ahead. I'll be over later."

Rio started for the door. "Sophie, we on for tonight?"

He made it sound like a big deal, and she didn't mind a bit. "Yes, of course, Rio. Soon as I lock up."

He sauntered out the door, and Greg watched him go with a peculiar expression on his face, as if Rio had one-upped him and he didn't like it. Then he shrugged and gave Sophie his full attention, launching into the speech she'd expected in the beginning.

"I must tell you what a super lady that mother of yours is, Sophie. She can run rings around the rest of us. Her sales were the highest in the office for the last three months."

"Yes, Mom's a dynamo, all right."

"Well, obviously you're no slouch yourself, designing and selling all these garments."

How typical that the clothes would be garments to Greg and things to Rio.

Well, Greg was unctuous and Rio was . . . honest?

"They aren't exactly zipping off the racks," Sophie noted with dry humor, indicating the store empty except for themselves and Gina. "I'm not winning any awards for high sales of the month. It's not an inherited trait."

Obviously Greg didn't know how to respond to that, and the conversation lagged.

"Do you have a listing near here?" Sophie ventured next, beginning to feel uncomfortable with the silent Gina a few feet away, holding up intimate lacy lingerie, and Greg shifting from one Gucci loafer to the other.

Maybe he'd take the hint and leave.

"No, I simply wanted to get a feeling for this area. And meet you, of course. The way real estate is booming, it won't be long before all these run-down warehouses are bought up by developers."

Sophie shuddered. "And turned into contemporary disasters. I hope that doesn't happen in my lifetime. I love this area just the way it is."

Greg laughed as if she were joking. He glanced over at Gina, still doing a minute inventory of Sophie's stock, and raised his voice as he said, "It's almost lunchtime, can I take you lovely ladies out for a bite?"

Sophie refused right away, but to her amazement, Gina did a slow and careful survey of Greg for the first time since he'd arrived, and in a laconic, husky voice, she accepted the invitation.

Greg seemed rather nonplussed. Sophie wondered if he'd included Gina in the invitation just to be polite, but he was every inch the gentleman as Gina slithered over and put a hand on his arm.

In fact, as Gina's musky perfume battled with Greg's powerful cologne, Sophie could have sworn they were made for each other. Much as she liked scent, she was going to have to air out the store after they left.

How could Rio be so natural, and Gina so contrived?

"You've got some terrific things here, Sophie," Gina complimented in an offhanded way, as if she were a queen bestowing a favor. Then she added, "Also, some of them are not so great, but I guess it's a case of whatever the general public wants, huh?"

They left, and Sophie pawed through various dresses and jumpsuits, racking her brain in an effort to figure out which outfits Gina had thought not so great and why. She stopped herself after a half hour. For heaven's sake, why should she let Gina's opinion bother her?

Sophie thought it over and came to the conclusion that Gina had a characteristic she envied. Gina had an air of absolute self-assurance.

Well, maybe it could be developed with practice.

Sophie took a deep breath and phoned her bank manager, Ms Penny Hawthorne, after writing down what she wanted to say so she wouldn't end up babbling like an idiot.

Ms Penny Hawthorne had once been one of Harriet's clients. Harriet had sold her an expensive town house, and when Sophie started the business, her mother had introduced them. It was the old game of scratch my back, I'll scratch yours. Although Sophie's business account was anything but lucrative.

Sophie always found the other woman cold and intimidating. She read off her request for more money, hoping it didn't sound as if she were reading. "Ms Hawthorne, I need an extension on my line of credit in order to . . ."

There was a long, pregnant silence. Then the cool, controlled voice said, "I have your last financial statement here in front of me, Ms Larson. Unfortunately, it appears that the Unicorn's sales aren't increasing enough to warrant a larger line of credit at this time. However, if you'd like to discuss it further, please feel free . . ."

Sophie hung up, feeling mad and inadequate and most of all, frustrated. She knew what she ought to do: change banks, shop around, take the initiative, be more dynamic when she presented her case and above all, she shouldn't do it on the phone. It was more difficult for a bank manager to turn down a client in person.

Sophie knew all those things. Harriet had taught her all the rules, but she could only do what her nerves would stand, and she'd just done it.

The velour caftans would have to wait another year. Now there was the nasty job of telling Bill she couldn't get the velour and listening to him rage.

SHE MADE ONLY TWO small sales that afternoon, and when the last browser left at twenty past five, she was quick to lock the door.

She washed her face and reapplied her makeup in the bathroom and wondered if she ought to go next door or wait here for Rio to come for her.

It wasn't a date, after all, she reminded herself. She'd decided last night not to date Rio, and it was the right decision.

This was just a discussion between business associates. Rio had said he needed a favor, and Sophie would grant it if she could, because Rio had done a lot of favors for her.

She hung around and waited for him until five to six, and then she decided to go next door, but when she reached the front of the store, he appeared at her door.

He was carrying two motorcycle helmets.

"Ever been on a bike?" he asked, handing her a shiny red-and-silver number. For a horrible moment, Sophie wondered if this was really how she wanted to end her life. The truth was, motorcycles scared the daylights out of her. But then she remembered Greg's attitude to bikes that morning and Rio's attitude to Greg, and she smiled and shook her head. "Never. But I thought we were only going to talk."

"We are, but not here. Put that helmet on, and we'll take a little zip along the highway. I've found fresh air clears my head at the end of the day. Good thing you're wearing slacks, although those shoes aren't the best."

They both stared down at Sophie's high-heeled sandals, and at last Rio shrugged.

"They'll have to do for now."

Sophie locked the door behind them, and there by the curb was Rio's blue motorcycle.

He was already shoving his helmet on, and Sophie gingerly tried to make the lightweight plastic thing go over her mop of curls without doing serious damage.

It was impossible. No matter how she tried to slide it on, the helmet resisted. Rio watched her clumsy efforts for a moment, and then he moved in front of her and buried his fingers in the thick hair on either side of her head.

Sophie could smell the clean, man scent of his body and feel the heat he radiated. His fingers touching her hair sent an erotic thrill through her.

Rio stroked her curls back with tender care, frowning and muttering under his breath as he concentrated on making the unruly mass fit under the helmet without hurting her.

"Maybe if we sort of gather it all back like this . . ."

With one hand he held her hair at the nape, and with the other he scrunched the helmet over it and gave a downward tug.

"There," he announced with satisfaction, and Sophie felt him thread the chin strap through the clasp and draw it closed under her throat. He trailed his fingers across her skin, which wasn't absolutely necessary. It was nice, though. Her shoulder bag was draped across one arm, and he took the strap and looped the bag up and over her head, adjusting it across her chest and settling it at her hip. Now she couldn't possibly drop it.

For a moment, she forgot the purpose of the exercise, losing herself in the heady delight of having him fuss over her.

But all too soon he winked down at her and stepped toward the bike, slinging one lithe leg over the saddle and balancing the contraption with an expectant look her way.

She had to face the fact that he expected her to get on behind him.

Her heart was hammering. She sidled over to the curb, put one foot on the pedal he indicated and lifted her other leg with as much grace as she could muster, swinging it over the back of the bike. She settled into the saddle, and Rio reached down and lifted her feet onto the foot pegs.

Once she was in place, she realized that there was a certain charm to the situation as long as they were sitting still.

For instance, her front and Rio's back were in intimate contact. Even her thighs were pressed against the back of his thighs, and there didn't seem to be anywhere to put her arms except around his middle.

She remembered the ride on the sewing machine and blushed, but he couldn't see her.

She rested her hands on his sides with polite, cool reserve.

"Hold on and lean the same direction I do, okay?"

Sophie swallowed. Her throat was dry and tight all of a sudden.

"Okay," she promised.

He did something vicious with his foot and one hand, and the engine roared to life. Sophie was aware of noise, vibration and a sense of leashed power. Then, with one easy movement, Rio steered out into the street. The bike tilted and righted itself with the motion of his body, and Sophie bit back the scream that rose in her throat.

She was about to die; she knew it.

Her arms snaked right around Rio's waist and she clung to him like a limpet, plastering herself against his back, aware only of fear and the awful certainty that death was imminent as the machine rocked and roared and bucked beneath her, coming to an abrupt halt at an intersection and then surging to life again.

Lean the same way I do, he'd instructed, and at first Sophie tried, but it was obvious Rio was intent on leaning the wrong damn way.

With every turn, he tipped their bodies over to the side in the same direction as the bike, and each time he did, Sophie knew they were about to fall to the pavement and lose most of their skin before they stopped skidding. It was going to hurt badly.

After the first three turns, she did the only thing she could think of to save their lives; she leaned as far one way as Rio leaned the other, compensating as well as she could for his stupidity.

The second time she did it, he pulled the bike to the curb and half turned toward her with a serious frown.

"Sophie, you've got to lean over with me into the curves, not the way you're doing. I know it seems all wrong to lean into the curve instead of away, but just trust me, can you do that?"

It was a lot to ask. Sophie realized she was trembling and her stomach felt nauseous. Being stopped was heaven. Maybe she ought to just get off here and take a nice safe bus home and forget she'd ever met Rio.

But before she could get her numbed and shaking limbs to obey, Rio had the bike moving again, weaving an expert and hair-raising path through the afternoon traffic and over the arch of Lion's Gate Bridge, taking the turn through North Vancouver that led to the Upper Levels Highway.

For the first half hour, Sophie kept her eyes screwed shut and her face pressed tightly to Rio's back, waiting for the inevitable moment when the bike tipped all the way over and her vulnerable bones and skin met the hard surface of the road.

To her utter disgust, in the midst of a near-death experience, she was still conscious of Rio's appealing torso, clasped in a viselike grip by her arms, of his smooth, incredible muscles and the easy grace of his body as he controlled the horrible machine beneath them.

In the midst of terror, she remembered wisps of her dream. And ever so gradually, she began to gain a tiny bit of trust in his ability to keep them upright.

She began to open her eyes now and then and raise her head a slight bit inside its plastic container, getting breathtaking glimpses of wide, winding highway running parallel to the ocean.

They were flying along, skimming what seemed bare inches above the surface of the road, mobile in a way Sophie had never dreamed possible. The cool, salt-tinged air rushed past, the scenery was three dimensional, complete with smells and wind sounds.

"How you doin' back there, honey?"

Rio had to shout to be heard over the wind, and Sophie saw his amused grin reflected at her through the rearview mirror.

Pride made her holler back, "Fine. I'm doing fine."

He terrified her all over again right then by letting go of the bike's handlebars with one hand and giving her clamped fists, somewhere in the vicinity of his belly, a comforting pat.

"Could you ease off a little on my gut, then? You're squeezing my belly into my backbone."

She forced herself to let her grip loosen a trifle, and he nodded his thanks and stroked her hand.

But an instant later, she didn't dare breathe as he pulled out with jaunty confidence to pass a transport truck.

Sophie had never felt as small or helpless or out of control in her entire life. She could feel the heat of the huge vehicle, smell the diesel exhaust, and almost—if she dared—reach out and touch the side of the monolith as they accelerated and glided past.

At last, Rio took a turn off the highway, which put them on a secondary road where the traffic was light, and after a series of hairpin turns that led up an ever-increasing incline on still another narrow road, they reached a park at the top of a mountain....

Rio drew into the parking area and cut the engine, leaning the bike on its kickstand and then swinging off.

He swept off his helmet and ran a hand through the mess of crushed curls beneath. He locked the helmet to the side of the bike and reached out to help Sophie.

She didn't think her legs were going to hold her up as he grasped her with a helpful arm and all but lifted her from the saddle to stand beside him.

She slumped against him for a moment, feeling as if she were still in motion. His strong arms supported her, holding her around the waist, clasped tightly against him.

"Little wobbly, huh? You'll get your land legs back in a minute," he assured her.

At last she was able to support herself. She moved back and reached up to wrestle the helmet off.

"I've never been so scared in my entire life," she blurted out.

Rio threw his head back and laughed. "I figured you were maybe a little nervous. You almost broke three of my ribs with that stomach lock you had on me. But you did real well there toward the end. You caught on fast to the rhythm of riding."

Was that what it was, rhythm? It had seemed the purest urge for survival to Sophie.

Now that they were stationary again, she started feeling little bubblings of pride in herself at actually having ridden on a motorcycle. She'd been a timid child and never really grown out of it, with no brothers or sisters around to dare or encourage her. It felt good to have conquered fear, even a little bit.

She mustered up an uncertain grin to match the wide one Rio wore as he went on holding her, even though her legs were fine again.

"Well, biker gal, want some fish and chips? There's an old guy with a stand in this park who makes the best fish and chips anywhere. It's a carefully guarded secret by those in the know, or the whole city would be up here on summer evenings."

"I'd love some." Sophie realized all of a sudden that she was ravenous. "Wow, I'm starving."

"It's the fresh air, does it every time."

Hand in hand, they made their way through groves of tall cedars toward a small concession stand attached to a green wooden bungalow. Several couples were waiting to be served, and other people were scattered around the cleared area, sitting on rough wooden benches enjoying their meal.

When it was their turn to be served, the grizzled man behind the counter reached out a hand to shake the one Rio extended.

"Hey, Rio, how's it goin'? How's your pop doin' these days?"

"He told me to tell you he's got a new batch of wine ready and waiting for you to sample. Vinny Travisano, this is Sophie Larson."

Sophie gave the vigorous little man a shy smile, and he saluted her with a kissing motion of fingers to his lips, an obvious compliment to her.

With a flourish, he produced two newspaper-wrapped bundles of deep-fried cod and thick home-cut potato chips.

Sophie balanced their mugs of coffee, and she and Rio made their way over to a vacant bench that seemed to hover on the very edge of a cliff. From this vantage point, the shoreline, ocean inlet and distant mountains spread out in breathtaking grandeur.

They devoured the simple and delicious food, talking about the beauty of the landscape, laughing at the gulls that swooped and dove for every discarded morsel.

Sipping the fresh coffee Rio had gone for, Sophie at last remembered the original point of this meeting. "You said you had to talk to me," she reminded Rio. "What about?"

He set his cup down on the bench at his side and looped his arms across the back support, a sober expression on his features.

"Ah, it's that sister of mine, Gina. She's driving the family crazy, that girl. First, she quit school in her senior year, and nobody could talk her into going back. She was gonna be a model. She talked Pop into paying out a bundle of money for some course. She seemed to be doin' fine, and then one day she up and quit that, as well. When I asked her why, she says it's because they treat her like a piece of meat, like she's got no brain."

Rio sighed and gestured with his hands. "I understand what she's sayin', but what did she expect? So from there she gets a job as a waitress in some fancy restaurant. One of my buddies let me know that the owner was all the time comin' on to Gina, making life tough for her, y'know?"

Sophie nodded, fascinated by the epic unfolding in Rio's graphic script.

He sighed again, letting his hands fall to his sides. "So I went over there one night, thinking I'd have a few words with the creep, sort of let him know Gina wasn't out there all on her own, and damned if I don't see the guy tryin' to make out with her right there in front of everybody?"

"What did you do?"

"Do?" Rio raised his eyebrows and his hands. "Nothing. I didn't have to. Gina picked up a heavy ashtray and almost brained him. There was blood all over his fancy suit, and the guy was screaming like a nut case, threatening to sue her. So I had a few choice words with him, a little reminder that dozens of people had seen him pawing her and that we were the ones who had a lawsuit if we decided to pursue it —she'd lied about her age of course. I got a check for Gina's wages and we left. So she's out of a job again, and now she's startin' to hang around with older guys, talking about taking off to New York. That's no place for a kid like her."

"Kid? How old is Gina, anyway?" Sophie had guessed her to be twenty-four or five, and she was shocked when Rio said, "She's just turned seventeen." He noted the expression on Sophie's face and nodded. "Yeah, she looks and acts lots older and smarter than she really is. She's a good kid. I figure eventually she'll get it together, but I'm scared silly she's gonna get herself in bad trouble before her brain develops enough to match her body. Which brings me to what I wanted to talk over with you." He hesitated and Sophie waited.

Finally he blurted out, "See, I wondered if you could kinda ask her to work for you in your store, Sophie. I could tell she loved your store right off the bat, and she's all the time on about clothes and designing."

Sophie felt all sorts of resistance to that idea.

First of all, she couldn't afford it; and second, Gina made her uneasy; and third, baby-sitting Rio's sister wasn't exactly what she'd had in mind as a hobby; and fourth, it was getting harder and harder to keep this thing with Rio on a strictly business level the way she'd decided in the beginning.

She stared to shake her head no, and Rio hurried on, "Hold it, okay? Now before you say a flat no, let me tell you all of it."

He was sitting to one side now, facing Sophie, and he reached out and took both her hands in his, palm to palm, folding them so their fingers interlaced, then moving his fingers in slow, deliberate cadence over the back of hers.

Rio was a toucher. It was almost as if he believed words weren't adequate unless bodies made contact. She could feel his warm, callused flesh against hers, and there was no question touching him was going to make it harder to refuse.

"I know she'd be a pain at first. You're used to working by yourself in the store and she's a funny kid. She doesn't know how to act so she puts on that sophisticated air. I could smack her one for it right in the ear hole sometimes. But she's honest and reliable, Sophie. It might give you a little time off. You need more time off than you get. And she's awful persuasive, if that counts for anything in selling."

Sophie wasn't sure it did. Knowing what you liked yourself and guessing what would please another person were two very separate abilities. But she let Rio finish.

"Also, I'd insist on paying her wages myself. But I'd like it if she didn't know that."

Sophie wanted to object for honor's sake, but the simple fact was the Unicorn made just enough to pay her own living expenses, never mind afford an employee. If Sophie was even to consider this scheme, she'd have to accept Rio's offer.

And get more and more involved with him.

She pictured Gina again in her mind, the dramatic hairdo and the short skirt. The gum.

A mental image formed of the times she'd left Michelle to mind the store. Even chewing gum and with her underpants showing, Gina presented the better image, no question there.

But Sophie had never been tough enough to train Michelle. What hope would she have with Gina?

She remembered Gina's fast mouth, her outspoken criticism of some of the styles in the store, her off-putting manners. From what Rio had just said, Gina was difficult and headstrong, not the personality type Sophie would have chosen as an employee.

"With Gina, you've got to come right out and tell her what you expect and let her know who's the boss, or before you know it she'll have the upper hand," Rio said, as if he were reading Sophie's mind. "She's not easy, I know this is a lot to ask of you, Sophie. Don't feel you have to give me an answer right now, but promise you'll think about it, okay?"

"Okay," Sophie agreed with reluctance. Rio was putting her on the spot, and she wasn't sure she liked it.

"Let's take a walk. There's a path that goes along the cliff." Rio got to his feet and tugged at her hands.

For the next half hour, as summer's twilight began to fall, they ambled along the path, admiring the sunset and the calm and tranquil inlet far below them with its sprinkling of sailboats dancing here and there. There were two large yachts moored in isolated coves, and from their vantage point, Sophie and Rio could see the boat's inhabitants sunbathing on the deck and now and then diving into the blue-green water to cool off.

Sophie forgot about the Unicorn as they laughed and talked like old friends, imagining what it would be like to own one of those luxury boats and sail away to wherever they fancied.

"When I was a real little kid," Rio confided, "Nonna— that's what we call my father's mother—well, anyhow, Nonna used to take me down to Stanley Park every Saturday. We'd walk around the sea wall and make up stories about the luxury liners that sailed in and out of the inner harbor. She used to have this dream of sailing away on one someday, visiting all her friends and relatives in Italy. And I'd always promise her that when I grew up, I'd make lots of money, and her and I'd take a cruise to Italy and then the Caribbean."

"Is she still alive, your grandmother?"

Rio's expression grew tender and sad. "Nonna's seventy-six now. She fell last winter and broke her hip. She's been in hospital ever since. The doctors don't think she'll ever walk again."

"Rio, that's awful. I'm so sorry." Tears came to Sophie's eyes, thinking of the little boy making promises he couldn't keep to the old woman he obviously loved.

Rio paused in a glade of pine trees and drew Sophie into his arms. "That's what makes you nice, Sophia. You've got a tender heart."

He reached up to touch her disheveled hair, and his voice was husky, "You're beautiful, you know that, Sophia *mia*? First time I saw you, tryin' to open that door that morning, I couldn't stop looking at you, how your hair sort of glows in the sun, and you're all soft and curvy and sweet. You're everything a woman ought to be."

He dropped his hand and used it to press the small of her back, coaxing her into the hard contours of his body. His smell, his personal man smell, filled her nostrils and she breathed it in. How she loved Rio's smell.

"I'm gonna kiss you now, okay?"

It wasn't a question, because the last word was felt more than heard as his lips closed on hers, his arms cradling her so every piece of her body fitted some part of his. Her arms came up and encircled his neck.

Sophie couldn't separate the delicious sensations he created. His open hands moved on her back, cradling her buttocks and pressing her hips against his hard arousal, then stroking up each side until his fingers rested under each swelling breast.

And his lips. He had a master's degree at kissing, that was certain. He angled his head until his mouth fit hers. His tongue ravished her mouth, hot and curious. He delved and

stroked and teased until she returned each caress with one of
her own, shuddering with delight.

Excitement and desire exploded between them. Sophie was
trembling, and she could feel Rio's heart thundering against
her breasts.

"Sophie, my Sophia," Rio breathed.

Eagerness and impatience filled her body with awful need,
fed by the way his hand cupped her breast, and, through her
blouse, his thumb found the hard-tipped nipple and circled
it with maddening, slow strokes that made her undulate
against him.

He nibbled at her earlobe, explored the curve of her jaw
with his tongue and teeth, and then, with a deep, shuddering
breath, he stepped back, away from her, and she heard the
sound of a woman's laughter and a man's voice. Other people were coming along the trail.

"One of these days," he said in a low voice unsteady with
passion, "we'll be doing this in a place where nobody can in-
terrupt us. And then, Sophie . . . and then . . ."

He didn't finish. He didn't have to. His smoldering eyes met
hers in a promise that had her heart hammering with desire,
her body damp and throbbing, just at the thought of having
him love her.

They walked back to the bike, and this time Sophie managed to pull the helmet onto her head by herself. Rio lifted
her up and onto the seat, and in moments they were once
again dipping and swaying around the curves of the road.

But something had changed in her attitude toward biking.

Now she welcomed the tearing wind, the awful excitement of speed and freedom the bike provided. For the first
time, she understood how sensual a motorcycle was, how
primeval in its unleashed power.

She understood as well the depth of trust a rider must be-
stow on the person operating the machine. Her very life de-
pended on Rio's skill and reflexes.

Now she was comfortable with that knowledge. She trusted him.

She clung tightly to his body, and every now and then he reached a hand back and touched her, sometimes her arm, or her thigh, a reassuring small caress that linked them in the vortex of rushing air and speeding traffic.

Long before they reached the city, Sophie found herself feeling sorry for the people locked in their cars, seat belts in place, windows rolled up to allow the air conditioning to cool the inside of the vehicle.

She felt young and wild and free.

She felt dangerous and sexy.

She felt like Rio's woman, and she refused to allow caution to interfere with that delicious sensation.

6

SOPHIE HAD GIVEN RIO her address, and by the time they were nearing her apartment, she'd made up her mind to ask him in.

The bike pulled onto her street, and Sophie's heart sank. Parked in front of her building was her mother's distinctive silver Cutlass.

The bike purred to a stop and Rio got off. When Sophie had wrestled out of the helmet, she gestured to the car.

"It belongs to my mother."

Just as she'd anticipated, Rio said he wouldn't come in.

"Not this time," he said, leaning forward to plant a nice rough kiss on her mouth. He sounded as disappointed as she felt.

"I don't think your mom would appreciate having me join the party. I'll take a rain check though."

He got back on the bike and roared away, and Sophie made her reluctant way into the building.

"Hi, Mom," she called when she opened her door.

Harriet was sitting in an armchair in the living room, feet propped on a footstool, half-moon glasses perched on her nose, and the latest real estate printouts spread over her lap and across the low table in front of her. Her fingers were busy tapping out numbers on a pocket calculator.

She punched in several figures and then jotted the result in a small notebook.

"Hello, Sophie. You're certainly late. Where on earth were you? I wanted to spend a quiet hour or two with you, but now I'm going to have to leave soon." She glanced at her watch.

Sophie kicked off her shoes. "Did Mr. Wanless let you in?"

Mr. Wanless was accommodating in the extreme.

"Yes, he did, and I must say, Sophie, I believe almost anyone could talk him into letting them come in here. Your security in this building is atrocious."

"But Mr. Wanless knows you, Mother. He's let you in before."

"That's not the point. The point is, you either have good security or you don't. And here you don't. Sophie, why on earth are you wearing your purse that way?"

Sophie sighed and unslung her shoulder bag.

"To keep it from flying away. I got a ride home on Rio's motorcycle." Prudence told her not to go into detail about the fact that the ride had taken her halfway to Squamish and back.

Not going into detail had been a good idea, all right. Harriet's half-moon glasses almost dropped off the end of her nose, and her voice was scandalized. "Sophie, I'm appalled at you. Don't you realize how dangerous those things are? And riding around with that hooligan. I can't imagine what you see in him. Sophie, sometimes I don't understand you at all." Harriet gave a beleaguered sigh.

The feeling was mutual, but Sophie held her tongue. Why was there always this friction between her and her mother? They only had each other, as far as relatives went, and it would be nice to be able to relax with Harriet.

"Greg said he dropped by today to meet you," her mother said next.

"Yes, he did. Would you like a cup of herbal tea, Mom?"

Sophie felt it would be a good idea to derail this new subject before it got started, but Harriet refused to be diverted.

"No, thanks, dear. I poured myself a sherry, and I still have some here. I don't think it would have killed you to go out for lunch with him, you know. He said you refused."

He'd also left out the fact that Gina had accepted, Sophie deduced. Well, she wasn't about to break the news to her mother that the Agostinis had probably corrupted yet another innocent.

"Want to come in the kitchen while I put water on for tea?" Sophie made her way along the hall. After several minutes, her mother followed her into the kitchen, and the subject of Greg Marshall followed right along with them.

"He's a nice man, Greg, ambitious, good-looking, good family background," she recited as if it were a mantra. "He moved here a few months ago from the East. Men like that are at a premium these days, Sophie." Harriet was trying to keep her tone light and teasing, but it didn't work. "He told me you seemed worried about your business."

Sophie could feel her temper slipping.

"He did, eh? Did he also tell you he met Rio and that they had an argument about motorcycles?"

"Yes, as a matter of fact he did."

"Sounds like you and Greg had a nice heart-to-heart about me. Did the pair of you figure out what to do about it all?" Sophie filled and plugged in the kettle and shoved two berry-blush tea bags into the fat brown pot.

"Don't be so touchy, dear. I'd never gossip about you, you know that. I just mentioned that I was concerned about you, that was all. You did go through a bad time after that last breakup, you know."

Why did her mother always make her feel like an entry in red ink on the debit side of some human ledger?

Why did she allow her mother to make her feel that way?

Somehow, Harriet had managed to spoil the lighthearted joy, the sensation of being daring and attractive, that Sophie had felt when she came home after being with Rio. Harriet had replaced those delicious sensations with old, painful insecurities.

"Mom, if you like this Greg Marshall so much, why the heck don't *you* date him? I don't need you to pimp for me."

The words were out before she could stop them, and Harriet's well made-up face reflected intense shock, and then hurt...and something else that Sophie couldn't decipher. She turned deep red, and her features seemed to stiffen.

"Mom, I'm sorry. I didn't mean to. It's just that . . ."

But Harriet was preparing to leave, and she was angry. She slid into her suit jacket and drew a lipstick out of her purse, applying it to her lips without needing a mirror. She didn't look at Sophie once, and her voice was as glacial as her expression.

"Obviously you're not in the mood for company tonight, Sophie. I consider that a very rude remark. I suppose it's indicative of the company you're keeping. Now, I have an appointment. I must go." She swept out the door, closing it with a bit more force than was necessary.

The kettle was puffing out steam, and the air was electric with the residue of negative emotion.

Sophie slopped the water into the teapot and poured herself a cup before it was steeped. Her hands were trembling, and she felt ashamed of herself and defensive and frightened, all at the same time.

I don't need you to pimp for me.

What on earth had possessed her, saying a thing like that to her mother?

But she knew exactly what had spurred her on, and she was honest enough to face it, even though it contradicted all the fine resolve she'd mouthed to herself about not getting involved in any intimate way with Rio.

The truth was, she'd wanted more than anything to invite him in tonight, to sit with him in her living room and talk and laugh, to . . . she closed her eyes and swallowed hard.

To what, Sophie? Let's be honest here.

The images appeared in her mind like an X-rated movie.

To talk and kiss and stroke and fondle. To get naked with him and make hot love until neither of them could stand up, that's what.

And her mother had prevented it just by being here.

Sophie sipped her tea and thought for a long time. She owed her mother an apology over the pimp remark, and she'd make it first thing tomorrow.

But Rio was a whole other story. Where was this thing with Rio leading?

She'd decided that she'd never fall for a man again unless she could depend on him to be there for her when she needed him. He would have to give her just as much as he took if she was going to enter a long-standing relationship with him.

Up till the time she figured that out, it seemed she'd done all the giving and men most of the taking. After a lot of self-analysis, Sophie understood why she needed someone ultra-dependable: she'd never had anyone to fulfill that role in her life. There'd been only Harriet, and the demands of her job always came ahead of Sophie's needs.

Was Rio the man she was looking for?

Sophie thought it over and shook her head. No. Rio was the sexiest man she'd ever known. He was fun, he was unpredictable, he was generous and daring.

But a man like Rio with a failed marriage behind him, with a little daughter he hardly ever saw, with a barrage of relatives and a heritage foreign to Sophie, to say nothing of a store full of motorcycles and a host of weird friends . . . no, Rio wasn't exactly the man Sophie had envisioned in her future.

He wasn't the type to inspire lifelong trust in a woman.

There was always the suspicion that he'd climb onto his bike some day and ride off into the sunset if the notion struck him. Perhaps it was that very touch of elusiveness that made him irresistible.

Yet something about her own motorcycle ride that afternoon and the intoxicating feeling of freedom she'd experienced had given her a sense of bravado and adventure, as well.

Seeing that she was being honest here, Sophie had to admit that she wanted Rio sexually, with a hunger that defied reason.

So why shouldn't she just have a good time with him, without all those projections of commitment, marriage, fidelity, trust and forever? What was wrong with good plain fun, as long as she had no illusions about forever?

Surely just once in a woman's life, there was room for a fling, no strings attached. Rio would be her secret indiscretion, her moment of madness, no regrets, no recriminations, no guilt.

When she was old and wrinkled and safely married to a different, safer sort of man for forty-odd years, she could take out her memories of Rio and this one mad summer and feel satisfied that she'd missed nothing in her life.

And she would regret nothing, either, Sophie decided with firm resolve.

It felt as if she'd made a momentous decision, so she went on and made another. She was definitely on a roll.

There were practical matters to consider if she was about to embark on an affair, such as privacy.

She decided that she was going to phone a locksmith first thing tomorrow and see about having a dead bolt installed on her apartment door. Then no one could get in without her knowledge and approval, such as her mother, arriving at an inopportune time, getting Mr. Wanless to let her in, only to discover two naked, sweaty bodies....

Sophie shuddered.

She'd tell Harriet the new lock was a result of her lecture about security.

Not all of her mother's ideas were bad, after all.

She went into the bathroom and drew her usual tubful of scented hot water. While she bathed, she pondered about the Gina thing.

She just didn't want to hire her. Gina made her nervous. Even knowing the girl was eleven years her junior didn't help.

Gina had a type of self-confidence that Sophie lacked, and age had nothing to do with it. It was unfortunate, but Sophie couldn't summon one positive thought about Rio's sister. The girl had been close to rude, and she'd acted as if she inhabited another planet.

But then Sophie thought about Rio and all the little, kind things he'd done for her. She owed him plenty of favors, and this was as good a way as any to repay some of them.

FULL OF MISGIVINGS, Sophie told Rio she'd give Gina a try in the store.

They agreed that Rio would pay his sister's wages, but only until the Unicorn began making enough money to afford an employee.

If it ever did.

Also, Rio didn't want Gina to know that he was subsidizing her, so Sophie promised to keep it a secret, wondering just what she'd gotten herself into when Gina ambled in to work the first morning half an hour late, dressed in a minuscule denim mini skirt that revealed miles of shapely leg and a shocking view of lacy black panties when Gina dared to bend even a little. She was chewing gum, and she looked as bored as she had when Sophie first met her.

"You can put your purse in here," Sophie instructed, showing Gina the back room, aware more than ever before of how messy and dingy it looked. Gina stared around and wrinkled her nose, which made Sophie cringe. It also made her more determined than ever to lay down hard and fast ground rules with this girl, so as not to be bullied by her.

"Gina, the store opens at ten, I'd like you here on time after this." Sophie gulped. This was awful. "And I'd rather you didn't chew gum while you're working."

Might as well start off with all the things she couldn't stand. If Gina was going to walk out, she'd have to do it right now. "Also, some of my customers are quite conservative, usually the ones with the most money. I'd rather you didn't wear minis quite that short."

Gina shrugged as if it were nothing to her whether her skirt touched her bottom or dragged on the floor.

"I only drink herbal tea," Sophie explained next in a defensive tone, "so if you want coffee or soft drinks you'll have to bring some. And we eat lunch in. I can't afford to close for an hour, so you're stuck here from ten in the morning till six at night."

Might as well get it straight right here and now that the Unicorn was anything but a gold mine.

Gina was bright, Sophie had to admit that after the first half hour. She learned everything quickly, and she spent the next half hour tidying racks, arranging the stock according to size and even coordinating the colors.

When a customer came in, Sophie realized that Gina had been making herself familiar with the stock as she tidied up.

"I'm looking for a dress I could wear to a wedding, but which would also do me for other occasions. Something not too fussy?" The timid young woman looked ready to bolt.

Sophie began a swift mental search through her dresses, but before she could suggest anything, Gina went into action.

"Soft colors would be good on you. You're the delicate type. There's a dress back here that reminds me of a flower garden, and here's another one in peach. This shirtwaist style would go anywhere. And there's this two-piece outfit in printed rayon. It looks like a dress, but it would work with other things in your wardrobe. . . ."

Sophie watched with reluctant admiration as Gina paid close attention to the woman without seeming to hover, making intelligent suggestions yet giving her the opportunity to choose between three different styles.

As the woman tried each outfit on, Gina rearranged it with a twitch here and a tug there, draping and blousing, and as if by magic, the outfits each took on style and a certain dash despite the wearer's mousy demeanor.

Without gushing, Gina reassured her customer about her hesitant final decision. She'd decided on the rayon blouse and skirt, and Gina convinced her that a simple silk camisole in a plain shade of old rose would enhance the versatility of the outfit, and yes, she could wear a strapless bra under it if she felt more comfortable.

The woman bought that, as well, not flinching at the price.

The transaction was completed with painless ease, and difficult as it was for her, Sophie stood back and let Gina add it all up. It was a sizable amount, and Sophie felt the thrill she always felt when the Unicorn made a good sale.

But she had to struggle with a feeling of resentment, because Gina had carried the whole thing off without visible effort and without any help from her.

Gina was a born salesperson. Sophie felt she'd told the girl everything that was wrong with her; she owed it to Gina to pay her a compliment on a job well done.

"You did great on that sale, Gina. I'd never have thought to suggest that skirt and blouse. I'd have gone for something more elaborate and probably put her off," Sophie admitted when the woman left the store.

Gina shrugged and turned away, but underneath her perfect makeup, her cheeks flushed with pleasure. Apropos of nothing, she announced, "Y'know that Greg Marshall guy I went to lunch with the other day? You got plans for him or anything?"

Sophie shook her head no, not daring to wonder what plans Gina might have. Would Rio have to challenge Greg to a dual at sunrise...?

"Good thing, because he's a perfect nerd. All he talked about was real estate, but I fixed him. I ordered practically everything on the menu. Listening to garbage comes high these days."

Sophie felt the first twinge of affection for Gina.

"SOPHIE, YOU KNOW what you oughta do around here?"

Sophie sighed and counted to ten.

"What, Gina?"

A week had gone by since Gina started in the Unicorn, and Sophie alternately blessed and cursed the day Rio had introduced her to his sister. Gina was enough to tax the patience of Mother Teresa.

Sophie was also beginning to wonder if she'd ever see Rio again for longer than ten minutes; he'd been too busy all week to do more than stick his head in the door, ask if she wanted the window washed or the flowers watered, and dash away again. He always managed to clean the dog mess for her, though.

Freedom Machines was becoming a success story; there were ever-increasing numbers of people in the store during business hours, and Gina had announced that Rio was teaching a motorcycle training course three evenings a week in order to advertise his business.

Sophie had to admit to herself that she missed having Rio drop in the way he did before he got busy.

It was ironic, but having Gina working for her gave Sophie more free time than she'd had before . . . and having Rio nearby made her less eager to be away from the store.

After that first day, Gina was lounging by the door each morning when Sophie arrived to open the store, snapping out caustic remarks at the mailman or making shy Adam Kelly from the shoe store quiver in his old-fashioned boots when she sidled over and tried to strike up a conversation.

"That Adam's kinda cute," she remarked to Sophie. "He's sorta like a rabbit, he twitches his nose the same. But wow, he's a disaster when it comes to picking stock. Is that store a joke, or what?"

Gina was a lot less generous about Herb. She took an instant dislike to the talkative mailman, and the more she tried to insult him, the more Herb tried to make friends with her and the longer he hung around each morning.

In fact, she seemed to have a devastating effect on most of the male population; an enormous number of phone calls came to the store asking for her, until Sophie put her foot down and insisted personal calls at work had to be emergencies.

She also told Gina in no uncertain terms that the diverse collection of males who wandered in those first few days had better be customers. Sophie wasn't running a rendezvous.

Gina accepted criticism with sublime nonchalance.

"Okay, Soph," she'd drawl. "You're the boss."

After all that, Sophie couldn't bring herself to tell the girl not to call her "Soph."

That was the minus side of the ledger. On the plus side, Gina was an absolute wizard at salesmanship.

She managed to sell, full price, garments that Sophie had privately labeled hopeless and was planning to relegate to the mark-down rack.

During quiet moments, Gina would take an arm load of clothes into a dressing room and try them on, and Sophie gave her a generous discount on anything she wanted to buy, because it soon became evident that whatever Gina draped over her lanky curves turned out to be the exact outfit at least half a dozen other young customers wanted the moment they laid eyes on her wearing it. With her tall, angular body, she could make a potato sack look like a designer original. Even Bill had started listening when Gina suggested they try a certain style. To Sophie's surprise, he adored Gina, and Bill took it upon himself to cut and sew samples based on her ideas, which sold as soon as they hit the Unicorn.

All of this went to Gina's head, and she became convinced that she knew better than Sophie what the Unicorn needed in order to succeed. She gave Sophie the benefit of this wisdom a dozen times a day, and Sophie began reminding herself that stabbing Gina with the long-bladed scissors really wasn't a good idea. The girl would bleed all over the rug, and Sophie couldn't afford a new one. And Rio might be upset.

"What this place needs is a line of stuff that would attract all the females from Rio's place next door, Sophie. You've seen how many women wander over here because they're bored senseless while their guys are talking bikes?"

Gina prowled among the racks, studying things and dismissing them with a supercilious flick of her hand.

"I guess you've got an okay line here, Soph, but it's geared more to boring than to bikers, if you get my drift. We could put in stuff that would just walk out of here. We wouldn't have to bust a gut trying to sell it."

Sophie's blood pressure was on the rise, but she restrained herself. There was maybe a kernel of truth in what Gina was saying. She'd noticed there'd been a lot of browsers, but not many sales from the motorcycle crowd.

"So what do you suggest, Gina?"

The caustic note in her voice didn't even register on her employee. Gina's eyes became slits, and she rattled off, "Lycra, snappy colors. A line of ready-mades in leather, pants and skirts and tailored jackets, they're big right now. T-shirts, oversize pure cotton without any junk on the front. Jumpsuits in wild shades, made of silk, like old-fashioned pilots used to wear, y'know? Wow, that's a great idea. Bill and Michelle could make 'em. They'd go like pizzas. I can't find them anywhere else in town."

Sophie snorted. "I'd need a ton of money to start putting in stock like that, Gina. Do you know how much leather costs even wholesale? My bank manager wouldn't go for it."

"You can't sell it if you haven't got it," Gina singsonged.

Sophie thought of her starchy bank manager and her refusal to let Sophie buy even the velour she needed for Christmas.

"The business can't afford it," Sophie added automatically.

"Way I see it, you can't afford not to. You're losing sales by not having the stuff young people want." Gina jerked her thumb at the wall separating the Unicorn from Rio's premises.

"You oughta discuss this bank manager thing with Rio, Sophie. I know he got turned down by a bunch of snooty banks when he wanted to start up, and I heard him telling Pop that he just kept shopping around till he found a manager with some smarts. Why don't you ask him who this money man is that he deals with and go talk to him?"

Now why did that sound like something Harriet would suggest?

It made Sophie furious. "Gina I told you—"

"You want me to ask him for you? I'll go right now. . . ."

"Gina, if I wanted to ask him, I'd do it myself. Now go over to the Sweat Shop and pick up the skirts Bill has ready, and then price and hang them on that front display rack. Then take the carpet sweeper and go over this floor," she ordered in a no-nonsense tone.

She had to get this outrageous, mouthy, brash young upstart out of the store, make a pot of soothing spearmint tea and do deep breathing. What had ever made her think Gina didn't talk very much?

But over tea, Sophie had to admit, even though it almost killed her, that Gina could be right about the stock. It was past time to add some new life to the Unicorn. And she knew she should change bank managers.

Maybe she would talk to Rio.

If and when she ever saw him again.

THE LOCKSMITH she'd called a week before, Mr. Beech, finally arrived that evening. He spent half an hour installing the dead bolt on Sophie's door and another forty minutes scaring her half out of her mind with tales of murder, rape and mayhem, all of which wouldn't have happened, Mr. Beech insisted, if the victims had installed the proper security alarms.

He tried talking Sophie into getting a security system that would cost more than her rent every month, but in case of emergency would ring in some central area, bringing armed men to her door in seconds, ready to fight to the death to save her virtue or even her stereo.

When Sophie managed at last to ease him out with a check for the dead bolt, she felt at risk for the first time since she'd lived in the quiet neighborhood.

She squinted up and down the shadowed hallway, then slammed her door and locked the new lock, double-checking it before she headed into the bathroom for her ritual soak in the tub.

She was up to her neck in bubbles, having a determined mental discussion with her bank manager, when the banging began on her door, a sudden, strong thumping that suggested seven-foot giants with insane eyes and instruments of torture.

Mr. Beech's horror stories sprang into her mind with embellishments, and she spilled gallons of water scrambling out of the tub, heart thumping with unreasoning terror.

It was now half past eleven, and no one came visiting this late. Even if they did, nobody Sophie knew would try to knock her door down quite this way.

Sophie tugged an old cotton robe over her wet body as the banging came again in strong, determined thumps.

A poker. If only she had a poker . . . but the best she could manage was a butcher knife from the wooden block on the kitchen counter.

"Sophie? Sophia *mia*, you in there?" The deep voice belonged to Rio.

The knife fell to the floor and Sophie almost sobbed with relief.

She struggled for long moments with the dead bolt, forgetting how the darned thing opened and then at last getting the hang of it quite by accident.

"I'm not sure how to work this yet and you scared me half to death," she snapped, glaring at Rio when the door finally swung open.

She was furious with herself for being silly, and equally furious with him for catching her soaking wet, without makeup and wrapped in her oldest robe, while he stood there looking gorgeous in faded jeans and a white short-sleeved T-shirt that outlined every muscle and sinew.

"Hey, I'm sorry." His eyes went over her damp body, leaving sensual tremors in their wake like footprints in sand. When his gaze returned to her face, his voice was none too steady.

"I guess it's kinda late all right. I was heading home and I got thinking how I hadn't seen you much lately, and I sorta came by to . . ."

His voice trailed off, and Sophie felt her breath catch in her throat. It was late, she was barely dressed, and there was hot desire already zapping back and forth between them.

She was at a crossroads. If she invited him in, anything was liable to happen and probably would. Did she really still want that?

It seemed a long time since she'd made her decision about having fun with Rio.

So did she still want it or not?

She decided she probably did.

Correction there.

She did want it, and that was that.

7

THE TRUTH OF THE MATTER was that Rio had finished his class early and gone for a beer with two of his students.

Restless, he'd made an excuse and left, riding his motorcycle to Sophie's street and then passing her apartment building three times without stopping, just to see if he could.

Feeling strong and virtuous, he'd roared off at last, all the way across town to the basement suite he rented from his parents.

There, he locked up the bike and went inside, flicked the TV on and off again and indulged in a stream of curses foul enough to peel the paint off the wall.

Unable to stop himself, he slammed out again, unlocked his bike and rode like a dervish all the way back to Sophie's apartment.

He'd been riding up and down the street in front of her place now for over an hour, half wishing some suspicious soul would call the cops. They'd come and haul him away for the night, and by morning he'd have come to his senses.

Maybe. Avoidance didn't work so hot with him. He'd been avoiding Sophie for the past week, and it wasn't working at all the way he hoped it would.

If there was one thing he didn't need in his life right now, it was this feeling that was growing inside of him, this tenderness, this aching longing, this hunger for Sophie Larson.

It had sneaked up on him when his back was turned and his defenses were down, and that was a dirty trick to play on a guy doing his best to get through his life without making any more major tactical errors.

What was it about her that got under his skin this way? Her breasts, her behind, her legs, some horny and ignoble part of his mind listed. Hadn't Pop once, in Italian, told Rio there was nothing crazier than a horny man?

Then why was making out with her such an issue with him, for cripes' sake? He'd had other women, and the enjoyment was mutual, the understanding clear that this was only for now.

Maybe that was the problem. Maybe he should sit Sophie down and have an honest talk with her.

Before he could change his mind again, he wheeled the bike to the curb and walked into her building. An old man in the hall told him which apartment was hers.

There was no damn security in the building at all. Anybody could walk in. It infuriated him that Sophie was at risk.

She seemed to have pretty secure locks, though.

She held the door wide and he came through it, and then she blurted out the first thing that came into her flustered head. "Come in, can I get you a coffee . . . or maybe there's some sherry. . . I was having a bath."

He closed the door behind them and with an easy motion, he secured the bolt.

"Yeah, I figured maybe you were." His white-toothed grin came and went. "You're all wet." He reached out and tousled her wild, damp curls, then took his hand away and followed her as she led the way down the hall and into the living room.

Sophie switched on only one lamp, off in a corner of the room. She loved the effect of shadows on the dozens of satin and velour pillows she'd made, the faded old rug and overstuffed couch with its pattern of intertwined roses. It was a room designed for lamplight.

He moved around, studying the books on her shelves, picking up a faded photograph and putting it down again. He reminded her of a wild animal, familiarizing itself with a place it had never been before, pacing with restless energy.

"I wondered what your house would be like," he said at last. "Somehow I didn't figure you for chrome and lots of glass, and I was right." He moved in a circle and came to stand very close beside her, looking down into her eyes.

"I like it here, Sophia. It feels good, it's comfortable, it's a real home. You've got a knack for making things look nice, just like you do at your store."

She felt flattered, a little giddy, a lot nervous. It seemed strange, having the real, live Rio here after she'd fantasized about him so often. But he wasn't acting the way he did in her fantasies. Every time he came close, he moved away again.

He was far too close now, though. The scent that had come to represent Rio filled her nostrils with its unique blend of man, machines, soap and fresh air.

Her eyes seemed to gravitate to the thick patch of dark hair that showed at the front of his shirt, and she wondered if he could hear her breathing speed up.

He moved still closer, not touching her but making her feel as if he were. He was frowning again, and his voice was a deep rumble in his chest, his words disjointed and anxious sounding.

"I wanted to come in here the other night, y'know, when you asked me. It wasn't just your mom being here that stopped me. And since then, I've been staying away from you, but that isn't working, either."

The admission that he'd been avoiding her was painful. She swallowed hard. "Why, Rio?"

He paused to draw a deep breath and let it out with a whoosh. Sophie was frowning at him, not sure now what was going on. When he'd appeared at the door, it had seemed clear-cut and simple, her decision alone to invite him in and let things progress in a natural way.

How wrong she'd been. It seemed he wanted only to talk.

"I'm not doin' so hot at this, am I? How about we both sit down here, and I'll try to explain."

He threw himself down on her sofa, looking a bit desperate as his eyes traced the shadow of her cleavage.

She drew the neck of her robe together and sat in the armchair facing him, making sure vulnerable parts of her were covered.

Still, the sexual magnetism between them filled the air with static that affected them both.

"Damn it all, I can't stay here now, either, unless I tell you how it is with me," he said in a jerky tone. "See, I don't want any games with you."

His hands were punctuating every sentence.

"There's this feeling between us. Before it goes any further, it's only fair to explain what kind of guy I am," he blurted. "See, there can't be any misunderstandings between us, Sophia."

She nodded and waited. He was sure to stop repeating himself soon and get on with it.

"Sophie," he said at last. "I've got this five-year plan, and I'm determined to stick with it. I told you before, I busted my ass as a laborer on construction sites to get enough money in the bank for a year, to cover alimony, support for Missy, and the little bit of rent I pay my parents for their basement suite. I figured that would give the business time to kick in."

Sophie listened. It was obvious Rio was having some sort of crisis and needed to talk. She waited without comment until he started again.

"I took a course at night school in business admin, and I mortgaged my soul to finance Freedom Machines. The first day I met you, I didn't have thirty dollars of my own in the bank or in my pocket."

"Are you trying to tell me you need money, Rio? I've got a little bit in an emergency fund you can have...."

He sprang to his feet, horrified.

"God, no! That's terrific of you, but that's not what I'm saying at all." He should have studied speech instead of business. Now he had the kid offering him money.

"I just thought..." Sophie began. "Sit down again, okay?"

He did, deciding that maybe she wasn't that far off base thinking he needed a loan. He drove a motorcycle not only through choice; it was inexpensive transportation. He lived as frugally as possible, spending little on fancy clothes or lavish entertainment. He wasn't exactly the last of the big-time spenders on a date. A beer was about his limit.

"What I'm telling you is that if this plan of mine works, I'll be a free man, financially, within five years."

"That's great, Rio." Sophie was getting more confused by the moment. It was beginning to sound as if he was here to sell her life insurance, for goodness' sakes.

"Five years from now, I plan to take a whole year off, and go on a tour of Europe on my bike. I'm gonna enter the Paris-to-Dakar motorcycle race and win it, Sophia." His eyes were glowing with an internal vision. "I'm gonna ride across the Alps and visit Italy and all my relatives."

"Like you were going to do with your grandmother," she whispered.

Pain came and went on his features. "Yeah. That was Nonna's dream, and she went and got too old before I could take her with me. But I'm determined to do it alone."

She was beginning to have a cloudy notion of what he was really saying.

"See, I know what marriage and families and kids and responsibility do to a guy. I got married because Carol was pregnant, and because she looked like a movie star, and imbecile that I was, I thought that gave me status. She married me because in those days I drove a hot little sports car and dressed like a dude and played football for Vancouver's best team."

He gave Sophie a wry look. "Great reasons for a marriage. I soon learned it would have taken a millionaire to buy her the things she figured she needed, and she decided she could do a whole lot better than me."

He'd worked two jobs and still came out of the disaster with a ton of bills to pay. Carol had decided to take the kid and all the furniture, plus what was left of the bank account and leave. He hardly ever saw his kid from the day she was born until she was three. He was amazed when one day this little thing was walking and talking.

"It was a bad marriage. But I've seen good marriages, and even in those, people give up their dreams. Take my pop. He's struggled all his life, pouring cement, getting old before his time, just to support us. He adores his family, but when the old man gets his nose in the wine, y'know what he talks about?"

Sophie shook her head no.

"Learning to fly a plane some day, for cripes' sake."

And Zio Genaro. The guy had seven kids, he'd never owned a decent car in his life, but he knew every race-car driver who ever entered the Grand Prix.

"I see the middle-aged guys who come into my store and drool over the bikes. They're never gonna be able to buy one. They're mortgaged to the hilt and their wives would take a fit."

Dreams. Rio had decided after his marriage failed that he wouldn't settle for only dreams. The secret to making dreams come true was financial security.

"So I thought about all that, and I designed this five-year plan. What I'm sayin' here, Sophia, is that getting tangled up with me wouldn't lead anywhere. I've got nothin' to offer you, not now, not in the future."

He made a hopeless sound in his throat and turned his head away. "I'm not much good at being just your friend, either. When I'm close to you, I need to touch you, see."

"Rio."

He gave her a sheepish, sidelong glance.

"Did it ever occur to you that maybe I feel exactly the same way?" There was passion and impatience and even anger in her voice, and he turned back to face her, surprised at her vehemence and her words.

"Did it ever occur to you that I'm not plotting two-point-five babies and a cottage somewhere with you? That maybe I want exactly the same thing you want, no strings attached?"

"Me, you mean? You sayin' you want me?"

The straightforward, humble question went right to the core of what she was feeling, and it simplified everything.

"More than anything in my life," she whispered.

"God, Sophia." He reached over and gathered her into his arms.

He was holding her in a grip that threatened to cut off her oxygen, and she tried to loosen his arms enough to breathe. His tense muscles felt like steel under her hands.

"But I can't give you . . ."

She made a sound in her throat that might have been a laugh or a sob.

"All I'm asking you to give me is your body, idiot."

His mouth came down on hers, and he unlocked his grip on her ribs. She felt him shudder as he ran his hands up her sides to her rib cage, not touching her breasts but lingering just beneath them.

She gasped as his fingers and palms touched her ribs, learning her shape through the thin fabric of the robe, making circles on the small of her back, dipping down until he cupped her bottom in his hands.

"Sophie, I never wanted a woman this much before, you're so warm. . . ."

Hot. She was hot.

"Soft . . ."

He pulled her into his lap, supporting her with his hands until she straddled him, his hardness grinding against her. She was naked under the robe. Her warm, moist parts were pressed tightly against his jeans.

She settled on him, not caring how heavy she was. Rio had lifted her before, there was nothing to hide from him.

"Sophia *mia*, I dream of tasting you, being inside of you...."

Sophie felt his tongue on her lips, flicking and searching out curves and hollows, teasing the inner corners of her mouth with its tip.

She was burning. She had to feel his bare body against her.

Her hands tugged at his shirt, pulling it out from beneath the belt and snug-fitting jeans. He made a twisting, accommodating movement, and the shirt came free.

She dropped it to the floor and savored the feeling of his heated skin, the teasing coarseness of hair, the leashed power of his strength.

His mouth ravaged hers, and their breath came in matching gasps of sound. She slid her hands up his bare torso, a little shy, feeling the smooth skin of his back, running her fingertips through the curly mat covering his chest, aware that between her legs his hardness had created a pulsing ache that grew more intense with each kiss, each caress.

She wriggled and moaned, and his nipples were hard and throbbing beneath her exploring fingers.

"Let's take this off."

He worked the knot free at the waist of her robe and moved the garment down over her shoulders, trailing small, biting kisses over the bared flesh.

As her robe slipped from her, Sophie suddenly became conscious of her totally naked body, and all the old insecurities about not being slender enough rushed over her.

He was about to see her, and she wasn't thin. Her thighs were too heavy. She could pinch far more than an inch on her hips, her breasts were full instead of girlish and rounded. Panic began to fill her and she was grateful for the subdued light. She clutched for the robe, trying to keep some of herself covered.

But Rio seemed to worship every generous inch of her.

There was no mistaking the expression in his eyes, the way his hands touched her, the sincerity in his voice.

"Let me see you. Let me see how beautiful you are, lush and sexy. I've always dreamed of making love to a woman like you."

She let the robe go, and Rio cupped her ample breasts in his palms and ran his roughened cheek and then his tongue over the lavish, hardened nipples before he drew first one, and then the other, deeply into his mouth, tugging at her with a slow, regular rhythm that echoed in the aching spot between her legs.

"You're gorgeous, Sophia." His voice was husky, his words so earnest she couldn't help but believe him.

"This body of yours, all curves and soft skin, like velvet, here—" his hands slid down and over her belly, and his breath caught "—and like silk here. Sophie, I need to touch you."

He stroked her hips and reached behind to caress each curve of her bottom.

"You've got the sexiest rear I've ever seen. I've wanted to touch you, there...and here..." He slid a finger between the curves, and the sensation made her writhe and gasp. She rocked against him, controlled by the urgent pulsing deep in her abdomen.

He shut his eyes for a moment and held her immobile in his struggle for control.

"Easy, lots of time. We've only just begun."

She pressed her lips to his ear, shyness secondary to the spiral of need consuming her.

"Rio, please, can you take your pants off. . . ."

He slid her onto the couch and stood up. Without one wasted effort, his boots and socks were off.

With one more writhing motion, he stripped off his jeans, and Sophie caught a glimpse of sexy black bikini briefs before her eyes came to rest on his naked body.

Rio was glorious. His skin was dusky and smooth, sprinkled all over with silken dark hair. He was lean and strong, with long arms and legs and powerful shoulders, and the throbbing proof of his desire made her breath catch in her throat.

That part of him was lavish.

"Let's make a place here, on the floor. . . ."

He was tossing big soft pillows down onto the rug, and then he drew her into his arms and lowered them both to the nest he'd created.

"I want to look at you. I've imagined what you'd look like this way. Lie still."

His voice was thick and dark with passion as he drew back a little to study her, and Sophie was aware of his eyes, hot and liquid with desire, the golden specks in their pupils seeming to glow.

They caressed her, those eyes.

Having Rio look at her brought a unique rush of pride in herself that she'd never known till now. He made it plain that he found her body irresistible, and so powerful was his delight in her that Sophie herself absorbed it and preened just a little under his gaze.

She moved, impatient for him, but he wouldn't let her rush. His perusal was hot and slow, and everywhere he looked, Sophie felt as though he'd touched her. In a half whisper full of sensuality, he told her what he would do to bring pleasure to every part of her, and she felt herself growing liquid and pliable just at his outrageous promises.

At last, with a soft groan, he encircled her with arms, legs, body. She could feel the heat and power of his erection pulsing against her thigh. She could feel his heart hammering against her.

He kissed her now, long and deep, and when his lips traveled to suckle at her breasts, his fingers went down to her soft nest of curls and found the place she needed touched.

She opened and arched against his hand, and he cupped her and made a satisfied sound in his throat. He murmured soft encouragement as his clever fingers incited and inflamed her.

It took a while for her to realize that the tender words were in Italian, but it didn't matter.

It was the timbre of his voice that mattered, rough and warm and thick with the need to please her, soft sibilant phrases that sounded more romantic than anything she'd ever heard before.

She hated interrupting the mood, but good sense insisted she must.

"I'm . . . I'm not on the pill, Rio." For a moment, tension replaced lassitude.

"Shh. I'll take care of it. I'll always take care of you, *cara mia.*"

Her concern vanished, and once again her body responded with a will of its own. He knew exactly how to pleasure her, where to touch soft and then harder.

He seemed to know the very instant when the uncoiling wildness within her became unbearable, and he straddled her without stopping her headlong rush, hard thighs between hers, taking only one interminable moment to make certain she was protected before he glided into her wet softness with one long, powerful thrust.

Immediately he pulled back and thrust again, harder, deeper.

She cried out when he entered her, and the delight of having him full and throbbing and moving inside her started the climax she'd been building toward.

She clung to him, repeating his name over and over, and felt herself sink further into the pillows as he plunged deeper, out of control himself now and breathing with heavy gasps.

He hovered at the apex, and then with a shuddering sigh he gave himself up to ecstasy.

Through her own mist of delight, she sensed the extent of the power he kept leashed inside of him, and she felt awed at the physical wonder of his strength and life force.

There was something primitive and earthy in Rio that allowed him to give himself over totally to loving her, with no part held back.

Because he was free and natural, he allowed her freedom, as well.

She watched his face contort and heard her name on his lips as his roar of fulfillment echoed through the apartment, and she felt omnipotent and tender together.

He collapsed on her, unable to support himself.

She was grateful for the pillows cushioning them. She cradled his weight, loving his temporary weakness.

Gradually he came back from where he'd gone.

"I'm crushing you, I'm sorry, *cara mia.*"

With great care, he rolled to the side, holding her with his arms and legs so that their bodies were still joined.

"You comfortable? You warm enough?"

"Yes, oh, yes. I feel wonderful, Rio."

He gave a sigh of pure contentment and pressed a kiss on her forehead.

"Me, too."

She snuggled close, and for long moments in time they floated, dreamers in the night.

RIO HEARD HER BREATHING deepen and change as Sophie fell asleep in his arms. He lay still, careful not to wake her, savoring the feeling of her ripe body nestled closely to his.

She was silken and voluptuous, his Sophie. She was . . .

His Sophie?

He oughta go careful here. This peculiar and unfamiliar mixture of emotions she unleashed in him could only lead to trouble.

After all, it wasn't as if he hadn't experienced great sex before. With Rio, a woman's pleasure was more important than his own, and in certain circles, he had a reputation, delightfully earned. He'd always privately believed that great sex was a lot like riding a motorcycle. It demanded endurance, physical dexterity, the ability to sense in an instant what a particular situation required and thorough knowledge of the machinery.

But this had been different.

He'd lost control somewhere along the way, given himself up to joy and tenderness, forgotten technique altogether.

She had a kind of innocence that made him feel protective of her. She gave him the impression that she needed him in ways that went far beyond the physical. She was...he searched for the word...she was vulnerable, that was it. For all her liberated views, she was still vulnerable.

The arm underneath her head had been asleep for a while now, and he stirred a tiny bit, trying to rearrange it without disturbing her.

She opened heavy-lidded gray eyes and looked straight into his, and she smiled in a sleepy, contented way and kissed him, her full breasts grazing his chest, sending erotic messages to every nerve ending.

Rio could smell the rich aroma of their loving mixed with that perfume of hers that smelled like vanilla, and he took control of the kiss where she left off as his body grew hard and hungry for her once again.

The more he loved her, the more he desired her.

It didn't make sense, but in a little while, sense was the last thing he was concerned about making.

GINA WAS SLUMPED against the side of the building when Sophie arrived at the Unicorn the next morning. She was chewing gum, and she reached over for the key as Sophie struggled to open the stubborn lock.

"I'll get it. You have to pull in on the handle like this." The door opened like magic.

"Did ya hear what happened at Mr. Krakowski's jewelry store a couple blocks over? Got broken into. He lost the only valuable stuff he had, which happened not to belong to him. He was repairing jewelry for people, and it wasn't covered on his insurance. Poor old guy, he was barely making a living as it was."

In the short time she'd been working at the Unicorn, Gina had somehow managed to get to know most of the other business proprietors in the area by name. She absorbed information like a sponge and very little escaped her notice.

Sophie felt bad even thinking it, but if there had to be another break-in, this was the best morning for it. She'd been afraid that Gina would take one look at her and say in that throwaway tone of hers, "So, you spent the night foolin' around, right?"

She felt as if everyone she met must know, because it was impossible to move fast. Her body ached in all sorts of mysterious places, and her mind kept going back to the night before. Actually the night before had extended until seven this morning. That was when Rio left her apartment.

They'd moved from the living room floor to her bedroom, but neither of them had had much sleep.

He'd used her shower and razor this morning, insisting she eat the toast and coffee he made for her, even feeding her small bits dripping with cherry jam so that he could wipe her lips with his tongue.

But there wasn't time to go back into the musky-smelling bedroom and pursue the feelings that aroused. He had a dozen things to do before he opened the store, and he needed an early start.

She needed a lot of time to make herself look as if she hadn't spent the night in his arms.

Even Rio looked a little dissipated when he left. His dark eyes were heavy lidded, and he stretched and yawned a lot over coffee, but the warmth and closeness of the dark hours had been just as strong as ever between them when they parted.

Sophie felt drained in a delicious way. This wasn't going to be one of her more productive days, and she was grateful that Gina was around to deal with customers.

"Go over to the Sweat Shop and pick up the orders for me, would you please, Gina?"

She needed a few moments alone, a cup of tea. But Gina was barely out the front door when an insistent tapping came on the back door, and when she opened it, Rio was there.

He shoved a warm paper sack that smelled delicious into Sophie's hand. When he realized Gina was out, he stepped inside and drew Sophie into his arms for a quick, thorough kiss.

"I'm still flying a mile off the ground," he murmured in her ear. "I've gotta go. There's a couple guys in the shop, but I just wanted to tell you . . ."

Her heart was racing.

"What, Rio?"

"That last night was magic. That—"

Whatever else he'd been about to say was interrupted by the bell over the front door. It was Gina. She had an arm load of skirts and tops.

"Rio, hey, I wanted to talk to you. Sophie has this dipstick for a bank manager. She wants to expand the stock here and this person's right from the Dark Ages, like no go on credit. What's the name of that sharp dude you went to for working capital?"

Sophie felt like throttling Gina, but Rio casually drew a pen from his shirt pocket and jotted a name and phone number on the back of an envelope lying on the work table.

"This guy used to be in business himself before he went into banking, he's okay. You want me to come with you the first time and sort of introduce you? I'd be happy to." He raised an eyebrow Sophie's way.

She shook her head. Gina picked up the paper and headed to the front of the store.

"Sophie, about us." Her heart skipped a beat and her stomach contracted. Was he going to tell her it had been a one-night stand?

"I'm sick about this, but I won't be able to see you for three, maybe four nights. I promised this customer I'd rebuild a motor for him, and I've got classes to give."

The regret in his tone almost made up for the disappointment she felt.

She was moving into his arms when Gina reappeared.

"Hey, I called and got you an appointment to meet this guy, Sophie," she announced with casual aplomb. The appointment was for that very afternoon.

"I gotta go. Let me know how you make out with the bank manager. I'll call him right away and tell him you're a friend of mine," Rio promised as he disappeared out the back door.

Sophie was trapped.

Gina opened the bag Rio'd brought over and studied the contents, then turned a knowing eye on Sophie.

"So you and my brother are an item, huh?"

Sophie felt herself turn magenta.

Gina picked out one of the pastries, an elaborate concoction of almonds and sweet dough and cream, and studied it.

"You can only buy these one place, over on Commercial, and then only if you know the woman who makes them. These are still warm from the oven, Commercial's a long way away. If Rio's going to all this trouble to bring you a snack for your coffee, watch out."

"Why... why should I watch out?" Sophie's voice was strangled, and she turned her back to Gina and made a fuss about making tea.

Gina shrugged. "Rio's too easy to fall in love with. Even being his sister, I can see what women see in him." She bit into a pastry. "Mmm, are these good or what? See, in the beginning it's all moonlight and roses and pastries. But it's not so great when the whole thing ends and you get your heart broken. Not that I think he does it on purpose or anything, but it sure happens a lot."

The pastry stuck in Sophie's throat, and she burned her tongue on the tea.

"Well, I'd better see about clearing off some of those back racks," Gina said. "We can set up a corner, sort of like a feature area, for the Lycra and stuff. Too bad we can't call it leather and lace, but I don't think that has the right note to it, d'you?"

Sophie was still thinking about Rio. It took several minutes for Gina's question to sink in.

"What Lycra and leather and lace?"

Gina gave her a long-suffering look.

"The stock you're going to put in after you see the bank manager today. Honestly, Soph, pay attention."

THE AMAZING THING was that the whole problem of changing banks and bank managers was a lot more simple than Sophie had thought it would be.

The manager, Brett Carlyle, listened to Sophie's less than professional explanation of why she needed a larger extension of credit than she was presently getting, worked out complex figures from the financial statement she'd remembered to bring and told her there'd be no problem extending an amount that was almost double what she had now. He made two brief phone calls, and her accounts were miraculously transferred to his bank.

She hadn't even had to face a confrontation with Ms Penny Hawthorne.

LATER THAT WEEK, Sophie met Gina at the entrance to the cavernous Showmart building, where the clothing wholesalers and Vancouver's designers marketed their samples to the retail market. Sophie had decided that because the whole thing was Gina's brainstorm, Gina should come along on the buying trip.

Try as she might, the girl had been unable to treat the outing with her usual nonchalance. Gina was out-and-out delighted.

She proved to be a tough and discerning shopper, although Sophie had to restrain her as to quantity.

Between them they chose a few innovative designs in leather, a basic stock of Lycra exercise-and-leisure wear and, at Gina's insistence, a line of pop jewelry by one of Vancouver's own designers.

When the totals were added up, Sophie knew there was still enough in her account to order the velour Bill had wanted for the Christmas robes, as well as pure silk parachute cloth for the jumpsuits Gina insisted would sell faster than Bill could make them.

The deliveries on the ready-made clothing came that very afternoon.

Sophie and Gina worked with furious energy and not a few arguments, rearranging the store to best show off the new items, and they lost track of time doing it.

Rio came in after he'd locked up his store.

"Hey, you two gonna sleep here tonight? It's after six. I'm turning this sign around to Closed and taking you both out for a burger, how's that sound?" He glanced around. "You got a lot of new junk here, huh?"

Junk.

Gina and Sophie rolled their eyes at each other.

"C'mon, you both need solid food, let's go. We can walk over to Gastown."

Gina shook her head.

"Not me, Rio, I've got to go to Nonna's house and do her hair, you know she got out of the hospital today and tonight everybody's coming in to see her, remember? You are coming, aren't you?"

Rio nodded. "Yeah, I'll be there a little later."

"Why not bring Sophie along? Come with him and meet my grandmother, huh, Soph? Nonna would love to meet you."

Rio looked a bit taken aback, but recovered fast. "Sure, we'll do that."

Before Sophie could say a word, Gina hurried out, calling over her shoulder, "That's settled then; I'll tell her you're both coming over in an hour or so. See ya later." The door slammed behind her.

"Rio, I don't think this is a good idea. . . ."

He moved close and kissed her.

"Too late, Sophia. My baby sister's probably on the phone now, telling Nonna you're coming. Boy, are you in for it. At least half my family's gonna be there. The others would be too if plane fare from Italy wasn't so expensive."

"If you'd rather I didn't—"

He put two fingers over her mouth. "The only reason I hesitated is because I had other plans for us tonight, and meeting half the Italian community wasn't part of my plot."

The way he looked at her made it clear what his plans had been, and Sophie felt the immediate surge of desire that Rio always stirred in her.

"I've missed you like anything, Sophia *mia*. I never cursed any motor as much as I cursed this one I was working on."

He moved to the front door and checked that it was locked, and then took her hand and tugged her into the back room.

He unbuttoned her blouse and slid if off, eyes kindling when he saw the gossamer lace on the top of her teddy. His fingers fumbled with the closure of her slacks, and Sophie couldn't stop herself.

She helped him with her zipper and then with his, and soon they were naked, rolling around on mounds of fabric scraps Sophie had dumped from several black plastic bags in order to make them a bed.

Late sunbeams filtered through the high window, but the room was dusky and filled with shadows as Rio straddled her body, running his hands up and down her as if she were a sculpture he was seeing with his fingers.

"I've been hot all week, just thinking about doing this to you."

He trailed kisses from her neck to her navel, wetting her skin with his tongue, teasing her with its delicious roughness in places where she was most vulnerable.

When his head dipped even lower, Sophie reached down in alarm to draw him away, but he resisted, and soon the world was only Rio's lips and tongue.

Now her hands pressed his head to her instead of away, and his clever mouth and hands drew her up and up until she arched and soared, moaning for him. A pleased growl sounded in his throat.

At the last moment, he moved up and entered her with one burning, violent movement, drawing away and plunging again until she couldn't stand any more.

Everything in Sophie's body contracted, hesitated, poised on the brink. Then she exploded, a bursting series of waves that seemed never ending, and her voice filled the high-ceilinged room with a lost and savage cry of rapture.

8

NATURALLY THEY WERE LATE getting to his grandmother's party.

When Rio led Sophie into the modest little house off Commercial Drive, there were already at least fifteen people crammed into the small kitchen.

Sophie was worried sick about how she looked. Could anyone tell what she and Rio had been doing for the past few hours? She had the awful feeling that the truth was written on her face for everyone to read.

There hadn't been time to go all the way home to freshen up. She'd washed in the store's tiny bathroom and tried her best to cover up the traces of whisker rub on her cheeks and neck.

She took as much care with her appearance as possible. But it was difficult to hide the afterglow of lovemaking; her eyes gave her away, the pupils huge and drugged looking.

They signaled fulfillment.

And there had been the matter of clothes. As usual, Rio was in jeans and a knitted shirt, so he'd looked fine after he dressed again.

The shirt and slacks she'd been wearing were a crumpled mess, so she simply chose a new rayon skirt and matching shirt off her own racks, a dark print with brilliant poppies scattered all over it.

She'd thought she looked pretty good when she climbed onto the motorcycle behind Rio to come over here, but now all these people made her nervous and insecure.

The crowd hailed Rio at the top of their lungs, both in rapid Italian and fractured English. There seemed to be a fair bit of teasing going on, with knowing looks and lots of laughter and exaggerated remarks about Sophie's beauty that made her blush scarlet.

Several older women kissed Rio with rough affection, and he introduced them as his aunts. He exchanged warm hugs with various uncles, who also pounded him on the arm or the back.

"Rio, how she go?"

"Gina's gone for more cream, Rio. She'll be back in a minute. Your momma and poppa are coming. They're picking up Zio Genaro. He doesn't drive now—they took away his license when he hit that stop sign, but they'll all be here in an hour...."

The cheerful, noisy voices bombarded them on every side, asking questions about the business, explaining where other members of the family were, demanding that Rio introduce Sophie to everyone.

"I will, I will, but first we go see Nonna, yes? Where is she?"

Yes, yes, everyone agreed.

Of course, Nonna first. It was a celebration in Nonna's honor, wasn't it? She was in the front room.

Holding Sophie by the hand and carrying a package he'd retrieved from the saddlebags of the motorcycle, Rio led the way to the living room where another group of noisy relatives crowded around a tiny regal woman seated in a wheelchair.

The crowd parted to let Rio and Sophie through, and again Rio was kissed and hugged and patted by numerous people, men and women alike.

Rio's grandmother had blue-white hair, a black silk dress, gnarled hands and eyes Sophie recognized right away. They were Rio's eyes, heavy lashed and coal dark, passionate and impatient.

"Ah, my Mario, *bambino*," she sang, holding her arms out and drawing him down, almost unbalancing him as he bent over and took her in his arms.

Sophie watched and smiled with misty eyes.

"Nonna, hey, Nonna, leggo, you're gonna break my neck, what did they feed you at that hospital. You're strong like a bear," he howled in mock pain, and everyone laughed with uproarious good humor.

But over Rio's shoulder, Nonna's eyes were taking minute stock of Sophie, and they didn't miss a single thing.

"This is your young lady, Mario? This is who Gina works for?"

"Yeah, Nonna, this is Sophie Larson. Sophie, my grand-mother, Teresa Agostini."

"I'm happy to meet you, Mrs. Agostini." Sophie's hand was taken in a blue-veined claw.

Nonna's eyes traveled up and down Sophie's form, and then she studied Sophie's face. The whisker burn seemed to grow fiery hot and turn scarlet under Nonna's scrutiny.

But the old lady nodded with approval.

"Welcome, welcome to my home, Sophie. And you will call me Nonna, like everyone else does, yes?"

Sophie flushed with pleasure. "I'd be delighted."

"Mario, where are your manners? A glass of my best homemade wine for Sophie, some biscuits, and—" she re-trieved a wineglass from a small table beside her "—just a tiny bit more for me. It's a celebration, no?"

Rio took the glass, but first he handed Nonna the pack-age.

"This is for you, Nonna."

It was a ceremony.

"Ah, Mario." Nonna held the parcel out for everyone to admire, head on one side, eyes fierce and shining.

"Mario, Mario, always such a thoughtful boy."

"It's . . . open it, Nonna, okay?"

With childlike enthusiasm, she tore the paper open, and the buzz of conversation around them faded into shocked silence.

Inside the box were jazzy, bright pink athletic shoes with tartan laces, the kind joggers wore. For an instant, Sophie had the awful feeling that Rio had given his grandmother the wrong parcel.

Nonna had broken her hip; she hadn't walked for months. It was doubtful whether she'd ever walk again.

But in another moment, Sophie understood what Rio was trying to do, and incredible tenderness filled her for the wonderful, caring man at Nonna's side . . . tenderness, and wonder at his insight, his determination. His bravery.

It would take intense therapy to get Nonna on her feet again, therapy that would be painful and require much courage and dedication on her part.

Sophie remembered Gina telling her that Nonna was refusing to try, despite the whole family's urging and pleading.

The gift of runners was a symbol, a way of saying, *you can do this, Nonna, I have faith in you, but you have to make the effort.*

The old lady knew what her grandson was doing.

She lifted the jaunty shoes out of their box, and for the first time, tears sparkled in the shiny depths of her dark eyes and then overflowed.

She looked up at Rio with a pathetic expression, and she sighed, a massive sigh of weariness and defeat. She shook her head at him, no, no, no.

Rio knelt beside her chair. "Yes. I want you to wear those shoes for my birthday next May. We'll go walking in the park and look at the boats the way we used to do. Yes, Nonna."

"I can't, Mario. I'm too old now, I can't."

"Nonna, you were the one who taught me I could do anything as long as I tried hard enough and wanted it to happen. We all love you, Nonna. We need you up and around, bossing us the way you always did."

She fondled the shoes, and the room was silent for a long, tense time. At last she looked up at him and gave a shrug and a little nod.

"All right, *bambino*, all right. I will try, that's all I promise. I will try once more, just for you."

"Not for me. For yourself, Nonna, okay?"

Rio took the wrinkled hand in his and bent to kiss it, and an intense look passed between grandmother and grandson, a look that settled what was to be.

It was then that Sophie made a big mistake.

She fell in love with Rio Agostini.

DURING THE NEXT HOUR, she met Rio's parents.

His mother, Anna, was a handsome, plump woman with a lovely, quiet smile and Rio's habit of touching to communicate.

His father was tall and rope thin, with a weather-beaten peaceful face and the scarred hands of a man who used them to earn his living. Sophie could see traces of Rio in each parent, but Gina wasn't at all like either.

Obviously they were fond of each other and of their son and daughter. Anna took Sophie aside to tell her what a difference it had made in Gina to have the job at the Unicorn, and to thank her for giving the girl a chance.

Sophie felt embarrassed, remembering how reluctant she'd been to hire Gina and how well the experiment had turned out. She'd already told Rio she hoped to be able to pay Gina's wages herself this month. Gina was more than earning her way.

Rio and Sophie spent another hour and a half drinking wine and talking. Talking was a thing this crowd did to perfection. The noise level rose steadily, and at times Sophie was certain her eardrums would never be the same again.

Rio's Auntie Rosamunde gave Sophie her recipe for cannelloni, and then Auntie Iris got into a big argument with Rosamunde about the cheddar sauce on it. One insisted on homemade hollandaise, the other said a mix made no difference.

Rio was borne off by several of the men who wanted to see the motorcycle he was riding. Sophie was taken under Nonna's wing, and the old lady had someone locate a photo album full of pictures of weddings fifty years old and babies long grown.

Rio was there, a cocky, adorable little boy, always grinning at the camera and usually none too clean. In one taken by a lake, he was holding hands with a simpering little girl in a swimming suit.

Nonna shook her head and clucked her tongue. "That Mario, even then he had an eye for the women. That was Nick Kiloski's girl, she was always crazy for him, remember, Anna?"

Sophie felt like spilling her wine on the page.

Nonna was clever at cross-examination.

This picture was taken when Vinny and Genaro had that job in the bush one summer.

What kind of work did Sophie's papa do?

No papa? Ah, poor child.

Here was Anna, when she worked in the grocery store.

Did Sophie's momma work? Momma was in real estate? Ahhh. Hard on momma to raise Sophie alone. But of course she was remarried by now, a nice husband to take over the worries? No? A spate of Italian and much gesticulation among the women.

But surely Sophie had family, aunts, uncles, cousins?

No family, either? Tsk, tsk, tsk.

Sophie must bring her momma over to visit Nonna. Sophie's momma should meet Cousin Rudy. He was a widower, a fine-looking man for his age, too, maybe, who knows...

To Sophie's everlasting relief, Rio came back about then and suggested they leave.

Leaving this gathering wasn't simple by any means.

First, Rio was made to promise that he'd bring Sophie back often to visit. He was given innumerable business tips. She was kissed and hugged by almost everyone and had her cheeks pinched until they smarted. One of Rio's livelier uncles kissed her more than once, with a lot more fervor than necessary, and his hand strayed from her back down to her hip.

Rio extricated her and let out a stream of curses when they were finally outside.

"That old lecher, he's seventy if he's a day, pawing at you. I'm sorry, Sophie, putting you through that."

It was one of the best evenings she'd ever had.

"YOU HUNGRY? I'm starving. We'll go eat now." Rio was unbuckling the helmets from the holders on the bike, and he fitted hers onto her head with gentle ease and balanced the bike until she was settled behind him.

"Rio, I couldn't eat a thing after all that wine and those almond things...."

He ignored her. They rode through the cool city night over to the Italian business district. Rio parked the bike in front of an obscure little restaurant called Il Travatore and led Sophie inside. The rich aroma of tomato sauce and Parmesan and meatballs proved that Rio was right. Sophie was starving.

The foyer was actually a roped-off part of the kitchen, and behind the barrier were three majestic women, slapping pasta into place for lasagna, tasting rich sauces that steamed on stove tops, draining spaghetti into huge colanders. During all of this, they talked—shouted, actually—at one another in volatile Italian.

"Are they having a fight?" Sophie whispered.

Rio laughed and hugged her to his side.

"Nope, they're talking about a dance at the community center and how much fun it was."

"Rio, welcome, long time no see."

A dapper little man with white hair and a carnation in his buttonhole hurried over to escort them to a table, taking special pains with Sophie's chair, fussing over their dinner napkins, suggesting the antipasto as an appetizer.

"Mr. Rosselini, this is Sophie Larson."

The proprietor bent over her hand with old-world charm, dark eyes liquid with silent praise of her beauty before he hurried away. Sophie decided the entire North American continent ought to be populated with Italian men.

"Mr. Rosselini owns this place, he knows my pop from the old days. They came to Canada together from Italy."

Soon a carafe of wine appeared, and a tray of antipasto.

Rio tenderly tucked a linen napkin the size of a small tablecloth around her neck, then fed Sophie bits of food from the platter.

"This shrimp, you've gotta taste this, Sophia. Ah, the sauce, open your mouth. Just let me give you a bite of this cauliflower so you can taste the sauce."

With Rio, eating was a sensuous experience, a ritual that demanded close attention, a concentration of energy and an intimate sharing she'd never experienced before.

He slathered butter on thick chunks of hot crusty bread and insisted she savor it. He ordered a particular tangy red wine because he thought she might like it better than the one they were drinking.

It occurred to Sophie that Rio ate the same way he made love, with meticulous attention to detail and a sensuous, fiery delight in taking and giving pleasure. He had a monumental life force, a sense of joy that came from living entirely for the moment, that she'd never found in a man before now.

And he also had a five-year plan.

She kept looking at him during the meal, seeing as if for the first time the way his eyes crinkled at the corners when he laughed, the way his ears fitted close to his skull, the square, competent shape of his large hands, the appealing dent in the middle of his chin.

There was nothing about him that didn't please and thrill her.

He was easy to fall in love with.

Rio, she kept repeating in a silent, muddled litany all through the meal. *I never meant for this to happen. I don't know what to do about it. It scares me half-senseless. And there's nothing I can* do *about it except keep silent.*

After they ate, Rio took her dancing.

The club was named Galla d'Or, and it was small and smoky, intimate and romantic. The music was supplied by a jolly man with a handlebar moustache playing an accordion, and a younger, doleful-looking fellow playing a guitar.

Rio was a superb dancer. He held Sophie against him and led her with absolute confidence around the tiny dance floor.

He pressed his lips closely to her ear and sang the Italian lyrics of the passionate, slow waltzes, and although she couldn't understand the words, their message was clear.

The songs were all of love.

Now and then he broke off and whispered in English precisely what he planned to do to her body when at last they were alone.

IT WAS AFTER MIDNIGHT when they climbed back onto the bike. Sophie had the feeling that a lifetime had passed since they left the store that afternoon.

She felt too exhilarated to even be nervous as they dipped and swayed around corners and across bridges. She was aware that everything had changed tonight.

Yet nothing at all had changed. It was only inside of her that the changes had occurred.

She'd think about it all tomorrow, however. Tonight, there was only Rio.

He parked the bike and led her inside to her door, taking the keys and unlocking it for her, leading her in and drawing her into his arms the instant he'd closed and locked the door.

He trailed kisses over her forehead, down her nose, to her lips, and desire uncurled in a silky ribbon between them.

By the time he released her, she'd forgotten about being tired. Her body was awake and throbbing in all the places that ought to be the most exhausted.

Rio looked down at her and swore under his breath, and then, in a sudden fury of passion and need, he stripped her clothing off and made love to her there on the antique rug.

Her last coherent thought was about how seldom they made it to a bed.

AT THE STORE, Gina was far too enraptured with the amazing way the new stock was selling to even notice that Sophie wandered through her days in a slow-moving, soft-eyed trance, body aching from Rio's imaginative and energetic attentions.

But Rio incorporated his caring into daytime hours, as well.

Even with the pressure of his own accelerating business, he always found time to do special, small things that touched Sophie, keeping her sidewalk clean of the dog mess, weeding the tubs of flowers out front and fertilizing them, even cleaning the old brick on the front of the building with a power washer he rented early one morning.

He fixed the lock on her front door, taking the old rusty workings out and painstakingly cleaning and oiling them before he put them back. For the first time, Sophie could open the door without any effort at all.

Gina had proven herself a genius when it came to stock. The Unicorn's sales more than doubled, and Sophie was thrilled about it. She gave Gina full credit for imagination, and when Bill and his crew finished the first silky jumpsuits, three of them sold the very first afternoon they were on display.

The Unicorn could now well afford Gina.

Days were exciting and more rewarding than they'd ever been in the store. But it was the nights that Sophie waited for. Exciting as it was to have the store doing well, nothing about her business could match the wonder of having Rio with her at night.

He brought a few things over to her apartment—underwear, shaving gear, a change of clothing—so that whenever his schedule allowed, he could spend all night with Sophie.

She reveled in it.

She cooked for him, baked chocolate brownies and butter tarts and apple pie, and to her utter amazement, she lost weight.

Five pounds disappeared, and then seven. She ate whatever she wanted with Rio, but on her own she stopped snacking on candy bars and muffins and doughnuts.

She preened for him. She wore her prettiest teddies, her most provocative panties and bras and slips, and now they weren't only for her own pleasure.

Rio delighted in her burgeoning sensuality, and although she was still too shy to take the initiative in their lovemaking, she welcomed all the ways he found of pleasing her, ways that left her trembling and drained, while his dark eyes turned liquid with the joy of loving her.

He made a ritual of undressing her, taking off each silky garment as if she were a treasure he was unwrapping.

For the first time in her adult life, Sophie like her body, accepted her rounded contours with the knowledge that Rio worshipped every inch of her.

THE PHONE RANG at seven-fifteen that Friday morning, drawing Sophie out of her gentle dream. She had to extricate herself from Rio's tangled embrace before she could reach to the nightstand to answer it.

"Ms Larson?"

Sophie cleared her throat and tried to sound awake.

"Vancouver City Police, Ms Larson."

Sophie's heart began to pound. She struggled to a sitting position. Rio raised his head from the pillow, and when he saw the expression on her face, he swung out of bed and began tugging on his jeans.

The impersonal female voice went on, "You are the proprietor of a boutique called the Unicorn, on East Pendrell? We have a reported break-in at that address. Our officers are there now. Would you please attend as soon as possible, Ms Larson?"

On Rio's bike, it took only a short time to reach the store.

A police car was parked at the curb, and several uniformed officers came over to them as soon as Rio pulled the bike to a stop.

"Ms Larson? I'm Constable Hill. The person or persons who broke in did so through the back door. They broke the lock. Would you come inside with me and try and give us some idea of what was taken?"

A cry of dismay erupted from Sophie's throat when she entered the Unicorn, and Rio put a sympathetic arm around her shoulders.

The store had been ransacked, and instead of just taking what he wanted, the thief had turned the entire place upside down. Racks were overturned, the cash drawer had been wrenched from its runners, the glass unit Sophie had used to display the jewelry was smashed.

The most expensive jewelry was gone, as well as most of the leather skirts, pants and vests Gina was so proud of—and which Sophie hadn't yet paid for.

The wholesaler ran on thirty days net, and she'd naturally been taking advantage of that time lapse, rubbing her hands with glee because it looked as though the sales would more than cover the invoice amount plus the month's expenses.

In a daze, Sophie found invoice slips and made a list of what was missing.

Rio, face tight with suppressed anger and frustration, set about picking up and rehanging the scattered stock.

Soon, Sophie heard him questioning one of the police officers. They spoke in low tones, but Rio made it clear he wanted answers.

"These break-ins are happening more and more often around here. Can't you guys stake out the street or something and catch whoever's responsible?"

Frustration was evident in the officer's reply.

"I know it probably seems as if we're not doing much, but that's not the case. We've put on extra patrols and had officers walking the area. This criminal is well organized and seems to have an uncanny ability to choose the very time we're busy somewhere else to vandalize one of the businesses. Our biggest problem is manpower. We just don't have the funding or the personnel to do lengthy stakeouts."

Rio didn't reply, but he didn't look convinced by the policeman's words.

"Wow, Sophie, what happened? How'd they get in? Did ya lose much? Bet they took all that new fancy stuff you had in here, right? I thought to myself when I saw it . . ."

The excited blabbering came, of course, from Herb. He took his hat off and held it in his hand, as if doing so would allow him to see every devastating detail. His bulging eyes flitted here and there and everywhere, and Sophie knew he was taking mental inventory so that he could broadcast the calamity and the extent of her losses up and down the street.

It exasperated her.

It also infuriated Rio.

"This is a private matter, Herb. Is that Sophie's mail? Here, Sophie." With one smooth gesture, Rio rescued the neat bundle of envelopes and thrust them at Sophie, then took Herb by the elbow and steered him toward the door.

"Now, we're still busy in here, so if you'll excuse me, just stick my mail in through the slot next door."

He hustled the reluctant mailman out and shut the door behind him, but a second later, Gina came bursting in.

"What in the name of heaven is going on here? They stole what? *Maledizione!* My leathers, all the jewelry..." Gina flew from one spot to the next, cursing in volatile Italian and berating the policemen, Rio, Sophie and the entire neighborhood.

The spectacle of Gina totally out of control at least took Sophie's mind off her losses for a few moments.

The young woman's face flushed, her eyes sparked with anger, her hands punctuated every vehement word, and her voice was shrill as any harridan's could be.

Rio threw his hands in the air and exploded.

"Shut up, Gina, they'll hear you all the way down to the waterfront," he bellowed, but he had not the slightest effect on Gina.

One of the young policemen had been watching the performance with interest. Gina was wearing a saffron silk jumpsuit, one of the ones Bill had made, and the fragile fabric ebbed and flowed over her long, dramatic body like water over a waterfall, concealing and revealing at the same time.

He walked over to her and took her arm in a firm grasp.

"Miss, you're hysterical, now come along with me," he ordered in a quiet no-nonsense tone.

To everyone's amazement, Gina quieted down, gave the officer her long, narrow-eyed look and slithered along as he led the way outside. Rio walked to the door and watched them, hands low on his hips and a scowl on his face.

"He's just taking her into the coffee shop down the street," the other officer explained, and then he winked at Rio. "Marcel's got quite a way with the ladies. He'll get her calmed down, all right."

"Yeah?" Rio growled. "Well, if he values his kneecaps, he'll behave himself around her. She's my baby sister."

Sophie was beginning to see what Gina meant when she complained that Rio was overprotective.

Bill and Michelle were the next to arrive, and there were definite similarities between Bill's reaction and Gina's.

Bill came bursting through the front door, gripped his hair with both hands as if to tear it out and then cursed for a full five minutes in Greek, gesticulating with his hands and appealing to God as his witness.

"From that window I can see the whole street. If I so much as see anyone suspicious from now on, daylight or not, I will call and you will come immediately, yes?" The policeman hesitated, and Bill added, "In Greece, I assure you, such things do not happen. Thieves are caught, and they are punished. It's a much better system, believe me, just I remember one such time, it was in our village, and an old woman . . ."

Sophie was beginning to feel a bit sorry for the patient officer.

"Bill, how's your mother?" she interrupted to distract him.

Bill rolled his eyes and drew her over to a private corner where they couldn't be overheard.

"Sophie, you know what has happened? Just she has sent money now for this girl to come here from Greece. And everyone expects that I will marry her. Can you believe such a thing?"

Sophie made sympathetic noises, and by the time Gina came back from the coffee shop with Marcel, Rio managed to ease Bill and Michelle out the door and across to the Sweat Shop. Two other people who had businesses in the area dropped by.

It seemed that everyone was critical of the way the police were handling the break-ins, and the remarks directed at the officers were pointed.

At last, all the forms were filled in, and the marked car drove off from in front of the store.

Rio drew Sophie into the back room and held her close. She was trembling and there were unshed tears in her eyes. He kissed each eyelid and cupped her face in his hands.

"This has gone far enough now. I'm gonna make sure it doesn't happen again," he growled. But he left before Sophie could ask what he meant.

Gina and Sophie worked hard at clearing up the rest of the mess so they could open the store for business. They managed it by eleven, and Sophie had Gina deal with the customers, as well as curious shopkeepers from up and down the street, while she made a calming cup of tea and worked herself up to phoning news of the robbery to her insurance agent, her new banker and Harriet.

It was anything but a pleasant morning.

The insurance agent wasn't certain that Sophie's policy would cover her entire loss. He went grumbling on for an inordinate amount of time about what type of lock she'd had on the back door.

The banker was better, but of course he wasn't ecstatic about the loss of stock which, technically, he owned.

Harriet was distant. She seemed distracted. Although Sophie had called and apologized for the pimp remark she'd made to her mother, the atmosphere between them had stayed cool and Sophie hadn't seen Harriet since.

"I've warned you of the importance of location, Sophie. It's unfortunate for you, but it's the price you pay for staying in a run-down area."

Sophie hung up feeling furious and unloved and sick to death of being Harriet's daughter. Why couldn't she have been born into a family like Rio's, where a whole battery of relatives would probably arrive to sympathize and hold her hand at times like this?

The store didn't make a single sale all day, and Gina blamed the loss of the new stock and alternately sulked and raged.

When closing time came, Sophie felt as if she'd been hit by a truck and left to expire alone. She sent Gina home early and was about to lock up herself and leave when Rio phoned.

He sounded agitated.

"I wanted to take you out for dinner, sort of get your mind off the store, but Carol, my ex-wife, just called. You know how she is about not letting me have Missy very often. Well, tonight she's actually asking me to baby-sit. She has an important appointment and the baby-sitter cancelled." Rio sounded nervous. "I really want to see my kid, but it means I can't take you out like I planned."

Sophie was about to say it was all right, she'd see him the next day, and then drag herself home and fall into bed for sixteen hours, which was all she had energy to do. Instead she heard herself saying, "Why not take both of us out? Or better yet, why not bring Missy over to my place and we'll all make dinner together?"

What was she saying?

"Hey, that would be great. You sure, Sophia? You like kids?"

"Of course I like kids. Go pick her up and I'll see you, what? In about an hour?"

"Hour and a half. I gotta pick up the truck, then go get Missy. See ya later. And Sophie?"

Her heartbeat accelerated.

But all he said was a heartfelt, "Thanks, honey."

IT DIDN'T TAKE LONG for Sophie to regret her impulsive invitation. She hadn't had a lot to do with children, but the ones she'd met before were nothing at all like Rio's daughter.

Instead of a mumbled "hi" when Rio introduced her to Sophie, the child held out a small, clean, perfect hand and said, "How do you do?"

She looked around Sophie's messy living room. Was there subdued horror on Missy's face? The child sat down gingerly on an armchair, feet crossed, hands folded in her lap, little face as pretty as a doll's and just as devoid of expression.

Sophie felt as though she were in the presence of royalty, and it wasn't comfortable. She'd changed into cotton shorts and a loose T-shirt, and she had the incongruous feeling that Missy had already checked out her thighs and found them unacceptable.

How could a five-year-old child make an adult woman nervous? And how the heck were they going to amuse a five-year-old going on thirty like this one?

The traumatic day with all its tensions had been long and difficult, and Sophie felt drained and too tired to cope with this caricature of a little girl.

Still, she was determined to give it her best shot. For Rio's sake.

"Would you like some lemonade, Missy?"

"I'm not allowed to have sugar. Is it made with sugar?"

"Nope, it's sugar free. I believe in having diet lemonade with my cookies." It was a weak joke, but Sophie laughed anyway, hoping to stir a response in Missy.

Rio laughed, too, but Missy didn't even blink. She said in a prissy tone, "I'm not allowed to have cookies, thank you. Mommy says they're empty calories, and they wreck your teeth."

Sophie stared down at the heaping plate she held.

She'd hurried to a special bake shop on the way home and bought an assortment. She'd chosen hearts and gingerbread men and huge raisin-filled ones with green trim that she couldn't wait to try herself.

Well, so much for cookies.

It was going to be one hell of a long and difficult evening.

9

"Do you have television, Miss Larson?" the child asked after a long, awkward silence. Honestly, Rio wasn't being any help here, Sophie thought in disgust.

"Call me Sophie, Melissa." She'd already suggested that several times, but Missy ignored it. "The TV is just a tiny one. It's on the dresser in the bedroom."

"Do you mind if I watch cartoons on it, please?"

"Of course not," Sophie said with great and honest enthusiasm. "As long as your dad doesn't mind."

Rio didn't mind at all. In fact, he sounded as relieved as Sophie. He led the way into the bedroom and settled his daughter in front of the television. It was obvious he adored the child, yet didn't have a single clue what to do with her.

Rio had brought a bottle of wine, and now he heaved a huge sigh and poured himself and Sophie large glassfuls.

He was different around his daughter, more subdued, as if he was trying hard to be on his best behavior. Well, that wasn't surprising. Missy had the same disconcerting effect on Sophie.

Now Rio gave Sophie a lecherous once-over and a pat on the seat, letting her know he liked the way she looked in her shorts.

They exchanged an intimate glance, reminiscent of the hours spent in each other's arms the night before, and settled down to sip their wine. But after a little while Sophie felt uncomfortable as the sound of the television and its vapid cartoon figures filtered through to where they were.

She couldn't help but think how sad it was that Rio and his daughter didn't have a better relationship than they seemed to have.

Sophie had never had a daddy, and she'd spend untold hours as a little girl dreaming of what it would be like, of all the things that fathers and little girls could do together.

Yet here was Rio, a warm, fun-loving man, sitting in one room, with his own little girl in another, and no communication between them.

"What sort of things do you and Missy usually do when you're together?" she asked at last.

Rio shrugged, a disconsolate look on his face.

"Like I told you, I don't see her that much. When I finally put my foot down and insist on spending a day with Missy, Carol always gives me a lecture when I pick her up on keeping her clean and not letting her get hurt and not feeding her a bunch of stuff that'll make her sick, there just don't seem to be too many things we can do. Usually I take her to Mom's. She brings her Barbie dolls and plays with them, or she and Pop watch TV, much the same as now. I always figured if she were a boy, it'd be different. I wouldn't worry about all that stuff, and there's lots of things a guy can do with a boy."

Sophie's feminist hackles rose to full outraged attention.

"What sort of things would that be?" she purred.

"Oh, you know, toss a ball around, go roller skating, ride pedal bikes. Physical things."

Sophie thought of the way Missy was dressed, and her heart sank.

Still . . . maybe there was a way it could be managed.

"Wait here, Rio, I'll be right back." She raced out the door and down the stairs, and before she could have second thoughts, she knocked on Betty Mills's apartment door.

"Hi, Sophie." The two women had become casually acquainted by chatting in the hallway the past few weeks. "You wanna come in? There's coffee on."

"No coffee, thanks, I've only got a minute, there's something . . . I need to ask you for a favor . . . do you think I could borrow . . . ooh, heck."

This was harder than Sophie had thought it would be.

Betty raised her eyebrows and chuckled. "I don't have a man in my life to lend, so that can't be it."

Sophie grinned and the awkwardness vanished. "I seem to have one in my life at the moment, and he's got this little girl, and . . . what I wanted to ask, Betty, was whether Tara might have some old jeans and a T-shirt I could borrow for the evening. This kid is all dressed up and we wanted to play ball down at the park."

"No problem at all, as long as they don't need to be fancy. What size feet does she have? Sounds like you'll need a pair of runners, as well. Tara has half a dozen pairs."

In ten minutes, Sophie was back in her own apartment. In a paper bag she had runners that she hoped might fit, a clean but ragged pair of jeans, and a T-shirt with Snoopy on the front.

Rio gave her a questioning glance.

"You stay right there. I have to talk to Missy for a minute."

It took much longer than a minute, but by exerting some firmness, a few veiled threats and a lot of enthusiasm, Sophie managed to get Missy out of her fancy-dress outfit and into the play clothes.

Sophie wasn't proud of using bribery, but she did anyway, right after she made the mistake of explaining what she had in mind for the three of them to do.

"No, thank you," Missy said. "I don't like ball. I'm always scared the ball will hit me, so I never play. Mommy sent a note to kindergarten. Teacher says I don't have to. Besides, my hair gets all messy."

Sophie had the urge to mess that too-perfect hair, all right. Rio's daughter needed messing more than anyone Sophie knew.

"If you put these on and come and just try a game of ball, I'll—I'll make you any outfit you want for your Barbie doll. I'll show you the fabric scraps later and you can pick the material you like. And I'll fix your hair if it gets mussed, don't worry about that, I'm an absolute expert at hair."

How difficult could one outfit be for a doll, anyway? And surely someone who'd done their own hair with varying degrees of success could cope with a few ringlets.

"Ugh, these things are awful," Missy groaned, tugging the jeans on and shoving one bare foot into the runners. Sophie had decided even Missy's socks were far too fancy and pristine to mess up, so she stripped them off the child's narrow feet to add to the careful pile on the bed.

The shoes fit, thank goodness, and so did everything else, more or less. Sophie dug through her closet and found a tattered softball and a green Frisbee.

Missy walked out of the bedroom in the borrowed clothing like a martyr being led to the burning pyre.

Rio was stretched out on the couch, eyes shut, listening to a Willy Nelson tape on Sophie's machine.

When he became aware of them, he struggled up and his eyebrows reached for his hairline.

"Holy... where'd you get those clothes, Missy? And why did you change out of your own?"

"Because," Sophie said with grim determination, "Missy and I are going to the park to toss a ball and have a hot dog and fries from the vendor. You can come if you want to, aye, Missy?"

"I guess so." Enthusiasm was in the minus column.

Rio was silent for several long minutes.

"Well, I guess we could try. Let's go." Rio sounded about as enthusiastic as his daughter.

Sophie pondered the allure of a nunnery.

BUT THE IDEA WORKED in spades.

When the three of them arrived back at the apartment two

hours later, they were grass stained, mustard spattered, stuffed with junk food and giddy with laughter.

At least, Rio and Sophie were giddy. Missy was still far too restrained to lose control, but there had been several times when she actually let out a couple of squeals and a definite giggle or two.

For the first fifteen minutes, Sophie had cursed herself for having the worst idea of her life.

Missy refused to have anything to do with the ball or the Frisbee or the adults, and she sat down on a wooden bench with a pained expression on her face, obviously waiting for her father and Sophie to get over this silliness and take her back to the television.

But then a small miracle occurred.

Rio threw the Frisbee, Sophie missed it, and a gangly brown dog ran out of nowhere, took the Frisbee in his teeth and went racing off with it, tail wagging with pleasure.

Rio yelled and ran after him and, to Sophie's astonishment, after a moment's hesitation so did Missy.

The dog made a big circle, avoiding Rio, and took the Frisbee straight to the child. He allowed her to take it out of his mouth.

"Good dog, good boy," Missy was crooning as Sophie came puffing up with Rio behind her. "Isn't he beautiful?" she crowed. The dog was licking Missy's face, and she wasn't bothered one bit about it.

"Look how smart he is, Daddy. C'mon, boy, catch it again, here, Daddy, you throw it far."

Soon a spirited game was in progress, with Missy doing some of the throwing and the dog doing the catching, and Sophie and Rio applauding.

"She loves animals, but her mother won't have one around," Rio confided.

Sophie was beginning to wonder why Rio's ex-wife even had a child around, but she didn't say so.

They shared with the dog the masses of food Rio brought from the outdoor concession, and when it came time to head home again, Missy begged to bring the animal with them.

But a man came by on a bike just then and called in an exasperated tone, "Major, you bad dog, where've you been? I've looked for you for two hours now." He got off the bike and fondled the animal before he snapped a leash and collar on him and rode off.

Major went running away without a backward glance, and to Sophie's amazement, Missy accepted it without a fuss.

"I guess he just wanted to play with me, eh, Daddy? He's a good dog, eh, Daddy?"

It was touching to hear her address Rio as Daddy, in that natural and spontaneous tone of voice. And it was touching to see the tenderness and pride on Rio's face when he heard it.

THEY HAD TO GIVE MISSY a bath before Rio could think of taking her home, and Sophie found that doing the child's hair was a major production and one that she was anything but adept at. And then they went through a long half hour while the girl chose the fabric for her doll's clothes.

But at last Missy was at least a reasonable facsimile of her former self when they all piled into the truck to drive her home.

Sophie waited in the battered old pickup while Rio took Missy into the modern apartment building in the city's trendy west end. There wasn't a park in sight, and Sophie doubted there were many other children in the neighborhood. No wonder Missy was the way she was, Sophie concluded with disgust.

This was no place to raise a child. She'd never raise a kid of hers in a place like this, Sophie thought with indignation.

She'd have a house and a yard and a dog. . . .

She stopped the dreams with a jolt.

Sure, Sophie. And a white picket fence with a motorcycle in the backyard.

If she kept on projecting rosy futures for herself and Rio, she was going to end up with a broken heart. Gina had warned her, and hadn't Sophie herself gone into this relationship with the sole intention of having fun for once in her life and not expecting happy ever after? It was no one's fault but her own that she'd fallen in love with Rio.

Somewhere along the way, she'd gone off base, and she'd better get herself back on track in a hurry.

RIO CAME BACK ten minutes later, slammed the truck door with vicious force and spun the wheels as he pulled away from the curb.

"How the hell I ever got mixed up with that woman . . ." he growled. "She took a major fit just now because Missy told her about the dog. Carol's sure the kid's caught fleas. She accused me of being irresponsible and an unfit father."

"Just because of the dog?"

They stopped at a red light, and Rio massaged the back of his neck with one hand in an obvious effort to calm himself down.

"Partly that. Carol's scared of dogs. She says they're dirty, and she always figures Missy's either gonna get bitten or catch something. Then she does a total turnaround and says that the kid needs to be with me more."

Maybe this Carol wasn't so bad after all.

Sophie couldn't stop herself from saying what needed to be said. "I think so, too, Rio."

He turned and gave her a long, angry look, and Sophie knew he was thinking that she'd betrayed him and also meddled in a part of his life where she had no business being.

"What the hell do you know about it, anyway? You've never even been married."

That stung, but it also goaded her into continuing. "Rio, I grew up with just one parent, my mother, and I remember how it felt. Oh, she loved me, and she was a good mother, just the way I'm sure Carol is, but it would have made a huge difference to me to have a father who cared about me. It gives a little girl a different perspective. She learns things from her father she can't know otherwise. And kids get crazy ideas when their parents aren't together. She needs a chance to ask you about things, and she can't do that if you're never around, or if she doesn't feel easy with you."

Rio was defensive and still angry with her. "Don't get the wrong idea here, okay? I care so much about that kid, I get all screwed up inside worrying over her." His voice was rough and full of frustration. "If I'd been a part of her life, every day, since the beginning... But Carol left me when Missy was brand-new. Now I just don't understand her. I'm, well, sort of scared I'll hurt her or something. She seems so . . . grown-up."

Sophie thought of Missy's composure, her silences, her unnatural dignity, and felt compassion for the man at her side, as well as for the strange little girl.

Missy was one tough kid to figure out, that was certain.

"Then there's all this stuff about her clothes and her hair and her food," Rio went on, punctuating his words by banging a fist on the steering wheel.

Sophie realized she had to tread very carefully here, or they'd end up in a full-scale quarrel. And she didn't want that.

"Maybe you ought to have a talk with Carol and ask her to dress Missy differently when you take her out, more casual."

"Yeah, maybe I should. Maybe I should do a lot of things. I never thought of just sort of, hanging out with her, y'know, like we did today. Today was fun," he admitted with wistful sadness. His natural good humor seemed to be restored when he added, "That was because of you, Sophie." He reached an arm over the seat and looped it around her shoulders, pulling her close to his side as he drove.

Sophie thought it might have had more to do with the dog, but she didn't say so.

"I'm sorry I snapped at you. I'm a bad-tempered bastard when I'm around that ex-wife of mine."

They'd pulled up and parked across the street from the Unicorn before Sophie realized where they were, and she felt depression settle over her. Why was Rio bringing her back here again?

Today had been one of the worst ones in her entire business career. She didn't exactly want to spend what was left of Friday evening here, as well.

She turned to tell Rio so, but he was craning his neck up at the windows of the Sweat Shop.

"You got the keys for your factory? I'd like to have a look at it if you don't mind."

Sophie dug them out of her purse, and together they unlocked the street door and climbed the narrow, winding stairs.

"Rio, I don't get this," she puffed. "If you had a burning desire to inspect the Sweat Shop, why not come here during working hours, for crying out loud?"

He was behind her, and he silenced her by cupping her hips in his hands and caressing her bottom with light, teasing strokes of his fingers as she climbed from step to step.

It took her mind off what she was saying, that was certain.

"I'll explain, I promise."

When they reached the top, Sophie used a second key to open the thick iron door.

The huge factory space was gloomy in the twilight, and balls of fabric dust rolled across the wooden floor when they entered. An immense pile of velour lay crumpled on the floor near the cutting tables, abandoned until Monday.

Their footsteps echoed as Rio crossed the room to the windows and peered out.

There was a bird's-eye view of rooftops, dingy streets and the front of Kelly's Quality Footwear, the Unicorn and Freedom Machines, as well as the row of stores in the next block.

"Perfect," he breathed. "I'm gonna use this place for a stakeout, Sophia, if it's okay with you. See, I decided today that I'm gonna catch those bastards who broke in your store. From up here, you get a clear view of a good dozen businesses, and it's only a matter of time till they try it again—if not your store, then one of the others along here."

"Stakeout? Like the police? But what if the thieves have guns? They're criminals, Rio. It sounds dangerous to me."

"You got a phone up here, right? All we do is call the police emergency number if anything suspicious goes down. Look, Sophie, these guys have been getting away with this scam for months now. They're confident that they aren't gonna get caught. And the cops said themselves that this is small potatoes to them. They can't afford to put a man on surveillance around here."

Rio's fists knotted and his eyes narrowed. "I get raving mad thinking what they did to your store this morning, thinking about how hard small-business people work to earn a living, while these criminals just walk in whenever they please and take stuff, and wreck the place in the process. I decided today that I'm gonna get them, Sophia."

There was no dissuading him. Sophie tried, but he'd made up his mind.

"You can't sit up here half the night and run your store the next day," she argued. "You'll get too tired."

"I'm not doing it alone. We're gonna run this in shifts. I talked to two of my friends today. They're willing to take turns. And Bill's in on the deal, too."

"Bill Stanopoulis?" Sophie was surprised.

"Yeah, he's just as fed up as I am with these hits. Actually, it was Bill that came up with the idea of using this place."

"But surely there's no need to stay here tonight, Rio. After robbing my store last night, they aren't going to come around again for a while."

"Maybe. Maybe not. We talked it over today, me and the other guys and Bill, and we decided to start tonight, and not let up till we catch them."

If she couldn't dissuade him, Sophie decided with a sigh, she might as well join him. There were worse things than spending the night here with Rio.

At Rio's suggestion, she drove his truck two blocks away and parked it in an all-night lot. It was her own idea to search out a small deli in Gastown and buy supplies for the siege.

She staggered back up the steps and wondered how many trips up and down would constitute enough of a calorie burn-off to amount to a substantial loss on her hips.

The aroma of the long loaf of French bread and Black Forest ham wafted up from the bag, and Sophie figured that if she was lucky, she'd maybe hold her own on the weight deal.

Rio had been busy, as well. He'd moved a shaky side table over to the window, as well as an armchair with its stuffing hanging out and a straight-backed wooden chair. He was sitting backward on the wooden one, arms folded under his chin, gazing out on the darkening street below.

His eyes lit up when he saw the things Sophie unloaded.

"Hey, it's a picnic. Too bad I didn't think to bring any of Pop's wine. I'll remember tomorrow night."

Sophie made instant coffee for Rio and curled up in the armchair. Rio had switched on the portable radio Bill kept on the cutting table, and soft music filled the shadowy room.

"We don't want to turn any lights on once it gets really dark," Rio explained. "Lucky there's that streetlight right outside, there'll be just enough light in here to move around."

The gloom deepened, and there was a long, comfortable silence.

At last Rio broke it.

"I've been thinking about something you said when we were talking about Missy, that you'd never known your father, and it dawned on me that in all the time we've spent together I never heard you mention him before. You talk about your mom, but never your dad."

"I guess it's not something I talk about much," she admitted with a catch in her voice. "All I know is what my mother told me when I was a little kid, driving her crazy with questions about my daddy. Apparently, he was a Swedish ship captain. His boat was in Vancouver harbor for repairs. In those days she was a secretary, working for the port authority, and Carl Larson had business with her boss. I guess it was a whirlwind romance, because they got married within a month, and she made plans to quit her job and go back to Sweden with him. Her mother and father had been killed in an accident years before, and she had no relatives. She got pregnant with me almost right away, and the night she told him, he simply packed his seaman's bag and walked out, never to be heard from again. His boat sailed a few days later, and that was that. She never heard from him again. That's all she'd say about it when I was little, but after I grew up, she told me that she found out he was already married, with a family back in Sweden. She was far too proud to chase after him or lay charges or anything. She took her first real estate course while she was pregnant with me, and she never looked back. The strange part is she went on using his name, even though technically they hadn't been legally married."

As she talked, Sophie looked out the window rather than at Rio, wondering how old she'd have to be before she outgrew the insecurities that had plagued her all her life. She gave a sad little chuckle and added, "As a kid, I always had the feeling that I'd ruined my mother's life just by being born. I figured out that if I hadn't come along, old Carl Larson might have stuck around. So I used to try to be a really good girl and not cause her any trouble, to make up for it. Crazy, huh, the ideas kids get in their heads?"

"You must've been such a lonely little girl. I wish I'd known you then. I'd have been your friend." His voice was so low and tender she had to strain to hear it. The story she'd just told him made Rio's throat ache with hurt for the helpless child she'd been. Her childhood and his were worlds apart, and for the first time he realized fully how lucky he'd been, and still was, to have the family he had.

He also thought he'd give a lot for ten minutes alone with Carl Larson, old man or not. . . .

But an uncomfortable parallel was slowly forming in his mind between the story he'd heard and his own inept parenting.

"Sophie, are you telling me this because you figure maybe Melissa feels like you did sometimes?"

Sophie sighed. "Rio, I don't know if she does or not. Who knows what kids are thinking? I don't even have a picture of my father, but you're a big part of Missy's life. You can choose to get to know her better, spend more time with her, talk with her about things. The situations aren't the same at all. And I know one thing for sure, Melissa loves her daddy. That was obvious tonight."

The tight knot of concern that had been building in him eased at her honest words, and all of a sudden he could see what was possible with his daughter. It wasn't too late to change things, and he would change them. He'd start by having a long talk with Carol, without losing his temper.

His attention turned to Sophie. She was unfailingly generous, this woman. He was grateful to her, but gratitude was mixed up with far more powerful emotions as he studied the curve of her jaw, the impudent upturned nose, the tumble of silky curls outlined against the window.

"Sophia, you're a special kind of lady." He reached over and raised her palm to his lips to press a kiss there. He ran his tongue over her skin, using the hot wetness to slide between each finger in a slow, provocative dance.

Sophie's breath caught in a gasp of pleasure at the sensations he was creating in her, and on impulse she took his hand and imitated his caress.

Her half shy, half bold manner filled his body with liquid heat. He rose from the wooden chair and lifted her up and turned, then sank into the soft armchair with her balanced on his lap. He wanted to hold her close and in some clumsy way soothe the deep scars she'd revealed to him tonight. He wanted to thank her, but the hot rush of sensual need she stirred in him became overwhelming.

"I want you, Sophia. Do you feel how much I want you?" He moved his hips a little. His desire was evident.

She nodded and then twined her arms around his neck and kissed his jaw, letting her tongue slide across his whisker-roughened skin. "You taste good," she murmured. "You make me want you, too, Rio," she breathed into his ear.

He cradled her, stroking her shoulder and arm, but she took his hands in hers and held them still, gazing into his eyes with a look that was still a little bashful, and her whispered request took his breath away.

"This time, let me?"

She'd been almost timid about lovemaking in the beginning, his beautiful woman. But there was newfound confidence in Sophie as she began to trickle tiny kisses across his face, nibbling at his neck, letting her tongue rest on the wild pulse in his throat that belied the careful control he was trying to maintain.

"Let's take this off...."

She lifted the hem of his shirt and slid it up and off over his head. Then, with trembling, clumsy fingers, staring into his eyes with provocative intent, she tugged her own T-shirt off, as well, and in slow motion, unhooked the front closure on her lacy bra, tossing the garment aside.

The rosy nipples of her full breasts were swollen, and Rio made a sound of pleasure in his throat, dipping his head, longing to capture them with his lips. But Sophie stopped him.

"My turn, remember?" Now her voice was low and thick with desire, her gray-blue eyes heavy lidded. She ran her fingers over his chest, finding the male nipples nestled in his chest hair, fondling them with her fingertips before she squirmed around and took them in her mouth, one after the other, sucking them until they became hard.

Rio groaned and moved his thighs upward against the warm fullness of her bottom.

"Sophie, you're making me crazy. . . ."

Her hand slid down his sides, found the snap of his jeans and released it. She moved away enough to undo the zipper, and her fingers slid down and circled him.

"Be still," she ordered. In one slithery motion, she was kneeling on the floor in front of him, and her hair spilled over his lower body.

In a rapturous instant, the touch of her lips made the aching need in his blood accelerate until he was certain he'd explode. He couldn't control the mad urgency from building inside him, but neither did he want to. His desire leaped and grew, almost out of control before he stopped her at last.

"Enough," he gasped, holding her face between his hands and covering her mouth with his. "Enough, *carissima*."

He shifted and stood up, drawing her to her feet, lifting her into his arms, moving them from the chair toward the heaped-up pile of velour on the floor.

He settled her there and stood up, stripping his clothes off in a few easy motions, then kneeling beside her to pull her shorts and pants off, a little rough and clumsy in his desperate need.

"Sophia, my wonder woman . . ."

It was growing darker all the time in the cavernous room, and the soft music from the radio floated around them.

His hand slid down to the apex of her thighs and found her warm flesh, her throbbing center, and she surged against his fingers with moist, warm eagerness.

"I love the way you touch me, Rio," she murmured.

His hands trailed down her legs and back up, and his breath caught at the silky softness of her flesh, the lush and lovely fullness of her hips and thighs, pale against the darkness of the soft fabric that cushioned her. He wanted her with every ounce of his being, wanted to part and enter her without any delay. . . .

"*Carissima*, you're beautiful, so very beautiful. Promise me you'll make love to me that way again."

She nodded, and the love and caring in her face reached down and touched his soul.

She was a giving woman, welcoming him with eager hands and lips, and an overwhelming need to give to her came over him, more powerful than his own hunger.

"Be still, Sophia. Now it's my turn to love you. . . ."

Using every ounce of willpower he possessed, he subdued his own desire, trailing his lips in the path his hands followed across her soft abdomen, down to the nest of curls between her legs.

His fingers found the soft lips and parted them, sliding into her hot damp places, and with his mouth, he located her center and began to torture it with slow kisses and long strokes of his tongue.

Her hands caressed his shoulders and back, but as the fire grew in her, she gasped and tangled her fingers in his hair, urging him in broken phrases to join her before . . .

Rio felt his own hardened body surge in dangerous cadence with the first slow undulations of her hips, rising to meet the delicious torture he was inflicting.

Control . . . he struggled for control, feeling his hot need come perilously close to erupting as she twisted and half sobbed his name, lost in the sensual maelstrom he was creating.

Gradually her movements lost their languorous slow rhythm, and she arched high to meet his lips and tongue.

"Please," her soft voice begged him. "Please, Rio . . ."

He quickened the pace, harder, faster, and when at last the tumult began inside her, he guided her with sure and steady strokes over the edge of ecstasy, encouraging the waves that rolled over her and increasing their intensity, hearing her cry out with fulfillment.

Never before had he taken such joy in giving pleasure.

With the sound of her voice still echoing in the corners of the room, he slid up her body and entered her at last, into the burning depths that welcomed him.

10

A WEEK AND A HALF went by, time which Sophie would later look back on as daylight bridges that had to be crossed in order to get her to the nights she spent with Rio.

Several of those nights were spent up in the Sweat Shop, the others in her apartment. Bill and Rio's friends shared the surveillance duty as they'd promised they would, but Sophie almost wished she and Rio were doing it alone.

There was something about the dusty warehouse that separated them from reality, that reinforced Sophie's subconscious efforts to separate her feelings for Rio from the rest of her life.

Being with him in the Sweat Shop made it easy. On one level, they were watching the street in order to catch the criminals.

On another, they were secret lovers in a cave where no one could find them, sharing pizza, wine, conversation, laughter and inevitably, wild, tempestuous lovemaking during the hours they spent together. There was a fantasy quality about their time up in the gloomy warehouse.

THEY WERE THERE TONIGHT, and it was raining, the gray downpour forming a kind of curtain over the windows. They'd just made love, and Sophie was dozing on the pile of fabric.

Rio untangled himself with gentle care, telling himself it was a blessing nothing had been robbed while they were supposed to be on duty.

He slid into his jeans and slouched over to the window. He felt suddenly uneasy. Almost an hour had passed since he'd last checked the street.

His watch said just after eleven. It was still pouring outside, a steady coastal drizzle, and each street lamp had a miniature rainbow around it.

To his relief, the street was quiet. But as he watched a moment longer, a shrouded figure appeared down the block, with a large dog trotting along at its side.

Rio stared at the pair, tugging on his runners and his shirt as he charted their slow progress along the stores below.

He tensed when they stopped in front of the Unicorn, and he bent down and touched Sophie's shoulder.

"There's somebody in front of your store. I'm going down to have a look."

He bolted down the endless flight of stairs and opened the street door as quietly as he could. The pair were still there, and now Rio could see that this was the dog responsible for the morning mess in front of Sophie's door. The dog was intent on creating that mess at this exact moment.

Rio had cleaned up the disgusting pile too many mornings to stay calm when he caught the villain responsible. He was across the street in an instant, careless of whatever danger there might be.

"What the hell do you think you're doing?" His voice boomed into the rainy stillness, and the figure with the dog whirled around, crouching in a fighter's stance.

But as Rio drew close, he saw that the man was old. He had some kind of dark hood on, and a black plastic bag over his shoulders served as a raincoat. He had a dirty white beard, and the hand that held the dog's rope was shaking, but the quavery old voice was full of bravado.

"This here's an attack dog, mister. You come one step closer and I'll give the command."

Rio eyed the dog. It was huge, with the face of a German shepherd, the ears if an Irish setter and the general configuration of a golden retriever. Might be a trace of Saint Bernard in there, too, but Rio would bet his bottom dollar this was no attack dog. The silly thing was wagging its tail and lunging at the rope, eager to get to Rio and lick him to death.

But there was a pathetic dignity to the old man that Rio couldn't bring himself to shatter.

"Don't set him on me, I don't mean to hurt you in any way. My name's Rio Agostini, and I own that motorcycle shop there...." Rio gestured at Freedom Machines and made his voice stern. "My friend owns this one. Three or four times a week, I've had to clean up after your dog here, and believe me, I don't enjoy it."

The old man was taken aback. He shot a guilty look at the dog's deposit and an apologetic one at Rio.

"Never gave it no thought." His hand went to the dog's head in a loving gesture. "Brandy here sleeps in the day, same as me, and he needs to walk when we get up. I can't take him to no parks at night, too dangerous these days, so we walk along here where there's streetlights. Sorry, mister, we never meant no harm. I'll talk Brandy into going someplace else, how's that?"

"That would be great." Rio found himself wondering where this pair slept all day and how the old man managed to afford enough food for the monstrous animal he so obviously adored. He was a street person, judging from his ramshackle clothing, and none too well fed himself.

"Brandy looks like a fine animal," Rio lied. "How old is he?"

The old man puffed up with pride. "He's just a pup, not a year yet. Found him abandoned under the bridge one night, no bigger than my hand. Raised him myself." He released the rope a bit and Brandy leaped on Rio, paws on his chest, eyes almost level with Rio's own, whining and licking in a joyful frenzy.

"Keeps me warm when we sleep, that's why I named him Brandy. Sure seems to like you." Brandy's owner eyed Rio and then stuck out a grubby hand. "I trust his judgment. Name's Potter, glad to make your acquaintance."

Rio did his best to ward off Brandy's advances and shake hands at the same time.

"Gotta be on our way, the cook over at the Ovaltine Café gives me scraps for Brandy, and we're pretty late tonight."

Rio waited until the pair turned the corner before he made his way back up to where Sophie was anxiously waiting.

THE NEXT DAY Rio bought an immense bag of dog food and a bowl and stored it in the back of his shop. At closing time, he filled the bowl to overflowing and hid it among the flowers in one of Sophie's planters.

He scribbled a note and took it over to the cook at the Ovaltine and asked him to give it to Potter, explaining where the bowl was, and that it would be there each night as a reward for Brandy for keeping the sidewalk clean.

There wasn't a scrap left in the bowl each morning, and there wasn't a mess at Sophie's door again.

THE MIDDLE OF AUGUST, Rio had to travel to Seattle to attend a motorcycle trade show where he'd agreed to do a presentation. He was leaving on Friday and he wouldn't be back until Monday morning. He'd hired a friend to run Freedom Machines for the weekend.

"I wish you could come with me, Sophia," he kept saying in a wistful voice. "You could leave Gina in charge at the Unicorn. The business part of this trip is just during the day. You could shop or something if you didn't want to come along and look at bikes, and then we'd spend the evenings—" his smoldering gaze made an understatement of his words "—we'd spend the nights having fun. What d'ya say?"

Sophie longed to say yes, but the timing was all wrong.

She was having to struggle hard again to make ends meet after losing her stock. The insurance company had agreed to pay for only part of her loss, arguing that Sophie hadn't extended her coverage to include the newest items. Besides that, the settlement would take time to come through. In the meantime, she had all the usual expenses to pay.

She was too worried about her business to play hooky for even two days. She told Rio so with real regret. He was disappointed, but he also understood.

He kissed her goodbye after their stores closed on Friday afternoon, roaring away on his bike.

By the time Sophie got home, it seemed as if Rio had been gone a week instead of only an hour. Her apartment was a disaster area, which wasn't surprising; she and Rio hadn't wasted their precious time together doing much housework.

Sophie made a halfhearted effort at tidying the place up and ended up flopped on the living room sofa, wondering exactly where Rio was at that moment and cursing herself for not throwing caution to the winds and going with him.

SATURDAY MORNING, however, Sophie was glad she'd stayed in Vancouver, because the Unicorn was busier than it had been in weeks. From the moment she unlocked the door and turned the sign around to Open, women started trickling in.

The jumpsuits Gina had suggested Bill make were becoming a trademark of the Unicorn, with word-of-mouth advertising bringing in customers who'd never heard of the Unicorn before.

With the bank manager's reluctant agreement, Sophie had managed to replace some of the better selling items she'd lost during the robbery, and today these, too, were bringing in sales.

It was just past noon when Harriet breezed in the door. Sophie was completing a charge form for a sizable amount, and she was feeling good about it.

"Hi, Mom," she called in a cheerful tone.

She hadn't seen anything of Harriet for several weeks. But then, she hadn't seen much of anyone except Rio in that time.

Harriet waved a hand, nodded at Gina and, as soon as Sophie was finished the sale, suggested they go out for lunch.

"Mom, I can't leave Gina here alone today. It's too busy. Let's go in the back and share the sandwiches I brought, and if she needs me she can call," Sophie suggested.

To her surprise, Harriet didn't argue. In fact, the older woman seemed more distracted than usual, not even clucking her tongue at the disorganized chaos of the back room.

Sophie made tea for herself and some of Gina's instant coffee for Harriet. She was dividing her chicken sandwich in half when Harriet leaned toward her and said in a confiding tone, "Forget the sandwich, dear. I'm not hungry. I don't suppose you've heard the big news yet?"

Sophie tore segments from a roll of paper towel to use as serviettes and frowned at Harriet. Her mother had an air of suppressed excitement about her today.

"Heard what big news, Mother?"

"About this building. Greg will be contacting you at the beginning of the week, but I wanted to fill you in ahead of time."

Sophie sipped her tea, and an apprehensive feeling began to niggle at her stomach. She stared at her mother and waited.

"You know that real estate values in the city have risen incredibly during the past six months."

Sophie knew because Harriet kept telling her.

"When Greg was in this area a few weeks ago, he saw potential in a way I have to admit I missed. And he acted on it. He contacted the owner and made him an offer on this building."

The twinges of apprehension in Sophie's stomach were becoming full-scale warnings.

"Are you saying Greg Marshall is buying this . . . my . . . our . . . building?"

Harriet hesitated. "Actually, dear, the two of us joined forces. The property is valuable, in spite of its run-down condition. It was much more viable for several people to invest."

"So you and Greg Marshall went in together? The two of you own this building now?"

"Yes, dear, we do."

Sophie swallowed hard, and despite the tea, her mouth felt dry.

"So I guess I pay my rent to you from now on. Will you send me nasty warnings if I'm late?" She tried for a feeble joke, hoping it would stall the even worse news she suspected was still to come.

"For the time being, you could say we're your landlords. But that's what I wanted to talk about with you, Sophie. We didn't buy this—" Harriet waved a deprecating hand around at the shabby premises Sophie loved "—just to become, uh, slum landlords. We have plans to develop the building. We have investors interested, and we'll tear this old thing down and rebuild. We'll turn it into chic retail space at street level and town houses above. You know how the Gastown area was developed. This area is the next logical direction for Gastown to expand."

Sophie felt as if she'd been punched in the chest.

"Tear down this building?" Her voice was high and thin. "But, Mom, this is my store, this is where I have my business." She stared at her mother in disbelief. "Don't you have any idea how much this building means to me? Didn't you hear me these past two years when I talked about how I was fixing everything up, how I felt about this place? I'm just establishing a name for myself here. I can't afford to move, but what's more, I don't want to. Haven't you been listening at all, Mother?"

As soon as she said it, Sophie realized that, of course, Harriet hadn't been listening. How could she forget what she'd always known, that they were on trains going in different directions?

Harriet was looking a bit taken aback and embarrassed, but her tone was still brisk, and sure enough, Sophie's meaning had once again sailed right over her well-coiffed head.

"Sophie, surely you can understand that this is progress. You must be able to see that moving to a better area is the only solution for you."

Now Sophie wasn't listening, either. Her brain was starting to work.

"You know, Mother, I have a lease on this place with another three years to run." Maybe she was on the right track. Her voice gained in confidence. Sentiment might not penetrate Harriet's head, but cold hard facts would.

"And so does Rio. I'm sure he mentioned a five-year lease. And Kelly's shoe store, I'll bet he has a lease, as well. Don't you have to let those expire before you can do any developing?"

Harriet's face was becoming flushed, and she sat up straighter in her chair. "Of course we're aware of those leases, Sophie. We're not amateurs, after all. But they don't have to expire. There's always the option of buying them out, making a fair settlement in return for the remainder of the agreement."

The scenario was becoming clearer to Sophie with every word Harriet uttered.

"So you came here to talk me into selling you my lease, is that it?"

She knew it was. She didn't need to have Harriet confirm it.

Harriet made an impatient gesture. "Darling, you're always so dramatic. I'm not here to talk you into or out of anything, you silly thing. I'm here to sound you out about a perfectly wonderful business opportunity."

"Which involves selling you my lease."

"Sophie, we're prepared to be extravagantly generous. We'll not only make you a fair settlement, we'll also find you an alternate location and make restitution for your moving expenses."

"Boy, Mom, that's really big of you. You must plan on making an absolute fortune out of this." Sarcasm dripped from Sophie's words. "As long as you make a killing, you don't mind being generous with the losers."

Harriet was becoming impatient. "For heaven's sake, dear, you're my daughter. You don't honestly believe I'd be involved in anything that would take advantage of you, do you? I've got your best interests at heart, this is an opportunity for you, now you can move somewhere—"

"Decent," Sophie supplied. Her anger and sense of outrage were making her reckless. "Well, Mother, you can go straight back to that stuffed shirt, Marshall, and tell him to . . . to stuff the offer right where it'll do the most good."

She paused and fought for control of her voice. "I do the most good."

She paused and fought for control of her voice. "I happen to know that Rio won't go for this either, so even if Kelly does, it's two of us against one. I'm not moving just so you can tear down this beautiful old place and put up some awful concrete rat warren, and that's final."

She sprang to her feet, grabbed her handbag and marched out, right past a surprised Gina and half a dozen customers.

She crossed the street without even checking for traffic and used her key to open the street door to the Sweat Shop, locking it again after herself.

She took the stairs two at a time and had to slump over when she reached the top, in order to get her breath back.

She locked the Sweat Shop door behind herself, needing to feel she was safe from any intrusion.

The space was empty, as she'd known it would be, but it seemed as if she could still feel Rio's presence here and be comforted and reassured.

And boy, did she need comfort and reassurance right now.

She walked to the armchair by the window and sank into it.

Rio had sat here so often and cradled her in this chair while she napped, secure in his arms.

If only he was here to hold her now, to tell her he was on her side and would fight the real estate development right along with her.

The awful thing was, she felt betrayed by her own mother. It was as if Harriet had chosen the very thing Sophie loved...her store...and attacked it, not with malice, but with something far worse—total indifference to her daughter's feelings.

Well, Harriet and Greg Marshall wouldn't get away with this, and that was all there was to it. When Rio came back, he and Sophie would decide on a plan of attack, but until Monday, there were things Sophie could do on her own.

Such as go over and talk to evasive Adam Kelly, sole proprietor of Kelly's Quality Footwear, and find out whether he would join Sophie and Rio in refusing to relinquish the lease he held on the building.

THE FRONT WINDOW of Kelly's Quality Footwear was clean for a change, and the shoes displayed were far more interesting than his usual antiques.

Sophie pushed open the heavy old door and entered the shop.

It was actually clean inside, and there was a pleasant odor of leather and soap.

Sophie was surprised and pleased. Maybe Adam had awakened from his long stupor and decided to earn a living after all.

He wasn't quick to answer his door's summons, however.

The store seemed deserted until a dark curtain over an opening at the back moved a little, and Adam Kelly peered out at Sophie, an apprehensive look on his face.

Why did he always look like a rabbit about to bolt?

"It's just me, Adam. I want to talk something over with you. Is this a convenient time?"

Adam Kelly came out from behind the curtain, carefully closing it after him. His long, thin body was stooped at the shoulders, his horn-rimmed glasses as finger-marked as his front window and his clothing rumpled. He reached up to push back his lank pale hair.

"As good a time as any, I guess. What do you want to talk about?" He sounded defensive.

If this was his business manner, it was a wonder he stayed open at all, new stock or not, Sophie decided, feeling irritated.

"I've just heard something disturbing, and I want to talk it over with you," Sophie began. "This building's been sold, and the buyers plan to knock it down, and we'll all have to move, but I think we can block it because of our leases. . . ."

Kelly listened, and he seemed less than happy as Sophie outlined the real estate dilemma. But apart from asking a few vague questions, he said little.

"So are you prepared to join Rio and me in fighting them on the strength of our lease agreements, Adam?"

"Yeah, sure, sure," he mumbled in such a distracted manner that Sophie felt like taking him by the shoulders and shaking him to wake him up. "I'll give it plenty of thought," he mumbled next, making Sophie wonder if he'd even understood what she was asking him to do.

He stood in silence for a long time, as if he were going to say more and couldn't get the words out. Sophie waited, exasperated, and when the silence lengthened, she opened the door and stepped outside into the rainy drizzle, drawing in a deep lungful of fresh air. Just before the door sighed shut behind her, she imagined she heard a woman's voice, but that was ridiculous.

What on earth was wrong with that man?

THE REST OF SATURDAY dragged its way to a close. Sophie couldn't face the thought of spending the evening alone in her apartment, brooding over her mother's disloyalty. She took a bus downtown, had a hamburger and went first to one movie and then to another. By the time she got home, it was after midnight, and she lay awake until the early hours, thinking of her mother, and Rio, and when at last she fell asleep, she slept soundly until the phone rang at nine the next morning.

Sophie groped for the receiver, praying it was Rio.

It was Betty Mills from downstairs, and she sounded hysterical.

"Sorry to bother you, Sophie, but I'm desperate. A pipe's burst under my sink, and the caretaker doesn't answer his phone or his door, and I don't know where to turn off the water."

Sophie came awake slowly. "It's Sunday. Mr. Wanless always goes to church on Sunday, I think I know where the main shutoff is, though, it's . . ." she tried to get her sluggish brain to cooperate with her mouth and gave up. "It's too complicated to explain, just hang tough a minute, Betty. I'll come down."

Moments later in Betty's apartment, Sophie struggled with a rusted turnoff valve hidden in the back of a cupboard and managed to close it. There was water everywhere, and Betty and Tara were frantically mopping it up with towels. Sophie, dressed in the first thing she'd grabbed, a slinky jersey muumuu, now soaking wet in various places, knelt and helped them.

Wringing out one last towel into a bucket some time later, Sophie shoved her sleep-rumpled hair out of her face and sat back on her haunches.

"That about does it. You won't have to wash your floors again for a year, Betty."

The other woman, wearing sopping wet flannelette pajamas, gave Sophie an apologetic, grateful look. "I'm sorry for dragging you out of bed on a Sunday morning like this. I can't thank you enough. I honestly didn't know what to do next. I'd never have thought of looking in that cupboard for the damned turnoff."

"I only knew because this happened to me once. These old buildings are notorious for plumbing problems, and they always seem to happen when Mr. Wanless isn't around."

The two women looked at each other and then at Tara. The three of them were still crouched on the floor, and all of them were soaking wet and totally bedraggled.

"Would you look at us." Betty was the first to giggle, and Sophie joined her. Tara lost her anxious expression and laughed with them.

"The problem is, you're going to be without water until Mr. Wanless gets hold of the plumber," Sophie mused. Inspiration struck, as well as a way to fill an empty day.

"Why not bring your clothes up and shower at my place? And then—" she caught Tara's wide-eyed look and winked "—why don't we all go for breakfast at McDonald's?"

THE DAY WAS a total success.

After McDonald's, they strolled to a nearby park and rode on the playground swings with Tara. When they got home, the plumber was busy in Betty's apartment, so Sophie invited Tara and her mother up to her place, and together, they made spaghetti and ate huge plates of it for supper.

"It's been great spending the day with an adult for a change," Betty said as they lingered over coffee. Tara had curled up on Sophie's pillows and gone to sleep, spaghetti sauce still streaked across her flushed cheeks. Betty reached over and stroked her daughter's tousled hair. Her voice was wistful.

"I love this kid like anything, but it gets kind of lonely on Sundays with just me and her."

Sophie remembered lonely Sundays she'd spent herself, before Rio came along. "You been divorced long?"

"Three years now; Tara was only two. The first year, I was hurting too much to even think about dating anyone, and then—well, it's tough being single with a kid. I went out with one guy for a while. He dressed nice, had a condo, a water bed and a fancy car. But he always wanted me to get a baby-sitter. He never really accepted me for what I am—which is a single mother." She shrugged. "I've sort of given up on dating lately."

There was a long pause, and then she blurted, "You serious about this gorgeous biker of yours, the one with the little girl Tara's age?"

Betty's impulsive question caught Sophie unprepared.

"Serious? I, um, well . . . he sure doesn't have a sports car, or a condo." Or a water bed for that matter. "Rio's different than any guy I've ever known," she heard herself saying. "He's sort of tough, but gentle. He's honest and levelheaded. He accepts me totally for what I am."

Rio not only accepted her—he made her feel like a queen. She'd pretended for so long that Rio was only an interlude in her life. Wasn't it time to admit that he'd become much more than that?

She stared at Betty, and at last she nodded. "Yeah," she said in a quiet voice. "I guess I am serious about him. I'm . . ." It was hard to say out loud, and she swallowed hard before she got it out. "I think . . . that is, I know . . . I'm in love with him."

Inside of her, something she'd kept tied in a tight knot was loosened and eased just by admitting it aloud.

Betty looked at her with a mixture of admiration and envy.

"I hope I find someone like that to love someday, but it gets a lot more difficult when you have a kid. The other person has to fall for both of you, if you see what I mean? But of course you understand that? He has a daughter, doesn't he?"

Sophie thought of Missy. If she imagined herself and Rio with a future, then Missy was part of that future, as well.

"My mom raised me. She and I were alone. She never did remarry," Sophie heard herself confiding in a thoughtful way.

"Funny, but I never thought much about her being lonely or needing companionship." It was strange to start imagining her mother as a woman with the same dreams about love as Betty or herself. It was impossible to feel much compassion for her, the way things were between them now.

They talked a while longer, and when Betty left, Sophie felt as if she'd made a good friend, and for some reason the issue over the business property didn't seem as urgent as it had.

Rio would handle it. He'd take control and do something about it, just the way he had with the neighborhood break-ins.

She'd come to trust him, and it was a wonderful feeling. But she didn't delude herself over their future. After all, he'd told her plain and simple they didn't have one.

BECAUSE SHE FELT more relaxed, Sophie didn't immediately blurt out her concerns to Rio Monday morning. He didn't arrive for work until an hour after Sophie, and when he stuck his head in the door of the Unicorn, he was already late and in a hurry.

"I missed you like crazy, lady. Can you come out with me for lunch about one? Larry says he'll cover the store for me."

Sophie drank in the sight of him. His strong features were windburned from the long ride on the motorcycle, and they seemed more rugged than ever. His shining dark hair curled in wild abandon around his ears and down his neck. His broken nose added to rather than detracted from the macho image he projected, and he gave her a lazy, meaningful smile and a wink.

"Yeah, of course she can come out for lunch," Gina pronounced magnanimously, as if Sophie were her employee, instead of the other way around. "She'll be free about one."

Sophie rolled her eyes heavenward.

"I MISSED YOU, God, I missed you something awful," Rio groaned once they were seated in the quiet little restaurant in Gastown he'd decided upon.

He'd been going to play this cool, wait for her to talk about missing him, but it was so damned good to be with her again, he couldn't play games.

During the short walk over, he'd told Sophie about the ride down to Seattle, the hectic schedule the organizers had set up at the trade show, and the quaint hotel he'd stayed at.

He hadn't told her about the rowdy party after the show, where one pretty lady in particular had spelled out delicious details about what she'd do to his body if he took her back to his hotel.

He didn't tell Sophie that the lady in question had come knocking on his door in the small hours of the morning. Or that for the first time in his adult male life, he'd said a gentle no and then a firmer and less polite one, sending her away in a fit of temper. Then, he'd lain awake the rest of the night, worrying about the changes Sophie had made in him.

It was hard for him to accept that he was falling in love with her, but about dawn, he'd admitted that was what was happening. He just hadn't figured out yet what to do about it.

"I missed you, too, Rio. I need to talk to you."

He reached across the table and took her hand in his, running a thumb over her palm and feeling a rush of desire when she shuddered at his touch.

"So go ahead and talk."

"My mother came to the store on Saturday," she began. "It seems that she and Greg Marshall have bought our building and are planning to knock it down and put up some fancy development."

What she considered a bombshell seemed to hardly affect Rio at all. He raised an eyebrow at her and nodded.

"Yeah, Marshall made an appointment to see me this morning. That's why I was late getting to the store."

Sophie's jaw dropped and she gaped at him.

"You know about this already?"

"Yeah, this morning, like I said. What's the problem?"

He didn't even seem upset or angry. Sophie stared across at him, astounded at his attitude.

The waiter arrived to take their order, and Rio paid close attention to the menu for a few moments, discussing the soup and the type of bread the sandwiches were made from.

At last Sophie couldn't stand it any longer.

"Rio, did you remind Greg Marshall we're all under lease?"

He grinned at her, his usual wicked lopsided grin. "Damned right I did. I told him it's gonna cost him plenty to buy us out. You want some wine?" He gestured at the waiter. "A couple glasses of white house wine here."

Sophie was trying to understand what he meant.

"You told him we wouldn't move, didn't you, Rio? You told him there's no way we'll let them tear down that building, didn't you?"

His grin faded. "No, I didn't tell him that. Sophie, be realistic. This is just business here. They've bought the property. It's their choice to do what they want with it." His voice hardened. "As long as they play fair with the tenants, that is. We've all got leases to protect us from this sort of thing. We deserve a decent buy out. I've been thinking I could use bigger premises, anyway, if my business keeps going the way it is. And you could expand, too, Sophie, put in more stock the way Gina's always saying you should. As for Kelly's shoe store, a buy out on his lease would be the best thing that could happen to him. He's got to be on the verge of bankruptcy anyhow, far as I can figure."

She heard the words he was saying, but she couldn't take in their meaning. She had to swallow twice before she could speak, and then her voice shook.

"Are . . . are you telling me we ought to let them buy our leases? Are you saying you're willing to just move somewhere else, start all over again, sit back and watch them tear down our building without even putting up a fight?"

He frowned at her. "As long as we get generous settlements out of this, Sophie, I don't see the problem. Sure, it's a pain in the neck, having to relocate and everything, that's why I was gonna suggest we oughta get a lawyer, make sure there's no funny business going on. But the building—God, Sophie, it's an old warehouse. No matter what you do to it, it's still falling apart. You know what they say, you can't make a silk purse out of a sow's ear." He grinned, and when she didn't respond at all, he studied her, becoming aware for the first time of just how upset she really was.

Then, in a quiet, emotionless tone, he said, "What exactly did you expect me to do here, Sophie?"

"Expect?" Her voice was rising, and the waiter glanced at her with alarm as he set down bowls of soup and fat sandwiches. Their wineglasses were still untouched.

"Expect? I expect you to understand how I feel. You know how much work I've put into fixing up the Unicorn. You know I love that place." Her voice rose. "I don't want some fancy shop in a plaza somewhere. I want to stay where I am. My roots are there. I thought you knew that. I . . . I guess I expected you to help me stop my mother and Greg Marshall from doing this."

He studied her in silence for another long minute, and then said in a soft voice, "Are those really the reasons you're against this, Sophie? Or is it because it's your mother doing the developing?"

She felt more betrayed than she ever had before. She felt as if he were using against her things she'd told him in confidence.

"That's a despicable thing to say. I thought you had a sense of honor. I expected you to put my feelings ahead of some balance sheet where money decides every issue."

"Well, maybe you expect too much, Sophie." Rio was still trying to be reasonable, but the lack of sleep and her wild accusations stung him. "I never signed any contract that says

I've got to pass up a good business opportunity just so you can win some points off your mother, y'know."

Her voice was shaking so hard she could hardly form the words. "I thought I could depend on you, Rio. I thought you'd understand the principle involved here, but all you see is the chance to make money, to pick up a few dollars on the deal. A chance to . . . to get to Europe a few months ahead of your damned five-year plan, and to hell with anybody who stands in your way."

That got under his skin, because all the way home on the bike, he'd been thinking about his dreams and of how loving Sophie had changed them. He'd even figured out ways to take her and Missy with him on a tour of Europe someday.

"You're . . . you're just as bad as my mother," Sophie burst out, and at that Rio lost his temper.

"Don't you dare compare me to your mother," he roared. "It's time you cut the umbilical cord, Sophie."

By now, their raised voices were attracting attention from all around. The food sat untouched as they glared at each other, and Sophie knew she had to get out.

She stood up, almost knocking her chair over.

"You go ahead and take their rotten money, Rio. Obviously that's all that's important to you. But I warn you, I'm going to fight all of you on this, you, my mother, Greg Marshall . . . all of you."

She whirled toward the door, almost knocking down their horrified waiter.

"Sophie, you wait one minute," Rio hollered in a furious voice as he pulled his wallet out and tossed bills onto the table.

She heard him, but she kept right on going out the door.

11

RIO CHASED AFTER HER, cursing with fear as she ran across intersections without looking. Irate drivers honked and hollered at first her, and then him.

He caught up with her a half block from the Unicorn, grabbing her arm and hauling her to a stop.

His quick, hot temper had faded somewhat during the chase. "Sophia, enough now. What is it with you today? Let's talk this over quietly." He added without thinking, "You're being ridiculous about the whole thing, y'know that?"

She tore her arm out of his grasp and gave him a freezing look. "Go ahead and sell out to the highest bidder, Rio, but don't try to bully me into doing the same thing. Now let go of me."

He turned her loose. She stomped toward the Unicorn just as a motorcycle pulled to a noisy stop at the curb beside him.

"Hey, Rio, think you could take a look at the ignition on this bike? It stalled right in the middle of the bridge."

Rio watched Sophie's stiff back disappear into her store. He had half a mind to chase after her, haul her into the back room and kiss her anger away. But he'd never seen her quite this mad before and he wasn't sure how to handle it.

Maybe he'd give her time to cool down and talk with her later.

He motioned to the man on the bike to drive down the alley and into the back entrance of his store.

SOPHIE MANAGED TO SAY HI to Gina and two customers on her way into the back room to hide until she could regain some composure. Rio's betrayal had left her hurt and aching, and she needed to be alone.

She slumped into a chair, absently fingering the stack of mail Gina had placed in a neat pile on the table.

The top envelope was from the insurance company, and when Sophie tore it open, a check covering the remainder of the losses from the break-in fell out, along with a curt note saying the adjustors had changed their minds about allowing her full coverage.

This would pay off the amount due at the bank, with some over to replace the leather garments that had been stolen. How ironic, Sophie thought, that just when her business was starting to improve, the rest of her life fell apart.

The second envelope was lavender, with Sophie's name and the store address in Jessica Stanton's distinctive old-world script on the front.

"My dear girl," the note inside read. "I so enjoyed your letter, and I'm hoping you make good your promise to come visit me before the summer's over...."

Sophie stared down at it, thinking with longing how wonderful it would be to pour out all her troubles to Jessica, just the way she used to when her friend was next door. How wonderful it would be to get completely away for a few days, away from the Unicorn, from Rio, from her mother.

It would give her time to think.

She could hear Gina taking an order for a jumpsuit out front, making certain the customer paid a hefty deposit on the sale while encouraging the other woman to try on a dress she'd been admiring and explaining to still another woman that it was possible to have a hemline altered on a skirt.

Gina was more than able to handle the store for a few days without her. The insurance check eased the financial pressure. So what was stopping her from paying a visit to Jessica?

BY FIVE THAT AFTERNOON, Sophie was on the small ferry that connected the Vancouver mainland with the Sechelt Peninsula.

She'd phoned a delighted Jessica to say she was coming for a three-day visit, extracted a firm promise from Gina, with a death threat thrown in for good measure, that she was not to tell anyone—especially, particularly, not Rio—where Sophie'd gone.

She hurried home and packed a small bag, bought a dozen of the cheese bagels she knew Jessica was addicted to and caught a bus that brought her to Horseshoe Bay and the ferry landing.

But with every watery mile that separated her from Rio, Sophie felt more desolate and empty inside.

It didn't help to remind herself of Rio's treachery; all she could think of were the delightful hours they'd spent together during the past weeks, of the fun she'd had with him and the passion they'd shared.

Sophie left the boat's stuffy lounge and went out on deck, welcoming the brisk wind that whipped her hair like an eggbeater and brought tears into the corners of her eyes.

The sun was dropping low over the horizon, and the boat was threading its way among the small islands that dotted the inside passage of Georgia Strait.

Couples were strolling around the deck, and Sophie knew if Rio was there, he'd be saying outrageous things to make her laugh, or sexy things to make her blush. He'd be wrapping his arms around her waist from behind and telling her it was to keep her from falling overboard. He'd be there for her.

But when she'd needed him the most, she reminded herself, Rio hadn't been there.

He'd taken sides with the enemy.

JESSICA WAS WAITING for her when the ferry docked at Gibsons Landing, and Sophie hurried down the ramp toward her.

Jessica looked just the same as she always had. She was tall, close to six feet, and probably somewhere in her sixties, but it was hard to tell. Her long, rusty hair insisted on pulling loose from its chignon, floating around her square face in wisps and tangles. Her eyes were an astonishing shade of cornflower blue, and they danced with animation so that no one noticed the network of wrinkles around them.

She wore one of her tweed suits with a linen blouse and a brooch, and she strode toward Sophie in sensible shoes, wrapping her arms around her and hugging her with all the strength in her wiry body.

"My dear girl, I'm so glad you came. You have no idea what it's like, living over here like a recluse." She held Sophie away so she could look at her, shook her head and clucked her tongue.

"Well, it's obvious you need sunshine and some of my fresh eggs, and perhaps a good dose of salts, as well. You're the most peculiar color, child. Come on, Gertrude's over here. We'll be at the ranch in less than twenty minutes."

Gertrude was a decrepit yellow Volkswagen beetle that Jessica had driven since she bought it new twenty-five years ago.

Sophie climbed in and had to smile at the familiar one-sided tirade Jessica carried on with Gertrude.

"Come on, you stubborn, obstinate old cow, let's get this show on the road...."

In a moment, the car roared to life, vibrating and backfiring as if she were talking back to Jessica.

They puttered and backfired along the streets of the village and soon were past it, heading along a highway bordered by huge cedars, with small farms carved out of the wooded terrain here and there.

Jessica herded Gertrude onto a narrow dirt road that soon gave glimpses of water through the trees. Then they pulled into a treed driveway that led up a slight hill where a small green cottage nestled in an open meadow, overlooking a breathtaking view of the ocean.

"Jessica, it's heavenly," Sophie breathed.

Jessica snorted. "Only if you don't know about the leak in the roof and the faulty septic tank, or cleaning the chicken coop." But there was a contented note in her voice.

Sophie's suitcase was deposited in a tiny screened-in porch at the side of the house, which had a sofa bed and doubled as a spare bedroom in the summer.

Jessica had prepared a simple dinner of quiche, green salad and fresh strawberries. After they'd eaten, the women went for a long, rambling walk along the water.

Jessica wanted to know everything that had happened since she'd given up her business, and Sophie did her best to fill in the details, proud of herself for avoiding the subject of her romance with Rio.

They talked about the break-ins and about Bill, whom Jessica had loved, and Michelle, whom she'd disliked. Jessica asked about Harriet—she and Harriet had had a casual friendship.

Sophie skated over the subject of her mother and chatted on about the new stock she'd had stolen and about Gina, who Jessica couldn't wait to meet. Then Sophie deliberately turned the conversation to Jessica's new life and what it was like to live in this beautiful place without business pressures or problems.

"Lonely," Jessica declared at once, wrinkling her nose. "Uncomfortably lonely."

Jessie had been married twice, the first ending in divorce and the second leaving her a widow.

"When Andrew died ten years ago, I decided that was it for me. I was too set in my ways to adjust to anyone else again. I'd live out my days single." Jessica looked thoughtfully at the spectacular sunset now playing itself out over the water. "But you know, my dear, I've quite changed my mind. I like being married. I like having a man in my bed. I'm going to give matrimony another try."

She laughed at Sophie's amazed expression. "I'm not going to abduct some poor half-blind specimen from the local pub and keep him in shackles until he marries me, so don't look like that. No, there's a perfectly nice gentleman, Cecil Montague. He's the father of that young bohemian man who lives in the old school bus on the next property. He's been paying me court, and very nicely, too. He's asked me to marry him, and I believe I will."

Sophie was happy for her friend, but inside, she also felt a painful stab of envy for Jessica's old-fashioned system. In her world, two people met, courted and married. There was none of the open-ended uncertainty of modern relationships, no hint of here today and gone tomorrow.

Like Rio.

As dusk fell they wandered back to the cottage, and Jessica made them each a gin and lemonade. They sat on the tiny front porch, listening to the night birds and watching the sky light up with moon and stars.

"Now tell me all about this young man of yours," Jessica demanded all of a sudden. "There's no point in trying to keep a stiff upper lip, either, Sophie, because I'm quite well aware that something is not right with you. It's that dashing fellow with the motorcycles, isn't it. Rio something-or-other? You mentioned him in your letter."

The shell that Sophie had done her best to maintain all day crumbled at Jessica's astute guess.

"Rio Agostini," she whispered, and just saying his name aloud made her insides ache. "He's, um, I, we, oh, damn . . ."

"Clear as glass," Jessica sighed. "How about starting at the beginning and taking it point by point?"

Sophie did. She started with the day Rio moved in, and there were a lot of things she didn't spell out in detail.

Several times she blushed crimson in the darkness, remembering in vivid detail what she was leaving out.

After a long while, she'd told Jessica the story, including Missy, Harriet, Greg Marshall, and the quarrel she'd had that morning with Rio.

Jessica's first comment astounded Sophie.

"Your mother is a dreadfully lonely woman, you know."

"Harriet?" Sophie's voice was shrill. "Don't be ridiculous. She's far too busy buying and selling and making money to be lonely."

Jessica put a soft hand on Sophie's arm. "Dear, she's like that because she's terrified to stop and have a look at her life. She fills it with busy work. She substitutes financial success for love. Harriet fell in love once, with your father, and when it didn't work out, she never allowed herself to love again. She was too frightened to take a chance. She doesn't even dare show how much she cares for you. And of course she objects violently to any romance between you and your Rio." Jessica shook her head.

"Your father was probably dashing, romantic and of course from a different cultural background, just like Rio is. She's afraid for you, dear. She doesn't want you to get hurt the way she did."

Sophie opened her mouth to object, but Jessica was still talking about Rio.

"I like the sound of him, Sophie. And of course, you're quite wrong about this whole issue of the building being torn down. My goodness, I'd have welcomed an offer to buy out my lease, and you know how much I loved my store. But face it, that building eats money and repairs. Don't you remember how much our heating bills were in the winter, and how we were never warm, no matter how high we turned the thermostat?"

It was true. In the summer, Sophie chose to forget those shivery days in January.

"And then last spring, when we had that infestation of mice?" Jessica shuddered, and Sophie did, as well. She'd forgotten the rodents that jumped out of every crevice for weeks, terrifying her and sending her customers shrieking.

"But, Jessica, I just don't want to move, I've had to move all my life...."

"Yes, well, you're getting like your mother that way. Afraid of taking a chance. With you it's moving, with her it's men."

Sophie felt hurt to the quick. Jessica was her friend, and here she was taking sides against her.

"Sophie." Jessica's voice was insistent. "I'm sixty-two years old. Don't you think I'm afraid of things? I'm petrified at the thought of starting all over again with Cecil, of making a mistake. But life is choice, and I choose to take chances. I think this quarrel today with Rio wasn't just about the lease issue. I think you're frightened because you love him, because you might give him all you have and then find it doesn't work out." Now Jessica sounded angry. "Well, so what if it doesn't? You pick yourself up, you learn from it, you heal, you go on. But there's always the possibility... and a very good one at that... that it will work, that you'll end up living happily ever after. You'll never know unless you try, will you?"

Jessica's heated words settled into the night and into Sophie's brain.

The two sat in silence for a long time, and then Jessica said in a teasing voice, "Of course, my dear, this Rio of yours has his faults, certainly. For instance, he's risked your life on the back of a motorcycle, he's landed you with his sister, who sounds impossibly charming. He's ready to engage in physical violence to stop those abysmal break-ins, and from what you didn't say during spells of heavy breathing, he's a masterful lover. And he's good at making money.

"So he thinks you're off base now and then. Find it in your heart to forgive him. It's men's weaknesses that make them most endearing. I'm certain he has some strong points as well to balance all those faults. Now, let's go to bed."

Sophie lay awake for hours. Sleeping on the porch was just the same as camping out must be, with the cool night air and the moon and stars visible on all sides. It was exhilarating, and it was also lonely.

With a pang of nostalgia, she remembered Rio suggesting once that they go camping on the motorcycle this fall and how she'd hesitated.

She'd held back over so many things, and Rio had shoved her along, encouraged her to be brave, to take chances, to try new things. And he'd taken her comments about Missy to heart, seeing more of his daughter and doing his best to be a good father.

She thought over all the things Jessica had said tonight. Her friend was probably right about most of them, Sophie admitted with weary honesty.

When she heard the first birds singing before dawn, she made a decision, and then she fell asleep.

"OKAY, GINA, now quit playing games and tell me where she is or so help me, I'll . . ."

Rio had been making threats for the past half hour and getting nowhere. When she wanted to be, Gina could be more closemouthed than the CIA.

"She's out of town, and that's as much as I'll tell you. Soph said she needed time away, I assume from you. And this is a lesson for you, Mario. How many times have I had to cover for you, say I didn't know where you were when some poor lady was desperate to find you?"

"But that was before," Rio groaned. "This is Sophie we're talking about here. Sure, we had a little argument yesterday, but to just take off like this, without telling me . . ."

He was going to give her a piece of his mind for doing this. He felt hurt and outraged, as well as worried.

Where the hell could she have gone? He'd checked at her apartment, he'd talked to Betty Mills, he'd even called Harriet and had her insult him and then hang up in his ear. Then he'd finally concluded Gina was the only one who might know.

Gina snorted through her nose. "Little argument, all right. When she got back from lunch yesterday, she looked like she was about to use a razor on her veins. What'd you do, Rio, give her your speech about so long, it's been good to know you? Those other bimbos you used to romance were one thing. I could see your point when you dumped them. But Sophie's something else. Wait till I tell Nonna you played fast and loose with Sophie. Nonna really likes her, y'know. In fact, you can tell her yourself. You're supposed to go over there for supper tonight, remember? Nonna's spent the day making lasagna just the way you like it."

He was going to do his sister serious injury in another second. He flexed his fists and tried to hold on to his temper. The only hope he had of finding Sophie involved keeping Gina alive long enough to pry information out of her.

"Leave Nonna out of this. I'll talk to her myself," he growled. "And the argument had nothin' to do with splitting. In fact . . ."

In fact, he'd been going to sound Sophie out on the idea of living together or something. Maybe even getting married someday wasn't as bad an idea as he'd thought.

But then she'd gone nuts on him, and all over a stupid lease agreement.

"Then I bet it was over this building," Gina said with triumph in her voice. "I just knew she was gonna freak out when she found out you weren't ready to lay down in front of the bulldozers."

Rio narrowed his eyes at her. "How do you know about that?"

He shouldn't be surprised. Gina always knew everything that was going down.

"From Adam Kelly next door. He told me Sophie came over all upset about the plans to tear down this dump. The thing is, he didn't want to hurt her feelings, but he's tickled pink about the lease buy out." Gina shook her head in disgust. "Just when I got him to smarten that place up a little, too. Did you notice his window? I've been working on him for weeks to put in a line of cowboy boots and belts and things, and the minute he gives in, they decide to knock down the building. By the way, I sent him to your bank manager for a credit extension. Might as well have all the loans around here under the same roof, so to speak. I'm thinking of hitting up your bank manager for a commission what with all the business I send him."

Rio looked at his baby sister. She had to be a throwback to the family's Sicilian ancestors. Was there such a thing as a godmother in the Mob?

"Gina." He decided to try a different tack. "When is Sophie coming back?" She couldn't stay away long; she had a business to run. Mind you, with Gina in charge—well, he wasn't sure anymore. "I mean, she's got no car or anything, and if she needs a ride from the airport or the train station, I could pick her up, no problem."

Gina shook her head. "She got there fine. She'll get back. Hey, Rio, how's the stakeout going?"

Rio sighed. "Don't yap that around, okay, Gina? It's supposed to be kept quiet, because I've got a hunch that whoever's doing it either lives or works in this area."

Gina shrugged. "Michelle from the Sweat Shop overheard Bill talking about it on the phone, and of course she told Adam, and he asked me."

The logic of that totally escaped Rio and alarmed him, as well. He'd had his private suspicions all along that just maybe the break-in artist was uncommunicative Adam Kelly. After all, he had the perfect front, and he certainly didn't seem to be the businessman he was supposed to be.

"Michelle told Kelly about the stakeout? Why the hell would she tell Adam Kelly?"

Gina shot him the look she reserved for people she figured might have a few olives missing from a full jar.

"For heaven's sake, Rio, her and Adam have been having an affair for months now. I figured that out the first week I was here. And I don't go around blabbing. I didn't even tell Sophie about Adam and Michelle, and she practically walked in on them last Saturday. You'd think Michelle would have smartened him up about his store, but you know Michelle. I call her the Fog, 'cause that's what she wanders around in half the time. That's why her and Adam suit each other. They're both space cadets."

She stopped for breath, and Rio felt his head start to ache.

"And, oh, yeah, what I started to say was, Bill phoned over here this morning when he couldn't get hold of you. He said to tell you he can't do his shift tonight at the Sweat Shop because half his family is arriving from Greece along with the woman they've picked out for him to marry, and they're having a big dinner at The Greek Village."

Rio had been on duty the night before, and being up in the warehouse half the night worrying about Sophie wasn't his idea of how to spend a pleasant evening.

Well, he decided, he'd get Louis or Salvatore to take Bill's shift tonight, go over and have some of Nonna's lasagna, and then go home and try to get a good night's sleep.

Although come to think of it, for one reason or another, he hadn't really had a good night's sleep since he met Sophie Larson, and until things were settled between them, he didn't think he ever would, either.

He called Louie first.

"Hey, ho, Rio, how ya doin', buddy? Hey, about that stakeout we been doin', I can't make it tomorrow night, my old lady's on the warpath, figures I must be roamin' around on her I been away so many nights, so I promised I'd take her out to dinner. You know how it is."

Rio hung up and dialed Salvatore.

"Rio, how's it goin'? Hey, man, I was just gonna call you. I'm supposed to be watchin' the street for you day after tomorrow? I'm sorry, man, but I gotta beg off. I got infection in my eye and the doc says lots of rest, no late hours."

Bill, Louie and Salvatore, all bailing out on him at once.

That left guess who up in that damn warehouse for the next three nights at least.

Terrific. He could die up there, and who'd know the difference?

No Sophie, no buddies to do surveillance with him, and he was already so tired he felt as if he'd been hit by a truck. His life was taking a turn for the dismal.

Well, there was one sure way to make it worse.

He called Gina and got Harriet Larson's address, which Sophie had scribbled beside her mother's telephone number.

HE RODE OVER to the neighborhood of sleek new town houses right after he locked up his store that evening. He figured out which unit was Harriet's—no easy deal because they all looked the same—and he knocked on the door, then knocked again. Her silver Cutlass was in the parking space out front, so he figured she was home, but no one answered.

He was ready to turn and leave when at last the door opened about four inches, and from behind a security chain Harriet peered out at him.

"You. What are you doing here? We have nothing to say to one another, Mr. Agostini," she snapped in an outraged tone. "I thought I made that clear on the phone today. My daughter's whereabouts are none of your business."

Rio stuck his foot in the crack before she could slam the door and talked fast. "I want to discuss the buy out on my lease."

"Then I suggest you make an appointment during business hours."

"This concerns your daughter, as well as me, Mrs. Larson, and I want to talk to you now."

"Is Sophie in trouble? There hasn't been an accident . . ."

Harriet sounded almost panicky, and Rio was quick to re-assure her.

"Nothing like that. As far as I know, Sophie's fine, or my sister would have heard." Rio was fed up with this song and dance. He decided to put his cards on the table. "Look, Mrs. Larson, I happen to love your daughter, I assume you do, too, and both of us are hurting her right now, so we need to talk, okay?"

"This isn't a good time . . ." she began in a different tone, but a deep male voice behind her interrupted.

"Let him in, Harriet. He's right, you do need to talk."

There was a long moment of utter silence, and then the chain on the door was released and it swung open.

Greg Marshall stood just behind Harriet. Both of them were wearing terry cloth dressing gowns and looking flushed and tousled.

Unless Rio was slipping all his marbles, they'd just been engaging in something other than a discussion about real estate values.

Even if Rio couldn't add one and one and get sex, Harriet's face gave her away. She looked as guilty as Rio had felt when his father caught him in the garage with Rosie Brizito.

Of course, Rio and Rose had been seven and nine years old at the time, and they'd had even less on than Harriet and Greg Marshall were wearing now.

Rio put one mark on his side of the mental scoreboard he was keeping between himself and Harriet Larson.

He had a distinct upper hand for the first time since he'd met her, and he was going to take full advantage of it.

In fact, he was going to enjoy the hell out of this.

12

THE FIRST FIFTEEN MINUTES were bad. The second fifteen were worse. Harriet accused Rio of coming between her and her daughter and of seducing Sophie into a cheap, tawdry affair.

Rio kept his cool and gave her and Marshall what he hoped was a meaningful look. "Tell me, Mrs. Larson," he said with his sweetest grin, "what's the big difference between us? How come my relationship with Sophie is cheap and...what'd you call it? Oh, yeah, tawdry. But yours isn't? What's the difference between us and you two?"

That really got to her. "There's no comparison between Greg and I...."

"Damned right there isn't. Sophie and I never stooped to sneaking around."

Her face turned magenta, and Marshall the hero puffed up and said, "Now see here, Agostini..."

But Rio was fed up, tired of baiting them. He had no desire to drive this crazy lady over the edge. He only wanted to help Sophie, and this wasn't doing it.

"Look, Mrs. Larson. I phoned you before. You know Sophie's taken off somewhere because she's in a state over this real estate deal. When—" He jerked his head in Marshall's direction. He'd be damned if he was gonna call him "Mr.," and he wouldn't stoop to "Marshall." "When...Greg...here discussed the deal with me, I had no idea Sophie was gonna be against the whole thing. I mean, I shoulda known, but I didn't. Sometimes I'm kinda slow. I only saw the advantages to my own business without thinking too much about how she'd feel about it."

Harriet sniffed. "Sophie is being totally unreasonable about this, I have to admit that."

Rio gave her a vicious, narrow-eyed look that made her flush and drop her chin.

"Unlike you, Mrs. Larson," he said, sarcasm evident in every word, "I don't give a damn whether Sophie's being reasonable or not. I just want her happy."

Harriet had the grace to look embarrassed.

"Now I came here because as far as I can see, we've got two choices in this. You two can go right ahead with your plans, in which case I'll be forced to side with Sophie and fight you every step of the way. There's only three tenants, and if two of us object . . . well, if that happens, I plan to get a lawyer, involve all the groups that scream to the city about destroying old buildings and hold you up for the full four years and nine months left on my lease."

Greg became upset at that idea.

"That's preposterous, we couldn't possibly. . ." He bit off what he'd been about to say.

Rio finished it for him. "You couldn't possibly delay development that long without losing a bucket of money, right? So my other suggestion is for you two to back out of the deal right now."

Greg began shaking his head and talking fast about closure dates and airtight agreements and losing security money.

"Hold it," Rio ordered, gesturing like a traffic cop. "Hold it. I've got an uncle who's been in real estate since before I was born. I called him today and had a little talk about this whole thing. Now, you two put up security money when you made your offer, right? About seven percent, Uncle Giovanni figured. But being hotshot movers and shakers, you also made sure there was a subject clause in the agreement. Subject, I'd say, to the present tenants being agreeable in regards to the outstanding leases. Which means that you wouldn't lose much on the deal, maybe a small inconvenience fee payable to the vendor, maybe nothing. Am I right?"

Greg nodded with obvious reluctance, but Rio ignored him and focused on Harriet.

"Mrs. Larson, Sophie's told me that in her whole life, she always came second to your job. It hurt her when she was growing up, and it still hurts her now, which is probably why she's so upset over this deal. See, to her it must feel like the ultimate betrayal, you just buying the place without even asking her first how she felt about it." He met Harriet's defiant stare with one of his own. "Tell me, do you really give a damn about your daughter, Mrs. Larson? Because I'd say this is your last chance to prove to her that you care more about her than you care about a lousy commission."

Greg was silent, watching the two of them. Harriet stared at Rio, and he couldn't tell from her icy expression whether what he'd said had registered at all.

She finally said, "You told us this buy out on your lease would be an advantage to your business."

Rio nodded. "Yeah, no question there. It would be."

"If you fight this, it's going to cost you a lot of money, and at the end of your lease we'd win anyway. I don't quite understand . . ."

Rio had had enough. "Damned right you don't understand. I happen to love your daughter," he roared at the top of his lungs. "Unlike you, I care about how she feels in all this. I'd go to any lengths to make her happy. If it's important to her to stay where she is, then, goddamn it, I'll make sure she stays. Now I'm out of here." He took two long strides toward the door before Harriet's hand on his arm stopped him.

"Mr. Agostini, please don't leave just yet." She made a visible effort and for the first time called him by his first name. "Rio, I should say. Sit down, please, and we'll all have a drink and try to talk about this like civilized human beings." She raised a brow and attempted a smile. "Please?"

He looked at her and thought it over. He didn't feel very civilized at the moment. On the other hand, stomping out wasn't going to solve anything.

He moved over to an armchair and balanced on the edge of the seat.

"Greg, go in the kitchen and mix us all a drink, would you? Whisky, or rum. I think there's even a beer in the fridge."

"Whisky's fine," Rio said in answer to Greg's questioning glance.

When they were alone, Harriet sat down on the couch across from Rio, and with her head bent forward, stared down at her lap. She seemed at a loss as to what to do or say next.

"Mrs. Larson, I've got a date for supper. I'm gonna be late. I think I'll just . . ." Rio began. This was stupid, he really did want out of here.

Harriet raised her chin, and it was a shock to see the slow tears trickling down her cheeks in a steady stream.

"I . . . don't suppose . . . you could call me . . . Har-Harriet? I've always hated . . . being called . . . Mrs. Larson." She ignored the tears except to wipe her fingers across her cheeks in an effort to brush them away, gulping down the sobs that accompanied them.

Now Rio was truly out of his depth. When his female relatives or any of the ladies he'd romanced had cried, they usually did so with noisy sobbing and much nose blowing and accusations hollered out at the top of their lungs.

It made it much easier to comfort them, once they were through being angry with him. But this silent, tortured grief was awful.

Where the hell was Greg? This was his lady. He ought to be here patting her shoulder or something.

"Look," he said in desperation, "maybe I said some things . . ."

Harriet shook her head. "No. What you said was the truth. I know I wasn't a good mother to Sophie. I was always worried out of my mind about finances. I never took time for her."

Rio dug into his pocket, found a tissue and handed it over to her. She took it and blew her nose hard. Then she gave him a sidelong glance.

"But you're wrong about me not loving her. I do love her, very much. That's why I have my reservations about you."

Rio decided not to let her off the hook easy after all. She was one tough lady, and she had a lot of making up to do with Sophie. "You got a funny way of showing love, I guess," he remarked, and a trace of the old steel glinted in the venomous look she shot at him.

Greg arrived with a tray of drinks and handed them out, then took a seat beside Harriet, looping an arm over her shoulders and taking a hearty swig of his drink before he said anything.

"I've been thinking this whole thing over, and I'm inclined to agree with you, Rio, about Harriet and I backing off now before this goes any further. It's financially sensible. If you're determined to fight us, we could lose plenty." He sighed. "It's too bad, because everyone would have benefited in the long run by the redevelopment. How do you feel about it, Harriet?"

"We'll back out. But I want it understood that the only reason I'm doing it is Sophie." She gave Rio a long look. "I'd never change my mind just because of a fight over this lease issue with you. I refuse to be bullied. But I think perhaps you're right, Rio. It's time I proved something to Sophie."

Mission accomplished.

Rio bolted the last of his whisky and shot to his feet.

"I gotta go. . . ."

Harriet got up, as well.

"There's one more thing," she said, looking Rio straight in the eye. "You told me you love Sophie. Are you planning to marry my daughter?"

"I sure as hell am." Rio looked over at Greg and back at Harriet. "Are you gonna marry..."

What the hell. He decided not to push it. He might have a long life ahead with Harriet as a mother-in-law. He gave her a half salute and opened the door. "Skip it. Thanks for the drink."

Harriet wasn't quite ready to let him go. "If you're going to marry Sophie, I think it's despicable to have a date for dinner with another woman, Rio."

He shook his head. This lady was really something else.

"Harriet," he said with a sigh, "the dinner date is with my grandmother, at her house. Is that okay with you?"

She closed the door behind him, but at least she didn't slam it.

LATE THAT SAME AFTERNOON, Jessica drove Sophie back to the ferry.

"I'm sorry you can't stay longer, but I do understand. The sooner you settle things with your young man the better." She enveloped Sophie in a voluminous hug. "I do wish, though, that you'd had a chance to meet Cecil. Perhaps, dear girl," she suggested with a roguish twinkle, "we could plan a double wedding?"

AFTER THE SHORT FERRY RIDE, Sophie boarded a bus that took her to downtown Vancouver. Every minute of the protracted trip made her more impatient to be with Rio, to apologize to him for her temper, to share with him the insights Jessica had forced her to recognize in herself.

She wanted more than anything to be in his arms.

The one truth that shone like a beacon through all this was how much she loved him. Jessica had accused her of being a coward, of driving Rio away because she was afraid to try to keep him.

It was probably true, but she wasn't going to do that anymore. She was going to have a long, honest talk with him, tell him the truth about her feelings, and let him take it from there.

She was the first off the bus, and then she had to wait for her suitcase to be unscrambled from the luggage compartment.

The moment she had it in her hand, she found a telephone and started trying to find Rio. She called Freedom Machines first, then remembered he'd have locked up the store a good two hours ago.

He wasn't at his apartment, either.

Sophie hung up and dialed Gina's home number. Rio's mother answered, and after a long delay, Gina came on the phone.

"Rio? He's either at your mother's place—"

"My mother's place? Harriet Larson?" Sophie was certain she'd heard wrong.

"Yeah, that's what I said. Or he's at Nonna's having supper, or else he's already up in the Sweat Shop pretending to be James Bond. One or the other. I didn't tell him where you were, either, just like you said. And Soph?"

Sophie was still trying to figure out one good reason for Rio to be at her mother's house.

"I sold four jumpsuits today and two dresses. And Adam Kelly finally got in the silver belt buckles I told him to get, and I helped him put them in his window this morning. We washed it first. He's nuts about you, y'know."

Sophie was getting more confused by the minute.

"Adam Kelly?"

Gina snorted. "No way. Adam's nuts about the Fog. Rio's the one who's losing it over you. We got our own little dating game going on in that building, huh? Boy, he was some upset today when I wouldn't tell him where you were. Rio, I mean. The family's laying bets on the two of you for a wedding before Christmas. Auntie Rose needs to know early so she can make the fruit cake and age it. Well, I gotta go, Soph. I've got a date with that nice cop that came to the store that day, Marcel? He's Italian. Papa even likes him. See ya tomorrow."

Sophie stared at the phone, gave up trying to figure out most of it and dialed her mother's number.

A man answered. Sophie wondered if she had the right number, but in a moment, her mother's voice came over the line.

"Sophie, where on earth are you?"

"At the bus depot. Who answered the phone just now, Mom?"

"Greg. Look, dear, we have to talk, right away. I've changed my mind about your building. We're not going to buy it after all. I don't think I realized how much it meant to you, but I do now. Sophie, I . . . oh, darn, I don't want to say all this on the phone. Can't you come over here. Can we come and get you?"

What was going on? Harriet sounded flustered—and soft, of all things. And changing her mind about a lucrative real estate deal just because Sophie objected . . . It took a moment to put all the pieces together, but when she did, a rush of tenderness and wonder came over Sophie.

This had to be thanks to Rio. She didn't understand how, but he'd managed to make her mother listen for once.

"Mom, I can't come over just now. I have to find Rio right away. Do you know where he is? And Mom? I've changed my mind, I think moving the Unicorn somewhere else might be a good idea after all. So don't do anything hasty about backing out on your deal. Listen, we'll talk tomorrow."

The line hummed for a long moment, and then Harriet cleared her throat. "I won't do anything at all until we've discussed it, how's that? I'll be at the Unicorn bright and early tomorrow morning."

A male voice rumbled in the background.

"Greg says to give you his best. Heavens, we'll have to talk that over, as well. Greg, I mean. And Sophie?"

Why were all her conversations baffling tonight?

"Yes, Mother?"

"I believe Rio said he was going over to have dinner with his grandmother. He also said . . ." Harriet sounded as if the words were choking her, but she finally got them out. "He . . . said he's in love with you, Sophie."

Sophie looked up Nonna's address and hailed a cab. She couldn't face one more telephone call.

AN HOUR AND TEN MINUTES later, Sophie staggered out of Nonna's house and into another cab, dazed from Nonna's nonstop comments and advice, two large pieces of lasagna and several glasses of the old woman's potent homemade wine.

Sophie clutched the paper bag Nonna had shoved at her when she left. Inside was still another bottle of that same wine.

"To loosen Mario's tongue," Nonna had instructed with a huge wink.

Sophia gave the driver the address of the Sweat Shop and sank back in the seat, closing her eyes and thinking about the visit to Nonna.

The old woman was still in her wheelchair, but she'd demonstrated how she was starting to use a walker for short periods each day. She'd answered the door at Sophie's hesitant knock and all but dragged the younger woman inside, urging her into the kitchen and into a chair.

"Ah, Sophia, Sophia, thank God, I prayed you would come and here you are. God is good. We have to talk. It's Mario, he will not eat. He does not sleep, he looks . . ." She gesticulated with both hands and rattled off something formidable sounding in Italian.

Sophie interrupted her. "Nonna, I want to come and visit with you, but right now I'm looking for Rio. I thought he was here?"

"Sit. First, we have a glass of wine. It's good for the blood. My Mario, he loves you, you know that?"

Sophie accepted the brimming wineglass before it spilled all over her and took a bracing swallow.

"I—Nonna, I hope he does, but he's never told me so." She added with a touch of irony, "Everybody else has, but not Rio."

Nonna clucked her tongue. "These Agostini men. Silvertongued devils they are, until they fall in love. Then, they become tongue-tied, clumsy, slow."

She wheeled like a dervish around the kitchen, serving up a huge plate of food and smacking it down on the table beside Sophie, talking nonstop the whole time.

"Eat. You will need all your strength. I know this because Mario, he is just like his grandfather, my Joseph, God rest his soul. Joseph, he was a terror in our village in Italy, women, wine, songs—my father didn't want me to have anything to do with Joe Agostini, I can tell you that. So I ran away with him. It took almost a year to coax a marriage proposal out of him. My family was scandalized. But a better husband and father never lived than my Joseph, once I got him settled."

She refilled Sophie's wineglass and her own.

"Eat. Then go find this grandson of mine.

THE CAB ROLLED TO A STOP on the deserted street in front of the warehouse, and Sophie got out and paid the driver.

High above, the window of the Sweat Shop was open. The bang of the car door sounded and then the clatter of footsteps on the stairs.

Rio, full of Nonna's lasagna and drained from the events of the past days, had fallen into a deep sleep, slumped over in an awkward heap in the soft armchair. He came awake with a start, jerking to his feet and peering out.

It was dark outside, the area below lit only by the occasional street lamp, silent except for a far-away siren.

He cursed under his breath. He'd slept a long time.

The taillights of a taxi were disappearing around the corner to the north. Far down the street, Potter and his dog, Brandy, were ambling along the sidewalk on their evening stroll.

Someone was climbing the stairs to the Sweat Shop, clattering up the iron staircase.

It could only be Sophie, wearing a pair of her crazy high heels.

Elation and relief swept through him, and Rio swung away from the window to greet her, still groggy with sleep, when something else registered.

A tiny pinpoint of light had flashed and died away through the newly washed windows of Kelly's Quality Footwear.

A small flashlight?

He hit the stairs in four long strides, half-falling down the first two flights, catapulting past a startled Sophie.

"Honey, call the cops," he managed to gasp, taking the steps three at a time and praying he didn't fall and break his neck.

He exploded from the street door and was across the road in seconds. Behind him, he heard Brandy start barking.

The front door of the shoe store was undisturbed, but the display of silver buckles in the window was gone.

Rio headed for the side of the building and the alley entrance, and as he rounded the corner, a dark figure was already running full tilt down the alley, twenty feet ahead of him. The back door of Kelly's was wide open.

Rio put every ounce of will into the chase. He sprinted as hard as he could, but the desperate runner ahead was slowly widening the gap between them.

Rio started as a hurtling shape came up behind and drew abreast of him, paws pounding on the cement. Brandy whoofed with delight and snuffled Rio's pant leg.

Inspiration struck. Rio slowed his pace and yelled, "Get him, Brandy. Get him, boy." He pointed at the fleeing figure now thirty yards away and about to reach the end of the alley.

The dog had already sighted the other sprinter. With effortless ease, he lengthened his stride and pulled past Rio, loving the game of chase.

It seemed only seconds before he reached the man ahead, and Rio felt like cheering as the running man started violently, broke his pace and half turned to fend off the dog, now jumping and barking beside him. As Rio broke into a sprint, the man ahead tripped on something and went sprawling.

Rio was on him in an instant, throwing himself across the prone figure and pinning him to the cement as he struggled to get away.

"Got you, you . . ."

Brandy chose that moment to join the game, and he landed full on Rio, knocking the breath out of his lungs and almost making him lose his hold on the twisting figure beneath him.

"Get off me, you bloody fool," Rio hollered as Brandy licked him and pretended to bite his arm, growling and whining all the while.

The writhing figure under him was screaming, "Get the dog off, help, murder . . ."

A patrol car, siren blaring and roof light flashing, pulled recklessly up on the sidewalk a few feet from them, blocking the end of the alley. The doors burst open, and two officers jumped out and came racing over.

Potter hurried up to join the group, and Sophie arrived, panting.

"Hold it, hold it," one of the officers bellowed, standing over the wrestlers. "Who owns the dog? Call your dog, call your dog off...."

"Brandy, here boy, good dog, come here now." Potter was trying to catch him, but Brandy was out of control. The dog was bounding around in an ecstasy of excitement, growling and tugging at random bits of clothing.

At last Rio struggled to his feet, holding his captive by the back of the neck, and Potter, with Sophie's help, managed to restrain Brandy.

The police quickly took a firm hold on both men, and for the first time, Rio got a good look at the man he'd caught.

"My God, it's—"

"Herb," Sophie shrieked. "Herb, I can't believe this. How could you..."

"This madman attacked me," Herb hollered to the police. "I was just out for a walk...."

Rio lunged, eager to plant a fist in Herb's face.

"This creep's been breaking into stores for months," Rio stated. "He had a bag in his hand, and when I was chasing him he threw it away back there...."

"I saw him throw it, too. I'll go find it." Potter, who'd tied a length of rope to Brandy, hurried off.

"Quiet here. Everybody by quiet. Now who called us?" The police officers were still trying to make sense of what was happening.

"I did. I'm Sophie Larson, Officer. I own the Unicorn boutique just back there. I know both these men...."

"Here's the bag he threw away," Potter crowed. "It's got silver belt buckles in it, too." With a malevolent glare at Herb, Potter sidled over and handed it to one of the officers.

Brandy promptly jumped up on Herb and licked his face, and the mailman let out another shriek of terror. "Get him off me. . . ."

"It's my duty to warn you . . ." One of the officers was reading Herb his rights, and a police van arrived and took him away.

Rio heaved a sigh of relief. Now maybe he could get things straight with his woman.

"The rest of you will have to come down to the station and give your statements," the officer announced next, making certain he was out of Brandy's jumping range.

Rio's hopes for a quiet interlude disappeared.

With a maximum amount of confusion, everyone at the scene, including Potter and Brandy, was loaded into the back of a patrol car and driven the short distance to police headquarters.

Scrunched into the rear seat, Rio wrapped his arm around Sophie's neck and crushed her to him, pressing his mouth to hers—the first chance he'd had to let her know how happy he was to have her back.

He wasn't exactly at his best, though. What with sweat and rolling around in that dirty alley, plus getting mauled by the damned dog, he was afraid he didn't smell too good, but there was nothing he could do about it.

It wasn't much consolation, but Potter smelled much worse, which was why Rio made sure he sat between the old man and Sophie.

She kissed him back so thoroughly the smell couldn't be that bad.

Potter, trying to be dignified under difficult circumstances, gave them both a horrified look that clearly indicated he considered Rio some kind of sex maniac, kissing a woman in the back of a patrol car. The old man made a disgusted noise in his throat and pretended he was staring out the side window.

Unfortunately, Brandy took the kiss as an invitation and started whining and licking Rio's hair with his big wet tongue.

Soundly cursed and fended off by Rio, he tried to climb into their laps.

Rio wondered what the hell had ever possessed him to spend his hard-earned money buying food for such an idiot animal.

AT THE STATION, they wrote out their statements.

After half an hour, Potter had already asked for extra paper, covered two full sheets with a meticulous backhand and was still going strong. Both Sophie and Rio were finished.

Rio, beginning to feel as if a freight train had hit him and wanting nothing more than to get someplace quiet and dark and lie down with Sophie in his arms, tried to hurry the old man along, but Potter was savoring his moment of glory.

"I'm making certain they understand that Brandy is an asset to the whole community," he stated with immense dignity. "After all, he caught that villain, didn't he? Could I have another sheet here, if you please?"

Rio thought he deserved at least as much credit as Brandy, but he kept his mouth shut and went to get them all coffee from the machine.

He handed Sophie hers and thought how gorgeous she looked in her peach cotton dress and her flimsy high heels, with a streak of dirt on her nose and her hair flying in all directions.

He sat down beside her.

"Sophia, about the fight we had over my lease, I didn't understand how you'd feel, and I'm sorry. I . . ."

She gave him a smile that sent blood surging to all his extremities. "Oh, Rio, I was so wrong about all that. I think moving out of that old building might be the best thing after all. Maybe we could find adjoining premises again, though."

Rio's head was spinning. After doing battle with Harriet and Greg, and feeling proud and honorable about putting her needs ahead of everything, this was a major letdown.

"But Sophia, your mother—"

"Finished," Potter announced just then.

Rio took Sophia's hand in his and got to his feet. They could sort this out as soon as they were alone.

"I guess we can go now?" he asked the officer behind the desk.

The man glanced at them and frowned down at Brandy, who was sniffing suggestively around the corner of the desk.

"You gentlemen can leave. But the arresting officers have obtained a search warrant for the house of the accused. He's being held in custody until the search warrant is executed. They'd like Ms Larson to ride along while they search the premises, in case she can identify some of the items stolen from her store."

He jumped to his feet all of a sudden and frowned down in disgust at the floor, where a golden puddle the size of a small lake was spreading across the tiles.

"Is this your dog, sir?"

Rio closed his eyes and shook his head. He jerked a thumb toward Potter.

"Does this dog have a license?" the officer demanded next.

Potter's face flushed, and he puffed up with indignation.

"Brandy's an asset to the community—" he began, but the policeman interrupted.

"I'd suggest you get some paper and clean up this mess, and then get that animal out of here. Technically, I should call the pound and have him taken away."

Potter looked apoplectic, and frightened, as well.

Rio heard himself saying, "If you let Brandy go, I'll be at city hall first thing in the morning to buy him a dog license, Officer."

Potter shot Rio a grateful look and scuttled toward the bathroom to get paper.

Rio wondered how much a dog license cost.

He glanced up at the clock on the wall. It was now half past one in the morning.

He wondered if this was just a particularly bad dream.

"Rio," Sophie said in a soft, endearing voice. "Would you please come with me?"

Rio put an arm around her shoulders and saw the admiring glances being directed Sophie's way by every policeman in the area.

"Try and stop me," he growled, planting a kiss on her forehead and glaring at a cop who happened to be admiring her legs. The young man in uniform flushed and looked away.

Maybe it wasn't such a bad dream after all.

13

It was after three in the morning when the police car finally dropped Sophie and Rio back in front of the Unicorn.

"You want me to give you a lift home?" the policeman offered.

Sophie and Rio both shook their heads.

Sophie had left her suitcase and purse on the stairway of the Sweat Shop, and Rio had his motorcycle parked behind the building. Besides, they felt more at home here than they did anywhere else.

"Thanks for your help, then, folks. Good night."

They watched the marked car disappear around the corner.

Rio felt as if he'd joined the police force himself, he'd been with them so long tonight.

The visit to Herb Cole's house had been a revelation, though. The smartly painted bungalow was only eight blocks away, and the inside resembled a well-ordered pawnshop. Every nook and cranny was filled with goods, all of them stolen and neatly catalogued on lists.

Herb was well organized. There were coin collections, jewelry—Sophie recognized some that had belonged to Jessica—auto accessories, stereo equipment and tapes, books, cartons of cigarettes and tools.

In one tiny bedroom was an entire stock of expensive clothing. Among the items hanging there were the leather jackets and skirts stolen from the Unicorn, as well as a portion of the lingerie taken during the first break-in months before.

The officer with Rio and Sophie had been delighted.

"No wonder we had trouble catching this guy. He wasn't only stealing the stuff, but fencing it, as well. And living so close to the areas he robbed, he could disappear fast. Plus, he had a perfect cover, being a mailman. Good thing we got lucky." He beamed as if he'd captured Herb single-handedly.

Rio was feeling put-upon. He was beginning to wonder if anyone was ever going to acknowledge the fact that Herbert Cole was in custody because Rio Agostini chased him, hell-bent for election, down a dirty alley.

Not that Rio wanted any big deal made over it. But it would be nice to have somebody say thanks for all the sleep he'd forfeited, all the skin he'd lost tonight rolling around on asphalt.

And he'd really done it all for Sophie anyway.

Which made him realize that he hadn't had a chance yet to tell her he loved her or ask her to be his wife. He felt scared now at the thought of doing that.

What if she didn't love him enough? She'd said once that she only wanted his body. He might be pretty good in bed, but apart from that he wasn't much of a prize, with a mortgage on his business, a million nosy Italian relatives, Gina for a sister, an ex-wife like Carol, a kid like Missy—he thought that over and switched Missy from the debit side of the ledger to the credit column. He had a hunch Sophie and Missy would be great together.

Sophie was climbing ahead of him up the flights of endless, echoing stairs, her beautiful, rounded behind swaying from side to side, making him half forget how beat he was.

They picked up her suitcase and her purse, too out of breath to say much to each other.

The Sweat Shop was full of night shadows, and they didn't turn on any lights. They needed to talk, but neither seemed to know where to begin. Sophie walked over to the cutting table, and there beside the phone was Nonna's wine.

She found two chipped cups and filled them, handing Rio one and holding the other up in a toast. "To my knight in shining armor," she whispered. "I watched you race down that alley and tackle that awful man, and I've never felt so proud in all my life."

Rio felt as if he'd been knighted. Her words made up for everything that had happened and everything that hadn't. He couldn't seem to say anything, because of the lump in his throat.

He took a deep, steadying swallow of the wine and led her over to the old armchair, pulling her down onto his knee. She brought the wine bottle along and refilled their cups.

"Don't you ever go away again without telling me where you'll be," he finally managed to say in what he hoped was a stern tone. "Where were you, anyway? I nearly went nuts worrying over you." The soft contours of her bottom were pressed against his front and made lecturing difficult.

"At Jessica's, in Sechelt. The next time I visit her you'll have to come along. She's dying to get a ride on your motorcycle."

Who the hell was Jessica?

"I had a talk with your mother," he tried next.

Sophie drained her cup and refilled it.

"Yes, I know. That was sweet of you, Rio. She's kind of hard to talk to, and I'm afraid she's got some hang-up about you and I being together."

Yeah, he'd agree with that. Especially about him, but it was going to be tough for Harriet to be critical with Greg on the scene. Did Sophie know what was going on there?

"It was strange, but when I called Mother tonight, that awful Greg Marshall answered the phone. What he was doing at Mother's apartment is beyond me."

Rio wasn't going to touch that one with a ten-foot pole. Let Harriet struggle through her own confession. It would do her good.

Besides, there were more important things to discuss, and
he'd better get on with them, because he wasn't exactly feeling wide-awake.

The wine was making him dopey, but it also made it easier
to say things.

"Sophia," he began in a formal tone.

He considered it, but he was just too tired to get up so he
could kneel down in front of her. He cuddled her close against
him instead, letting his hand wander a little over her body,
breathing in the scent that was so much a part of her.

"Sophia, will you marry me?"

It came out fast and uneven.

He felt her become absolutely still. After a couple of
eternities, she said in a voice he had to strain to hear, "Why?"

"Why?" His bellow echoed around the Sweat Shop and
back again.

"Yes, why."

Terrific. His temper was starting to fray around the edges.
His nerves were shot. It had been a long night, and now she
wanted to know why, for God's sake.

"Because I'm in love with you, for cryin' out loud. Because
I love you so much I can't stand not being married to you.
Because I never thought past the next five years, or figured
out how empty it was gonna be, with no dreams left after I
got home from Europe, and you married to somebody else,
and Missy growing up without me, and Gina probably getting herself in trouble."

His headache was coming back.

"Sophia, be reasonable here, okay? I'm asking you to
marry me. Just give me a simple yes."

Or no? He couldn't say it.

She squirmed in his arms and made him wait one heartbeat, two . . .

"Okay, Rio. Yes, I'll marry you. I love you, too, Rio. I have
for a long time. But I needed to hear you say it instead of

hearing it from everyone else. Everybody tells me you love me except you."

He didn't bother trying to figure that one out. He kissed her instead, a long, delightful testimony to how he felt about her.

She snuggled closer to him, arranging her legs and arms comfortably with his, resting her head on his chest.

"We'll have a huge wedding, right, Rio?"

He groaned at the thought. Family weddings were events he'd just as soon avoid. There were endless arguments and Zio Genaro always got drunk and made an interminable speech, and Rio and his cousins played horrible tricks on the groom.

God, this time he'd be the groom.

But the bride would be his Sophia.

"And Bill will make my dress, and I'll have Jessica and Gina as attendants, and Missy and Tara as flower girls, and Nonna will be there, and we should phone Aunt Rose about the cake right away, and . . . Rio?"

Beneath her cheek, a gentle snore sounded, and then another.

In the street below, a garbage truck rumbled along, the worker's cheerful voices floating up and in through the Sweat Shop window. The first pale rays of sunshine filtered in, touching Sophie's arm with a warm caress.

It was morning in the city.

In a few short hours, it would be strictly business, up here in the Sweat Shop and across the street at the Unicorn.

Until then, wrapped in Rio's arms, she could dream of weddings.

COMING NEXT MONTH

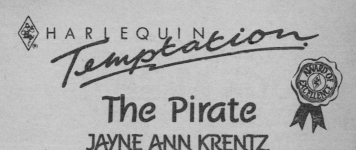

The Pirate
JAYNE ANN KRENTZ

At the heart of every powerful romance story lies a
legend. There are many romantic legends and
countless modern variations on them, but they all
have one thing in common: They are tales of brave,
resourceful women who must gentle and tame the
powerful, passionate men who are their true mates.

The enormous appeal of Jayne Ann Krentz lies in
her ability to create modern-day versions of these
classic romantic myths, and her LADIES AND
LEGENDS trilogy showcases this talent. Believing
that a storyteller who can bring legends to life
deserves special attention, Harlequin has chosen
the first book of the trilogy—THE PIRATE—to
receive our Award of Excellence. Look for it now.

AE-PIR-1A

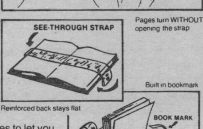

Harlequin Superromance®

LET THE GOOD TIMES ROLL...

Add some Cajun spice to liven up your New Year's celebrations and join Superromance for a romantic tour of the rich Acadian marshlands and the legendary Louisiana bayous.

Starting in January 1990, we're launching CAJUN MELODIES, a three-book tribute to the fun-loving people who've enriched America by introducing us to crawfish étouffé and gumbo, zydeco music and the Saturday night party, the *fais-dodo*. And learn about loving, Cajun-style, as you meet the tall, dark, handsome men who win their ladies' hearts with a beautiful, haunting melody....

Book One: *Julianne's Song*, January 1990
Book Two: *Catherine's Song*, February 1990
Book Three: *Jessica's Song*, March 1990

SRCJ-1R